WITH LOVE
from the
INSIDE

WITH LOVE

from the

INSIDE

Angela Pisel

G. P. PUTNAM'S SONS | *New York*

PUTNAM

G. P. PUTNAM'S SONS
Publishers Since 1838
An imprint of Penguin Random House LLC
375 Hudson Street
New York, New York 10014

Library of Congress Cataloging-in-Publication Data

Names: Pisel, Angela, author.
Title: With love from the inside / Angela Pisel.
Description: New York: G. P. Putnam's Sons, 2016.
Identifiers: LCCN 2016008052 | ISBN 9780399176364
Subjects: LCSH: Mothers and daughters—Fiction. | Women prisoners—Fiction. |
Physicians' spouses—Fiction. | Family secrets—Fiction. | Death
row—Fiction. | South Carolina—Fiction. | Psychological fiction. |
Domestic fiction.
BISAC: FICTION / Contemporary Women. | FICTION / Legal. | FICTION / Family Life.
GSAFD: Mystery fiction.
Classification: LCC PS3616.I867 W58 2016 | DDC 813/.6—dc23
LC record available at https://lccn.loc.gov/2016008052
p.   cm.

Printed in the United States of America
1   3   5   7   9   10   8   6   4   2

Book design by Lauren Kolm

To Greg and the four kids who share our home.

You're the reason I want to be there.

WITH LOVE
from the
INSIDE

GRACE

The police took "normal" away from me the moment they came rushing into William's hospital room. They dragged me from his crib while my helpless baby lay hooked up, struggling to breathe, needing his mother. I had been to doctor after doctor, but no one would listen to me when I tried to tell them something wasn't right.

"Bradshaw, your attorney is here to see you," an unfamiliar voice barked at me through the steel door, and snapped me into the present.

Tuesdays were my usual lawyer days, not Thursdays, so the news couldn't be good. I slid the pen inside my worn leather journal and tossed it on my cot. As I stood, the shooting pain in my back reminded me I wasn't sleeping at the Hilton.

The stark, cold walls and the constant clamor of cursing and flushing toilets wasn't at all how I'd pictured my life. It was a stagnant existence, every day like the one before and the one after. As unjust as I know that to be, nothing I could do will change my situation or my reputation. The latter, as crazy as it seemed, still mattered most to me even after seventeen years. I would prefer not to be remembered as the monster the local newspapers dubbed me, and especially not as a baby killer.

"Hurry up," a new officer growled through the narrow horizontal opening in the door. "Give me both your hands." His tone startled me, and I bit the inside corner of my lip, a nervous habit I'd tried and failed to break. This time I tasted blood.

I handled officer changes better than some on the row. Jada, I suspected, was right now sitting with her hands clasped around her legs, rocking back and forth like someone residing in a psych ward. She once told me that when she was little she never knew who her "daddy" would be when she woke up in the morning. I pictured a four-year-old Jada peering around the corner in footsie pajamas, surveying the situation—praying that whoever she might see at the breakfast table would be kind to her. A sanguine version in my mind, but Jada still panics, even more than the rest of us, when an untried voice gives her orders.

I placed my left arm through the slit and elevated my right shoulder a bit to get my other arm to cooperate. My limbs had gotten stiff and slow, and sitting in a cell all day didn't help. The officer pulled my wrists together, snapping the cuffs tighter than necessary before he pushed my arms back through the hole and unlocked the cell door. "Your attorney is waiting on you."

I avoided eye contact with him as he escorted me, kept my eyes on the floor, counting the gray concrete slabs to keep calm. My count was interrupted when Roni started screaming.

"Keep it down," the officer snapped, "or you won't get a shower this week, either." I knew by the sharpness in his voice that he meant what he said.

"Okay, Cowboy," Roni shouted back. "Okay."

Cowboy spelled backward is YOBWOC, and it stood for Young Obnoxious Bastards We Often Con (one of the many useless things I've learned in prison). I don't include myself in the "we" part of that acronym—I just do my best to get along—but Roni does. She's the one in here I've tried to connect to the most, the one I've tried to help. Maybe it's because she's young enough to be my daughter, but for her own sometimes inexplicable reasons, Roni chooses to make trouble whenever she has a chance, or whenever she has no chance at all.

Only four of the seven cells in this wing of the prison were occupied on death row, but only outsiders called it that. Those who resided here called it the Hell Hotel. On the inside, hope was something no one seemed to believe in except me.

Mainly, I just missed the ordinary. The uncomplicated, taken-for-granted things like the sound of my husband's house keys rattling in the front door at exactly two minutes before six o'clock, or the buzzer on the duct-taped dryer signaling a load of warm towels was ready to be folded; the gritty feel of the hot driveway on my bare feet as I walked to the mailbox to raise the rusted red flag, or sitting in my cold minivan making sure the windows defrosted before driving my daughter to school. Or burying my face in the space between William's chest and his rolled chin just to smell his sweet baby-powdered scent after he had a bath.

The officer squeezed my upper arm as he guided me through the vacant dayroom and buzzed us through one door and then another before we entered one of the attorney-client holding rooms. *Room* was a generous term, but at least it was bigger than my cell and offered some contact, meaning my attorney could shake my handcuffed hands if he so desired or slide a paper across the chipped Formica table without hitting glass.

Ben Taylor stood when I entered. He'd represented me for the past five years and had become one of the few noninstitutionalized faces I saw. His face today didn't look that good.

"Hello, Grace. Please take a seat." I sat down with my feet and hands still cuffed.

"Ben, how are you?" I was delaying, wanting to hear anything other than the news I feared he was about to give me.

"I'm fine." His slight southern accent made whatever awful words he was about to tell me sound more tolerable. Most of the guards and many of the inmates here had come from all over. Ben's soft tone reminded me of home.

"Have you found her?" I asked, hoping he would give me something to cling to.

"I'm sorry, Grace. My office still has not been able to get in touch with her."

After all these years, I still woke in the morning with a sweat-soaked shirt stuck to my skin, dreaming about my daughter sitting alone at her dad's funeral. Abandoned. I knew I couldn't make my daughter forgive me, believe me, or even come to see me, but I wouldn't stop hoping. I'd stopped calling many years ago, figuring the refusal of collect calls meant the expense was too much for her to handle. Eleven years, five months, and twenty-seven days separated me from the last time I'd heard her voice—the last time I'd heard anyone call me "Mom." A word I'd never longed to hear until I did.

"That's not why I'm here," he said. "I am afraid we didn't get the news we had hoped for. The court refused to hear the latest appeal."

I dropped my head and tried not to make my attorney, my only believer, feel any worse than I knew he already felt. Whatever hope I'd carried into the room had fled by the time I looked up.

My lawyer rubbed his forehead. "Grace, the judge has set your execution date."

SOPHIE

Sophie knew she'd made mistakes. The kind of mistakes an "I'm sorry" wouldn't erase and a "Please understand" wouldn't go far to repair. Not after all this time. The car in her driveway, her oversize lake house, and her bulging bank account made her life look perfect on the surface. By anyone else's standards, she should be fulfilled, ecstatic, but . . . maybe it was because she was turning thirty this year that her heart seemed to be catching up with her deception and she hated that feeling.

She sat where she did every morning after Thomas left for work—with her coffee on the veranda off the master bedroom overlooking the lake. This spot helped quiet her mind and energize her for the day ahead. At least it usually did. But this October morning felt different somehow.

She set her mug down and snuggled as deep as she could into her chenille bathrobe. The sharp chill in the air caused her hands to shiver and she looked down at them, wishing she still had the red snowflake mittens she'd worn as a little girl. Holes on both of them, right at the tops of her palms under the first two fingers, from hours of raking leaves in her backyard, just so she could jump in and bury herself in the pile, counting the seconds until her dad would find her. *Sophie, Sophie, come out, wherever you are.* After many minutes of pretending he had no idea where she was, her dad would fall into the pile on top of her. She felt like she'd never stop giggling. "You got me good this time, pumpkin," he would say to her.

Sophie tried to recall the last time she'd actually done something like that just for the fun of it, or experienced some overpowering emotion other than the flatline she had grown accustomed to. She did feel happy when she laid her head on her husband, Thomas, and watched his chest rise up and down as he slept, or when she put together puzzles with children at the hospital, but those feelings were short-lived.

She shook her head, scolding herself for the psychoanalysis, and decided to push whatever these strange emotions were back to her hidden and unexamined places. She controlled her life now. No one could take that from her, not anymore.

Her thoughts were interrupted by her vibrating phone. Seven new e-mails, two new texts, and one missed call. *Guess my walk down memory lane affected my hearing.* One text from Thomas, one from Mindy, and a call from a number she did not recognize.

She was typing a reply to Thomas when Mindy's text vibrated. *Not coming today. talk to you later. will still help with fund-raiser.*

She checked the clock on her phone. The time for figuring out her tangled lack of emotions had expired. She needed to get going.

SOPHIE HATED THURSDAYS. Ever since they'd bought a house in West Lake several years ago, Thomas had insisted it would be good for her to get to know some of the other women in the neighborhood. Sophie resisted at first—faking end-of-the-week migraines and even an ankle sprain—until Thomas noticed a pattern and forced the issue. "You've got to get out of this house and make some friends."

After a few months, she finally gave in and started attending the monthly meetings the women called "the book club." Sophie secretly called the women "the synthetics." A roomful of designer-dressed plastic ladies sitting around drinking margaritas while discussing the latest scandals lurking within their gated community. The books they were supposed to be reading never came up.

Sophie didn't exclude herself from that less-than-complimentary stereotype. On more than one occasion she'd presented herself to be something she was not. It wasn't that the ladies hadn't been nice to Sophie since she and Thomas moved into the neighborhood. Most had been welcoming—since the first day, actually, when a few of them brought a large welcome basket of wine and cheese and left it by the front door. It had a note attached: *Sorry we missed you! Dinner at the Parkers' Friday night?*

Before that first dinner at the Parkers', she'd changed outfits three times and ran to the bathroom to throw up twice, all before finally settling on a tweed blazer and dark blue jeans.

Mindy Parker (who happened to work at the same hospital as Thomas) had put Sophie at ease right away, and she and Sophie had developed somewhat of a friendship since that night. Maybe it was the way her house looked. Clean, but not perfect; functional, but not organized. Chocolate cookie crumbs and milk drops lingered on the kitchen counter and shouted that Mindy was not trying to impress anyone. Sophie envied that attitude. Mindy always let her two-year-old twin girls say hello and good night to everyone before excusing herself to tuck them in to bed.

Mindy's friend Eva, however, wasn't as genuine. Sophie could picture her as an eighth-grader, pointing and whispering at an unfortunate misfit unlucky enough to have inherited an older sibling's hand-me-downs. Sophie could feel Eva's eyes scanning her fashion selection whenever she walked into a room, and she always seemed a little too interested when Thomas told a story. Sophie wasn't normally the jealous type, but something about Eva's smile when she looked at him made her more than a little uncomfortable.

While Thomas socialized with all of the husbands they had met in the neighborhood on occasion to play tennis or a round of golf, Mindy was the only relationship Sophie had cared to foster outside of the book club and other cursory social events. Even that friendship had gotten only so deep. The less people knew about her the better.

ALL THE USUAL "BOOK CLUB" cars were present and accounted for when Sophie pulled her Land Rover behind Eva's brand-new red BMW. She could see Eva and three other women (all of whose names escaped Sophie) walking in, chatting with fast and flippy hand movements, and whispering about something Sophie wasn't quite sure she wanted to hear. Since no one ever seemed interested in discussing their assigned book, Sophie had turned the monthly meetings into planning events for her latest endeavor—a fund she had created for indigent children at St. John's Hospital.

To raise money, she was planning a Secret Chef fund-raiser that she described as: *A soon-to-be-annual wine- and food-tasting event that will boast the most culinary delectable dishes ever served in the South. The chefs and their restaurants will "surprise" the highest bidders with sensational award packages sure to satisfy even the pickiest palates*—or something along those lines. Sophie fine-tuned her pitch as she grabbed her laptop out of the back of her SUV.

"Did you hear about Stephen?" Eva said, before she had a chance to set down her bag or take off her jacket. Sophie, not sure if Eva meant to include her, didn't immediately respond.

"Did you hear me? Did you hear what's going on with Stephen?"

Sophie didn't want to appear to be out of the loop or to give Eva the satisfaction of knowing about whatever was happening first, so she quickly replied, "Yes, heard about it last night. Thomas told me. I can't believe it." A calculated response, since she had no idea what was going on with Stephen. But one thing she knew for sure—Eva loved to be the first to give details.

"Well, for those of you who *don't* know . . ." Eva launched into the gossip without taking a breath. "Stephen moved out. Mindy is devastated; they just put in a pool and all." One bejeweled hand flipped her shiny hair over her shoulder. "I can't totally blame him. Have you seen Mindy lately? Not exactly keeping herself up. Never met an ice-cream cone she didn't like."

All the ladies but Sophie laughed. She didn't run to Mindy's defense, but she didn't laugh. Did she get credit for partial loyalty? She hadn't talked to Mindy for a couple weeks and, granted, their conversations weren't all that deep, but problems with Stephen—she had no idea.

"Ready to get started?" Kate, the hostess for the day, said while narrowing her eyes in Eva's direction. She handed Sophie a mimosa and then subtly motioned for her to turn the conversation away from Mindy's personal life.

Sophie pulled out her laptop and began to go over the first item on her agenda.

"Wait, wait, wait," Eva interjected immediately. "I hear you're hiding something from us."

Sophie pretended to check the wall for the nearest outlet, praying that when she looked up Eva's fake eyelashes would be batting in someone else's direction.

"Sophie, I am talking to you." Eva shrilled the personal-pronoun part of that sentence when Sophie failed to turn around. "We read the newspapers, you know?"

Sophie bent over to plug the cord into her already fully charged computer, her face feeling like it could melt off.

Do they know?

This moment, the one she feared the most, had played out in her mind a million times before. All with varying degrees of who finds out what first and when. *How will she ever make them understand?*

"For God's sake, Sophie. What's wrong with you? You look like you chipped a tooth or something. You should be proud of Thomas," Eva continued, starting the hand-flipping thing again. "The story was all over the newspapers this morning. Michael called me from his car to see if I'd seen it."

"Thomas, in the newspaper?" Sophie braced herself against the wall, relieved her sinking sand stayed loyal for another day.

Eva let out an exaggerated sigh. "Your husband is operating on that little girl today. For freeeeee! You know, the one who got her face burned?"

Sophie vaguely remembered hearing the story on the news. Something about a six-year-old tripping over an electric skillet's cord.

"I had no idea." Sophie averted Eva's eye batting and tried to hide the fact that she hated it when Eva knew something about her husband that she didn't.

"I knew his hands were created to do fine things," Eva purred. "Don't you agree?"

The implied familiarity made Sophie uneasy and annoyed. *How would she know? Was she a patient of his?* Sophie studied Eva's plump red lips for signs of collagen.

"It's nice to know you find Thomas's hands attractive," Kate butted in with a stiff smile, "but let's get back to the reason we're here."

Eva started to backpedal, but Sophie cut her short. Using her mimosa as a microphone, she said, "Right, the fund-raiser." She tapped on the rim. "Is this thing on?"

"It may not be on, but it's sure empty." Kate grabbed the pitcher and filled Sophie's glass to the top.

Sophie took a long sip and summoned the version of herself she wanted everyone else to see. After the mimosas started to kick in, she pulled out her three-ring binder filled with to-do lists and due dates and started handing out assignments.

GRACE

Grace Bradshaw, Lakeland State Penitentiary, Death Row. It's how my mail—mostly legal correspondence from my in-and-out state-appointed attorneys—had been addressed for the past seventeen years. I knew, given my conviction and current occupancy in the ward where prisoners await execution, that this conversation had to happen at some point, but in all the time I'd been here, no one had *actually* been put to death.

The rumors about the governor must be true. The state was cleaning house, and they were beginning with me. The sound of something clinking together stopped my thoughts. My handcuffs. Ben heard it, too, and reached across the eroded coffee-stained table to stop my hands from shaking. Before he touched me, the officer standing guard snarled out a reminder of the limited-contact rule.

Ben's voice lowered. "Grace, I will not give up on you." He glanced over to see if the officer was watching before he put his hand under my chin. I noticed new lines on his forehead that had formed since the last time he'd visited.

"I promise I'll find a way to help. I took your case because I believed you. Now that I have gotten to know you better, I'm certain you don't deserve to be here. You aren't who they say you are."

Who they say I am. I'd struggled with that sentence from the moment I'd been accused. *Munchausen by proxy* was how the prosecutor explained my crime. As in one of those crazy mothers from horror movies who purposefully make their children sick for attention and sympathy. A catchy, devastating term that had made for quite the splashy headlines.

The twelve people of the jury sat stone-faced, fixated on every damaging word, while I remained motionless, trying to envision this monster he described. *A depressed mother who never wanted a second child, a lonely pastor's wife so crazed for attention she made her baby sick.* His summation—slow and deliberate, calculating but sincere—made William's death seem like a series of events I plotted for some sick reason.

The man elected by the courts to represent the people never once set foot on my lattice-framed front porch, nor did he care to ask me about the horror of losing a child.

He never witnessed me comfort a crying William in the way only my breast could. Never saw me pace around the family room, gently rocking my baby in my arms, praying he wouldn't get sick again. He didn't see me wet a towel to wipe the blood trailing down my daughter's skinned knee, then remain by her side until "Itsy Bitsy Spider" made her giggle again. I may not have won any awards for parenting, but I loved my children as much as anyone.

The jury bought the prosecutor's tale of how William became better in the care of others but sick again when I alone cared for him. The man with a different-colored paisley tie for every day of the three-week-long trial convinced twelve jurors of the culpability of one.

Who they say I am. I'd hoped the jury could see me as I was, sift through the fabrications and one misrepresented event. Instead . . . it was worse than I ever let myself imagine beforehand. *How could twelve out of twelve people vote to have me killed?* That thought still caused me panic.

"Five minutes." The officer held up his spread hand.

"Grace," Ben said softly, "I'm still trying to find her."

"I know you are, but it is hard to find someone who doesn't want to be found. I think I'm already dead to her."

"I have someone searching university records, past addresses, things of that sort. Is it possible she might have changed her name?"

I had thought of all these possibilities, a thousand times, and still did not have an answer to give him. I shrugged.

"Promise me you'll do one thing for me." I tried to control the shake in my voice. "Give her my journal when I'm gone."

"I'll escort Bradshaw," a familiar pleasant voice whispered to the other officer. I sat in a metal chair with my hands cuffed to a leather belt buckled around my waist. The restraints limited my physical movements, but my thoughts ran all over the place as I tried to process the news I'd received from my attorney.

I looked up into kind green eyes and the face of Officer Jones. "I'm sorry," Officer Jones said, a crease forming between her brows. "I know that wasn't the news you were hoping to hear."

In a more normal situation, like being told I could live twelve to fourteen months if the chemo worked, or finding out my husband of thirty-three years had died in a car accident, I would've fallen on her shoulder and sobbed until I had no tears left. I said nothing and gave her a small nod.

I get the feeling that Officer Jones likes me, or at least believes something good lives within me. We've never talked about my conviction because she already knew what I'd been accused of. Everyone did. My face, to hear some of the staff talk, used to be on every TV and radio station in the United States and in Canada, until finally the coverage died down and moved on to some serial killer murdering prostitutes in Nevada.

Officer Jones was one of the few female officers who worked on the row long before I arrived. I assumed she was in her late fifties, based on her seven grandkids, but I never dared to ask her personal questions.

Instead, we covered generic carpool topics, like her plans for retirement: "Just twenty-three months and fifteen days until this lady"—she would use both thumbs to point to herself—"is out of here."

I never thought I'd be the one leaving first.

"This isn't over yet. The governor can still stop this." She helped me stand and steady myself, a task that proved harder than I'd thought it would be. My legs wobbled.

The newly elected governor had run on the promise of swift justice. I wasn't sure it was wise to hope for his help.

I attempted to look on the bright side: Wasn't there some comfort in knowing the end of my story? A sense of control, perhaps, over writing my own obituary, filling in the exact date that comes after the hyphen. I could ballpark a pretty close time of death and maybe let people know about my state-run, graveside funeral. The problem was I wasn't sure who would come.

"Come on," Officer Jones said, "keep your chin up. You've never been one to give up on anything. Fight for that daughter you've been telling me about. Sophie, right? Fight for Sophie."

Hearing my daughter's name spoken in a kind way by someone other than my attorney was more than I could handle. I dropped my head into my shackled hands and began to cry.

I didn't speak with Officer Jones as she escorted me back. Instead, I did the only thing that calmed me when I couldn't stand this place anymore. I let my mind go to six-year-old Sophie in high pigtails, front tooth missing and a Christmas-morning smile, handing me a bottle of Sally Hansen's Hard As Nails purple glitter nail polish. *Please, Mommy, can we use this sparkly one?*

All the way back to my cell, I painted Sophie's fingernails one by one, with perfect strokes, blowing each nail between the coats until they were dry and her hands looked perfect.

SOPHIE

She'd just finished lighting the last candle when Thomas walked through the side door leading in from their garage. His phone plastered to his ear, he was still giving the nurses orders: "Up her pain meds to what we discussed. Call me if her temperature is over 100.5." He blew Sophie a kiss as soon as he saw her.

Eight-forty-five in the evening seemed to be his usual time of arrival rather than the exception these days. Sophie didn't complain; when Thomas was home he made her feel like she was the only person who mattered in his busy world.

Pad Thai, spring rolls, and steamed vegetables were arranged on coordinating black-and-red-and-yellow-flowered platters, while the take-out containers lurked in the trash can by the garage. She knew he didn't actually think she cooked all this herself, but she loved to give him that impression.

"Hey, baby." He kissed her on the cheek, then tossed his keys and cell phone onto the ivory granite countertop. "I'm starving."

"Hi, handsome. Save any lives today?"

"I improve lives—not save them." He grinned. It was a standing rhetoric the two had had since they'd started dating a few months after Thomas began his plastic surgery fellowship.

She knew Thomas loved his job. And she loved the way he described his work, even jokingly comparing himself to Frank Lloyd Wright. If his patients—or clients, as he liked to call them—wanted some additions, he could do that. If clients needed some subtractions, he could do that as well. No one was too young and no body too old to deserve a little renovation. Lately, most of his clients—and most of them were women—wanted additions on the upper floor.

Sophie didn't mind. Breast augmentation paid the bills, financed some pretty elaborate vacations, and allowed her to live in a house that had been featured on more than one regional magazine cover. She could overlook the fact that Thomas had touched more breasts than Hugh Hefner had.

"How was your meeting?" he asked, while he opened a package of soy sauce. "Talk anybody into helping you with the fund-raiser?"

"I did. I have most of the key committee chairs lined up. I still want to give Mindy something to do." She picked up her spring roll from her plate and peeled back the overly fried top layer. "Did you know she and Stephen were having problems?"

Thomas leaned back in his chair and tossed the empty packet of soy sauce in the trash. "I think I heard Eva say something about it when she was dropping off samples at the office the other day."

"Eva's working again?" She didn't know what to be more shocked about—Stephen and Mindy or Eva's access to Thomas.

"A couple days a week. The drug company gave her a salary she couldn't refuse. She's taking samples around to a few offices in the area."

Great, Sophie thought. *Not only do we have to live in the same neighborhood with Malibu Barbie, but Thomas gets to see her at the office, too.*

"Can you hand me a napkin?" he asked, interrupting her jealous thoughts. "I missed you today." His wide smile reinforced his words.

Most parts of her believed him. The other jagged misfit pieces still felt unworthy and lost, frantically trying to find their way back to where they fit and felt protected. To her once-unbroken place, her existence before her mom killed William and shattered Sophie's life.

Thomas's pager went off before dinner was finished.

"It's the hospital." He pushed his plate back and looked at the numbers on his pager. "Have a kid not doing so well."

"The little girl with the scars?"

"You saw the paper?" Thomas paused the twirling of his noodles around the fork.

"I saw Eva." Sophie leaned over and wiped some sauce off the corner of Thomas's mouth. "I knew my husband had a soft spot for children hidden somewhere inside there."

He hated treating kids, and Sophie knew it. Not that he didn't like children—they were just more challenging and he didn't like to make them cry. Most of their problems were a result of birth defects, accidents, or because of an incompetent ER doc who couldn't sew. The parents were usually overprotective and hovering, making Thomas's job even harder. The child would inevitably squirm, shift on the exam table, and eventually cry before Thomas would have to ask his nurse to hold the kid down.

"I'll call the hospital from the car. Come with me and you can see Mindy. I think she's on tonight."

"I'd love to," Sophie said as she stuffed down the rest of her spring roll. "May be the only way I can spend time with my popular husband."

THOMAS RAN AHEAD OF SOPHIE DOWN THE LONG, deserted hospital corridor. The phone call from the car hadn't gone well. Sophie had listened over the speakerphone as Anna, the nurse on two west, said, "Your six-year-old postsurgical graft patient in room two-sixteen, she's not doing so well, pulse is rapid and irregular, temperature 104.9. Her mother called the nurses' station because she seemed confused."

"Okay," Thomas replied, then paused. Sophie could tell by his silence he was trying to find the reason why the girl had gone south after a routine surgery. Before he could come up with any good explanation, the nurse shouted in the phone, "Dr. Logan, better get here quick; oxygen levels are dropping. She doesn't look good."

Sophie followed him as he rushed toward the girl's room, giving orders to the nurse on his cell phone. His six-foot-three-inch build exuded confidence and commanded respect. Even in a crisis, Thomas remained composed and certain.

Sophie paid attention to the way other women looked at him. The way they followed his instructions without hesitation or doubt. She noticed details like the way his graphite eyes tapered when he concentrated but became almost round when he had something important to say. His steady hands had propelled him to the top during his plastics fellowship, and then to a position at one of the top hospitals in the Southeast. He was as talented as he was good-looking.

Still, Sophie knew things Thomas would never know. Disgusting, never-discussed things, like the wrenching smell of feces and the shape it takes when rubbed on a dingy prison wall. Images a child should be protected from—those were the images that formed the backdrop of Sophie's last memories of her mom.

Thomas's Ivy League education had prepared him for many things, but Sophie's real life had taught her lessons you couldn't pay to learn. His childhood had consisted of playdates and lacrosse games, while her Saturdays in high school had been spent taking the bus back and forth to visit her mother. She was never sure whether she visited because of obligation or loneliness, but every Saturday, while other teenage girls were trying on prom dresses or squeezing into bikinis at the mall, she boarded the bus, robotically paid her fare, and stayed with her mom as long as prison visiting hours would allow—until one Saturday she didn't anymore.

Marrying Thomas had given her a fresh start, a clean slate. One that could be written on with the words of a life she was supposed to have, deserved to have. No one, she'd decided, would ever know her shame, or the scandal that had ripped apart a little girl's fairy tale.

Sophie hadn't consciously decided to fake her way into a more privileged world. Her fate had happened to her, set in motion the day Thomas walked into the Starbucks where she was working to pay her way through grad school. Her dad's life insurance had covered college and some of her current classes, but paying for an apartment and food was another thing. Her green employee apron, stained with God knew what, had been what she was wearing when she met her future husband. He would tell her a few months later that it was crazy love at first sight. For Sophie, it was like a dream come true. His dark, wavy hair and pin-striped blue-and-white Ralph Lauren dress shirt, tucked into perfectly pressed khakis, had signaled he was out of her league. She hadn't dated much, but the guys in her life didn't come in looking like Thomas or ride out driving the kind of car he did. She couldn't believe it when he asked her out two weeks and seven lattes later.

Now green aprons, taking orders, and listening to people complain about their coffee were a thing of the past. She was the wife of Dr. Thomas Logan and the daughter of no one.

THOMAS CONSULTED WITH THE NURSES ON DUTY while Sophie searched the hallway for Mindy. "Hey," she said, when Mindy finally appeared from behind a pile of charts on the unit secretary's desk. "You have a second to talk?"

"I will as soon as I'm finished drawing my meds." Mindy looked out of order and her flat-ironed hair seemed even more worn. Chunks had started to rebel and wave in the wrong direction around her rounded face. "I know someone who has time for you," Mindy said, as she pulled a rubber band off of her wrist and corralled her red hair (paprika red, as Mindy described it: "My stupid hair looks like a garnishment on a damn deviled egg"). She tied it off in a French knot, then pointed to the room located directly in front of the nurses' station. "He's been asking for you."

Max's face lit up when Sophie walked into his room. *Sesame Street* was just ending on TV. She reached for the remote, which was sitting on the table next to his bed, and turned it off before public television forced Max to watch some French chef make chocolate soufflé with a twist of rum.

Max, who had just turned three, still needed the rails of the bed up when he was unsupervised. Sophie lowered one and sat on the edge of the mattress beside her favorite hospital resident. "Hey, little man. How are you doing today?"

Max placed his index finger over his throat to cover the surgically created hole from a tracheostomy and with a raspy voice said, "Puzwle."

"Puzwle," Sophie teased. "What's that?"

Max, now sitting up and bouncing on his bent knees, pointed across the room to the circus puzzle he and Sophie had been working on for the past few weeks.

"Puzwle," Max said, giggling. "Over there."

"Oh, you mean *puzzle*," she said, gently poking Max in the tummy. "I'll get it for you."

She scooted Max back to the center of the bed, then retrieved the puzzle from the table under the windows. "Think we will ever finish this thing?"

Max held up both of his arms and wiggled every finger, making it impossible for Sophie not to pick him up and set him on her lap as they searched for the missing piece that would finish the white unicorn on the carousel.

She found the corner piece before Max did and slid it to the edge of the table, away from the distractions of the other pieces. Her plan worked. Max squealed in delight as he picked up the piece and said, "Horsie done."

Mindy, who was Max's nurse for the day, walked in just in time to witness his victory. "Good job, Max. You're such a smart little boy. Who's your helper?" She winked at Sophie. Max ignored her, intent on finding the piece that would complete the elephant's ear.

"Any news on finding this guy a foster family?" Sophie whispered, while Mindy prepared his medications. Max's premature birth had left him with underdeveloped lungs, which was why he had the tracheostomy. His mother, Sophie had heard, couldn't handle the responsibilities of caring for an infant with such severe special needs.

"Not yet, not with all his care. Going to take a special family for this one," Mindy said, then converted the first dose of medication into a bunny rabbit hopping toward Max's unwilling mouth. He'd been placed in a few homes, as far as Sophie knew, but nothing permanent. His need for constant suctioning and breathing treatments had worn the last family out. And his health didn't appear to be getting any better. Lately, he seemed to be in the hospital more than out.

Sophie had met Max quite by accident. His occupational therapist had been giving him a ride through the hospital gift shop in an oversize plastic green wagon and Sophie, who was volunteering in the unit, caught a glimpse of his big, gap-toothed smile when they went wheeling by. His messy blond hospital hair and large brown eyes captivated her heart, and her growing relationship with him eventually set in motion her idea to start her fund for needy children on the pediatric ward.

She'd convinced Thomas to be the figurehead behind the fund-raising effort, but not before he attempted to persuade her not to get too involved with Max. "He has social workers to help him," said Thomas. "Besides, I don't want you to get attached to him and get your heart broken."

Her heart was already broken, and maybe, in some small way, Max could help change that. She and Max had a connection, and if she couldn't help William, couldn't she at least help Max?

"Here comes Peter Cottontail," Mindy said in her best furry voice. As Sophie looked on, she noticed Mindy's left hand was missing her wedding ring. She started to ask her about Stephen, but before she could, a flurry of activity in the hallway interrupted their conversation. "Code red in room two-sixteen, code red in room two-sixteen," shouted a voice over the PA system. Mindy immediately got up to leave. "I think that's Thomas's patient. Be back as soon as I can."

Sophie tucked Max into bed and then closed his door. She didn't want him to be startled any more than she assumed he already was. However, Max, to her surprise, didn't seem to notice the hospital hustle and bustle, but busied himself making a pretend rocket ship out of a folded lunch menu.

She dimmed the lights since it was after ten and pulled his favorite book, *The Velveteen Rabbit*, out of his top drawer. "I like wabbits, not bunnies," he'd told her the last time she read it to him.

It was clear to her she needed Max more than he needed her right now, but at least he nodded when he saw the book and tossed the makeshift rocket to the floor.

He scoured his bed for his *Toy Story* blanket. Sophie helped in the search, undoing his sheets in three out of the four corners. The bed looked as if a tornado had blown through, causing them both to laugh when they noticed Buzz Lightyear and the gang had been hiding under the bed the entire time.

"Come here, silly boy." She picked up Max and carried him to the mauve recliner angled in the corner of the room. "Buzz Lightyear can try to hide, but he's no match for you."

She gave Max the book to look at while she attempted to reassemble the bed. When she glanced over at Max, his tired head was bobbing.

The commotion in the hallway seemed to have died down, so she picked up a sleeping Max and tucked him into his bed. She put his favorite blanket under his floppy arm.

"Sleep well, sweet boy, sleep well," she whispered into his ear before pressing a good-bye kiss into his chubby cheek.

Sophie walked down the hallway, trying to find Thomas. The sound of muffled voices led her to a small lounge at the entrance of the pediatric ward, directly across from the elevators. Through the slightly open doorway she could see Thomas talking to a young thirtysomething couple. She eavesdropped while she poured herself some coffee from the mobile cart parked in the hallway.

"You said this operation would be a piece of cake, Dr. Logan. You said our daughter would be okay," said the man, who was wearing faded blue jeans and a Blue Devils T-shirt. He spoke slowly, as if trying to process his own words.

"What went wrong?" the mother asked, her question drenched by her tears. She had both arms wrapped around a gray stuffed elephant and held it to her chest.

Thomas's face was pale and his white oxford shirt wrinkled. His suit jacket and tie lay beside him over the arm of the chair. Sophie watched as he searched for something to say. Her confident, capable husband appeared unable to find the words to make the situation less painful or to make any sense of it at all.

The expressions on the parents' faces would forever be embedded in Sophie's mind. Shock and sadness alternating with anger, then disbelief. A carousel of emotions Sophie had seen years before on the faces of her own grieving parents. A haunting gaze that could be replicated only by those who had lost a child.

"I'm not sure what went wrong with—with . . ." Thomas stuttered. "The autopsy will tell us more. I've done this procedure multiple times, and I've never had a bad outcome." His pager beeped, and Sophie saw him take it out of his pocket to look at it.

"Dr. Logan," said the father, his voice escalating. The man stood up, over Thomas, with his sobbing wife's head braced against the side of his trembling leg. "This bad outcome was named Isabel, and your bad outcome, as you like to call it, was our daughter."

GRACE

(*This journal belongs to Grace Louise Bradshaw #44607—Please see that my daughter, Sophie Pearl Bradshaw, receives this upon my death.*)

Dear Sophie,

I'm writing this journal so you'll have a piece of me to hang on to when I'm gone. Words, written in my handwriting, declaring our great love story. The beginnings before my end.

I pray the words written on this faded, white paper will find you someday, and maybe—just maybe—you'll let your heart love me again.

My legal fight appears to be over. I haven't lost hope, but I'm preparing myself for the inevitable. My execution, which will happen sometime in February.

I'm not mad at you. I understand why you stopped visiting. The embarrassment, I suspect, was too much for you to handle. Your dad made up reasons for your dwindling visits, saying things like "She has a big geography test" or "Her best friend Jillian is having a pool party," but I knew the truth. You needed me, and I wasn't there, in our home, living in a normal world that didn't include plexiglass with attached telephones and graffiti-covered metal dividers.

I'm writing to you on a thin mattress that covers the rusty off-

white bed frame in my six-by-nine-foot cell. My room, I like to call it, consists of a small sink and a toilet without a lid. I've wallpapered the space above my bed with photos from our life— a lovely life that I view as unfinished.

Life, or what little I have left, still matters to me. I'm not sure it matters to anyone else. It's hard to be a good friend to anyone on the outside when you're on death row.

Hanging right beside me at eye level are three smiling faces. You, wedged between a enormously pregnant me and your daddy, with both of your arms muddled together, trying to hold on to our squirmy three-month-old poodle. Do you remember? We're standing under the red-and-white awning of a borrowed RV. We'd spent the weekend at Hilton Head Island and I'd forgotten to rub sunscreen on your nose. I could feel William kicking and turning inside of me when the kind stranger snapped the picture.

The puppy, if you remember, had served as a negotiating tool in a minor squabble your dad and I had been having with you. For months, you wanted a puppy, citing the usual promises all kids tend to make. You told me at least three times a day: "It will be all my responsibility. I'll potty-train him. I'll walk him every day after school. You and Daddy won't have to do a thing. I already have a name picked out. I'm calling him Teddy." I'm sure you figured out that the pronounced dimples that appeared right below the corner of your lip when you begged for something usually tipped the scales in your favor.

It wasn't that I didn't want a dog. It was the adding of another thing to my to-do list. I didn't feel like myself and hadn't for the past few weeks. I was always tired and sick to my stomach. I knew your dad worried that my depression had returned. That wasn't it, but I couldn't argue the point much when something as simple as a coffee commercial sent me running for a Kleenex.

After weeks of throwing up at the smell of anything sizzling in a frying pan, I scheduled an appointment with our family physician. It was during that visit that I found out I was ten weeks pregnant with William.

I'd given up on having another baby. I knew Paul was right. The aftereffects of my first pregnancy had taken a toll on me and on our marriage. The baby blues from having you had lasted too long to be considered normal. I'd consented to see a psychiatrist after Daddy found you (I think you were around nine months old) crying in your crib, your onesie soaked halfway up your back with urine, while I sat in front of the TV, engulfed in the latest episode of Guiding Light. *I hadn't held you all day.*

"Pregnant?" I said to the doctor when he gave me the news. "That wasn't supposed to happen."

The doctor gently squeezed my left foot as he listened to me from the end of the exam table. He squirted something on his fingers and asked, "I take it this baby is a surprise?"

"A big one." I closed my eyes and tried to breathe slowly in and out through my nose.

He finished my exam and then sat down on the rolling stool beside me. I watched the black ink flow from his stainless-steel fountain pen, documenting the truth I didn't yet want to accept. Another baby. The ends of my fingers tingled as I struggled to catch my breath.

The truth is I never thought I wanted to be a mother. I never once had the desire to hold or dress or rock anyone else's baby, cooing at how cute and how tiny his or her fingers were. In no way did I ever share this intimate information with anyone, especially not your dad or the women in our church—most of whom already had their nurseries decorated with spindly monkey

*mobiles and matching safari borders well before their white sticks
turned blue.*

*"When are you and the pastor going to start your family?"
they'd ask me, when it was my turn to watch the newborns
during the morning service. I wondered if something was wrong
with me, or if I lacked the gene that made the women around me
feel whole.*

*My youthful lack of desire haunts me now, keeping me awake at
night questioning myself and taunting me for something I know
I did not do, could never do. I'm not sure why I'm sharing this with
you now, but I feel I have to. I probably won't get another chance for
you to know who I was before all of this.*

*After a few days the initial shock wore off. I couldn't help being
excited. Many times, Paul and I had second-guessed our decision
not to have any more children, but mentally I was now in a much
better place. I knew by the way you cuddled up against me on the
sofa and rubbed your bare toes against mine—I'd turned into an
excellent mother.*

*"PTA-perfect," Paul teased me. "Best blue-ribbon bake-sale
brownies in the entire school district." I hadn't needed medication
in years.*

*I prayed your dad would be happy about the pregnancy. I thought
about wrapping a Carolina-blue baby blanket and a box of Huggies
as a way to deliver the news but decided against it, fearing you
might walk into the room.*

*Instead, I thought of a more foolproof approach. I still get tears
when I think of Paul—his suit coat draped over his shoulder,
sweating, exhausted from another contentious elders' meeting—
going to the mailbox as he did every day on his way in from work
and finding a letter addressed to My Daddy.*

On yellow-and-blue polka-dotted stationery, I'd
written:

Dear Daddy,

I hope you don't mind, but sometime around early
September, I'm going to need a place to live. Also going to
need all the usual things, like a bassinet, rattle, bottles, and
lots of diapers. Don't know the exact day of my arrival, but
I plan to stay with you for many years. Hope that's okay.

Love, Your Kid (name and gender to be decided)

I sat on the front porch swing, watching to see Paul's reaction.
Minutes later we sat together, holding each other, crying and
thanking God for this unexpected miracle.
Eleven-year-old you, who had been eavesdropping from behind
the screen door, whined, "Does this mean I don't get my puppy?"

xoxox

MY DAILY ROUTINE DOESN'T VARY MUCH HERE. Morning wake-up is at
5 a.m. on the dot when the meal cart squeaks down the hallway. The
bright fluorescent lights pop on in stages, first flickering, then buzzing,
making it impossible for me to sleep. I roll out of bed with little time to
empty my bladder before a tray of two link sausages, a slice of wheat
toast, and one hard-boiled egg forcibly enters the slit in my front door.
The tray stays for thirty minutes before, finished or unfinished, I have
to push it back through and it makes its way on the clanky transporta-

tion cart to the kitchen dishwasher to get ready for a revisit at 10:30 and 4:00.

When I first arrived at Lakeland, I barely ate. The infirmary placed me on medical watch after my weight dropped by twenty-two pounds. I knew I didn't have a pound to lose, but I couldn't force myself to eat. How could I, after what I'd been accused of doing? I wanted to die. It's ironic how now the tables have completely turned.

The warden and the infirmary nurse followed the rules and made sure I didn't die. I found it morbidly humorous that the people who would eventually observe my death now forced me to stay alive, recording every morsel I put in my mouth, meal by meal. After a few months, the prison doctor put me back on antidepressants.

Every day after breakfast, I pick up my Bible and read a Psalm. I have to check and double-check to make sure my favorite picture of Sophie and William are being guarded between the pages of Psalm 91. A favorite of Paul's. My Psalm of protection.

Every morning I say this prayer for you: "Father, thank you for letting me sit beside you and talk about my Sophie. I trust you with my daughter. Please keep your eyes on her. I know your huge outstretched arms are protecting her, and she is perfectly safe. I will fear no disaster during the day because your faithfulness will protect her. Guide her where evil can't get close to her. Thank you for the angels that are guarding her and holding on to her for dear life. I know you are giving her the best of care. Thank you for giving her a long life and please, somehow, let her make her way back to me. Amen."

I bank on that prayer as others do an insurance policy. I have to trust that someone is taking care of you. I study the photo again before I tuck William, in his blue-and-white sailor outfit, and you, in your pastel-purple ballerina tutu, safely away.

I'm not mad at God, in case you're wondering. I hope you aren't, either. This IS NOT what I planned for myself, or for our family, but I've adjusted. I've turned my outcome over to the One who created me, and placed my hope in the only One who can save me. He gives my heart new guts when it doesn't have the strength to beat another beat.

"Stand for count," an officer yells at me through the door. I stand facing the door as I do every hour on the hour when I'm confined to my room. Not that I could be anywhere else, but those in command need to write down a number and make sure each inmate is still breathing.

"Shower day. Be ready in ten," he orders. I know he means it. Hygiene is a privilege and can be taken away. I found that out the first week when I was too slow to follow an officer's orders and I wasn't allowed to shower for two weeks.

I pull my dark-brown-and-gray "highlighted" hair into a loose bun, which is a style I've grown accustomed to since coming to prison. Calling the gray "highlights" makes it seem like a choice instead of a reminder that the pages of my calendar are turning even though I am standing still. I wish the prison commissary sold Clairol.

Grandma Pearl—I wish you could've met her—was the one who taught me how to cut, color, and curl hair at an early age. Lack of money made trips to a salon few and far between, and it's come in handy here, too. She also, as you well know, taught me how to sew. She made all my clothes when I was young, just like I made all of yours. You weren't so happy with the situation, as I remember, and made no effort to conceal your discontent. I tried to reason with you, explaining that Paul was the pastor of a small church with an even tinier budget, and I didn't get paid for cleaning our toilets and

*carting you back and forth to school, but you didn't get it. I'm not
sure you really ever understood, but I eventually stopped arguing
and stopped sewing. Our small savings bought you clothes we
couldn't afford, but I think it made you happy. We wanted you to be
happy. Are you happy?*

"Shower time," the officer says to me. I gather my soap and shampoo
and wait for my door to open. I can't change my situation, and I have
come to terms with that fact, but I'm not going to stop hoping. I'm not
going to stop praying. The rest of my days will be spent saving the only
thing I care about saving—my relationship with Sophie.

SOPHIE

Normal people cringe when the phone rings in the middle of the night. Maybe Sophie startled at unexpected calls when she was younger—she couldn't remember—but after being married to a doctor for almost five years, she didn't jump when the phone rang or when the annoying sound of Thomas's pager turned her dreams into a random game show in which she was constantly running toward a beeping sound she could never quite reach.

Thomas, usually exhausted from a hectic day of surgeries, slept without acknowledging the first round of *beep . . . beep . . . beep*. After two minutes—and yes, Sophie had timed this—if Thomas hadn't responded, a closer, longer, higher-pitched *beeep . . . beeep . . . beeep . . .* had him searching the nightstand for his pager.

If he was totally knocked out—or in a surgery-induced coma, as Sophie liked to call it—the pager would sequence through to its final passive-aggressive demand and launch into a solid ear-piercing *beeeeeeep*. Similar, Sophie guessed, to the sound family members heard when a heart stopped beating and the hospital monitor flatlined.

So early that morning when the pager went off, she assumed the usual—the hospital, calling for Thomas. Another consult, an infected suture, or a new nurse scared to make an independent decision. Whatever the case, he would listen, give orders, then roll over and they'd both go back to sleep. Thomas was good about keeping work matters at work.

But this time was different. Neither of them had slept well. Thomas had tossed around so much since returning from the hospital after midnight, the silk sheets had pulled off the mattress corners on his side of the bed.

He hadn't discussed the case with Sophie in detail, mumbling only generic things like "allergic reaction" or "possible infection," but she knew that he was bothered by this little girl's death, and not only on a professional level.

She hadn't seen him this way before. When his pager beeped at 4:51 a.m., she wasn't sure he'd ever fallen fully asleep. Something about last night had also triggered feelings and memories for her that she tried desperately to push from her mind. William's contagious giggle played in her mind like an old breakup song on the radio. She saw his face, too. His head full of white-blond twisted hair. The twinkle in his sea-blue eyes and how his neck disappeared when he belly-laughed. The smell of his miniature toes sprinkled with baby powder and the acceptance of his tiny fingers around hers. Fragments of her life Sophie had tried hard to forget.

"Geez, Sophie, I feel like I'm in a damn straitjacket," he snapped, as he grabbed the beeper and called the hospital back. "This is Dr. Logan. Somebody paged me," he said curtly to the voice on the other end.

Sophie flopped her head back against her pillow, then sat up. She hated it when Thomas became angry. He didn't get mad often, and rarely at her, but when he did she took the blame and tried to fix the problem. She motioned for Thomas to stand so she could tuck in the bottom layer of sheets around the whole bed.

"Wound care," Thomas repeated, still on the phone, "third-degree burns." He scribbled the patient's name on his hospital list lying beside the bed. "Okay, thanks. Can you put his nurse on the phone, please?"

"You doing okay?" she asked as they both returned to bed.

"Well, I need a haircut before we leave for my parents' house," he said with a slight grin, avoiding her question as he ran his fingers through his thick hair. Sophie loved his wavy, ink-black hair, and the more of it the better. She hated it when he cut his hair, and Thomas knew it. When it was long, slightly touching the neckline of his T-shirt, it accentuated the sharp angles of his jawbone.

"Stop torturing me," she teased. Her pleas were interrupted by another page.

"This is going to be a long day," Thomas said, and groaned. He looked at his pager and picked up his cell phone.

AFTER THOMAS LEFT, SOPHIE WENT on her usual morning run. She started down her brick-paved driveway and through the columned flagstone posts that announced their residence. She'd been slightly overwhelmed when she first moved into a house with such large columns: they made her think of big exclamation points that shouted, "Hey, these people live in a gigantic house!"

West Lake subdivision was considered, by anyone's standards, elite. It consisted of older homes that all had a European Old World elegance to them. Many of the homes were occupied by older couples, retired, who rode in golf carts and sipped sangria at the clubhouse. Some privileged couples were younger, some with kids, some not. All lawns were perfectly landscaped and most had circular driveways that highlighted a tiered fountain or sculpted trees that looked as though they were posing.

Growing up in her small town of Brookfield, Sophie knew no one who'd had a house half as nice as the ones that now surrounded her. Her parents' two-bedroom, one-bath house could have easily fit into the garage of most of these.

Her mom, to her credit, had made the most of what they had. Sophie imagined if the cards had been dealt differently, her mom could have had a show on HGTV demonstrating how to make curtains out of a pair of old blue jeans, or a hundred different ways to decorate with wildflowers and canning jars. Sophie's childhood was not luxurious, but there was a time when it had been beautiful.

Her only true childhood friend was named Jillian, and she hadn't talked to her since they both graduated from high school. Jillian, a part of the pre-Thomas era, knew all about Sophie's family and loved her anyway. Sophie thought about calling her but dismissed the idea. Too much time had passed, too many conversations missed. And a wedding invitation that never got mailed.

Sophie hadn't known whether she could trust Jillian to keep her secrets. To keep the lie that popped out of her mouth the first time Thomas asked Sophie about her family.

"Gone. I have no one."

"No one?" She saw sadness in his eyes. He touched her hand, and for the first time she put her hand in his.

"No." This part was true. "My dad died of a heart attack right before I graduated high school.

"My mom," her first lie to Thomas began, "died of cancer when I was twelve. No siblings."

She wanted to tell him the truth, but it was too soon. Too early in a relationship to delve into her story of murder and abandonment. She would accept his sadness instead of his pity, take his compassion to avoid humiliation. She planned to tell him; if this relationship progressed anywhere, she would tell him. But for right then, she'd told herself, she needed to move on. She had to forget.

One kiss turned into dozens, and before she could find a way to tell Thomas the truth, he had told his parents. About her, about everything. They showered her with gifts when Thomas took her to meet them over Christmas break.

Oh, what a tangled web we weave when first we practice to deceive, Sophie's mom used to tell her. She loved to quote famous people. Sir Walter Scott was her go-to guy for honesty. *Your word is everything,* her mother emphasized. Sophie wondered if her mom had choked on that adage.

She checked her watch to decide how far she could run this morning. She had time to run her usual three miles, three full laps around the outer streets of West Lake if she cut over through the country club and ran around the pond. Her legs felt heavy after she made her first lap—worn out from lack of sleep. She mustered the will not to give up and turn around so early in the workout. *Two more miles, and then tackle my marathon to-do list.* The sooner she finished, the more she could accomplish on the fund-raiser. She picked up her pace, sprinting faster than she ever had around the pond and up the steep hill that bordered the golf course at the club.

The chocolate-brown Lab who sat watch in the courtyard at the front of Mindy's house barked as she approached the top of the hill. She knew she should check on Mindy, but her mounting to-do list overshadowed her nagging sense of right and wrong.

Her mom's old lesson rang in her head: "Friends need each other."

"Hey, Murphy." Sophie panted as she slowed down and petted the top of the dog's head. He was the sole beneficiary of the bacon treat she had tucked in her Dri-FIT Nike running jacket. The bank teller handed out either lollipops or dog treats. Since Sophie didn't have a two-year-old, she took the bacon treat.

Murphy always waited for Sophie. As soon as he saw her coming up the hill, he assumed the give-me-a-treat position. Upper-class dog etiquette, Sophie had thought when he first demonstrated his new trick. His head pointed straight up in proper form while his tail remembered the pound he'd come from. His quick wiggle made Sophie smile. *Best part of my run,* she thought as she tossed the treat over her shoulder and started to move again.

"Sophie." She turned around and saw Mindy in a butter-colored bathrobe standing on her front steps. Her eyes were swollen. "Can you talk?"

"Sure. Long time no see," Sophie said in a lighter-than-appropriate tone. "You okay?"

"I hope to be." Mindy wiped her nose with a crumpled Kleenex. "He left me. Stephen left me. I don't think he's coming back."

AN HOUR AND A HALF later, Sophie returned home to an empty house and her bulging list of things to get done. She wished she'd known the magic words to help Mindy feel better, to stop crying, or at least to help her make sense of the situation. Phrases like "I'm sure this will work out" or "He'll cool down and realize what he's throwing away" hadn't seemed to comfort her. Stephen was probably gone for good, Mindy's life would be altered forever, and nothing Sophie did or didn't say would change that.

She took a quick shower and towel-dried her hair. If she let her hair air-dry, she could make a few calls before heading to Thomas's office. She hoped she could eat lunch with him before heading to solicit donors at the hospital. She pulled out her white button-down shirt and navy blazer, and sifted through the bottom hanging rack of her closet before pulling out her dark skinny jeans.

Okay, where to start? She glanced at the top of Thomas's organized desk sitting angled in the corner of the study. Medical journals, fountain pens, and paper clips all had their place and stayed in perfect order. Her stack of unopened mail, the latest issue of *InStyle* magazine, and the Secret Chef fund-raiser notes did not; all were perched on the red-and-white paisley chair, hungry and vying for her attention.

She decided to blow-dry in lieu of phone calls so she could simultaneously sort through the mail. She pulled a trash can close while she turned the dryer on at the warmest setting. *Flyer about tire sale, throw away. Water bill, keep. Pest control, keep. Heart Ball invitation—definitely throw away. Second thought, keep. Thomas said we needed to go this year.*

The last piece of mail came from an address Sophie didn't recognize, from a name she had never heard. Her hands started to tremble as she examined the hand-addressed envelope with the name *Mrs. Sophie Logan* written across the front. Someone from her hometown was trying to get in touch with her and apparently now they knew where she lived.

GRACE

"Bend over, Bradshaw," ordered the badge conducting the strip search. "Spread 'em and cough."

I had never been completely naked in front of anyone before coming to prison. My husband, of course, but even then I asked Paul to turn off the lights. Besides my doctor, he'd been the only one to touch me, to see my most intimate places. In here, every crevice was open to the elements and on display for officers, male or female, to examine anytime I left my cell. During those moments, shame replaced modesty and my self-worth took a beating.

My first strip search after coming to Lakeland was the worst. My identity no longer existed. The former Grace Bradshaw became prisoner #44607 and the second woman on South Carolina's death row. My peer group had one thing in common: we had all murdered someone, or at least been falsely convicted of doing so.

During that first search, I stood naked in front of two correctional officers while they documented every square inch of my body as though they were inspecting livestock at the county fair.

"Raise your left arm," said the female intake officer. She scrutinized my armpit, and I remembered I hadn't shaved.

"Now your right arm." She scribbled something with her red pen.

"Bend over, spread your cheeks, and cough," ordered the male officer helping with the search. "Cough again."

"Lift your breasts." He put on his latex gloves. "One at a time."

Was this happening to me? I started to feel hot and off-balance, like the floor was tilting and about to give away.

The male officer made a quick, deliberate swipe under each of my breasts.

"Turn around. Lean over," he said. My eyes focused on his unreadable, black-chipped name tag. "Put your head down and shake your hair." His fingers raked through my tangled, sweaty hair.

The other officer shook white powder over my head. "Lice shampoo." I tried not to inhale.

I no longer belonged to myself.

"Straighten up, spread your legs," he ordered. "Okay, now squat three times."

"Cough . . . cough again," commanded the female officer as she looked between my crouched legs, checking to see whether anything fell out.

"Any birthmarks?" asked the male officer.

I pointed him to the two-inch pear-shaped pale red spot that has occupied the space between my shoulder blades since birth. A favorite spot of my husband's. In here, another thing to document. Paul used to outline "the stork bite," as he called it, with his index finger just before he kissed me there.

The female officer moved from my backside to my front lower half, documenting the two-inch-thick raised scar below my left knee. She must have been describing it in great detail, judging by the amount she was writing. No one asked, but for the record, it happened in the sixth grade when I fell out of my tire swing. A birthday present from my dad after I proclaimed my old metal swing set too embarrassing for a twelve-year-old. *Hold still, Gracie girl.* He examined my injury while my mom dripped stinging droplets of Mercurochrome on my bleeding shin. *Why didn't that square knot hold?*

On both sides of my belly button were stretch marks that started and stopped like faded zebra stripes. Ugly to most, I supposed, but to me they were trophies. Reminders of Sophie and William and how they'd grown inside me. I'm not sure whether the officers wrote those down or not.

"No tattoos?"

I almost laughed. I hadn't even gotten my ears pierced until age twenty-five. I shook my head.

At the time, I didn't think I would ever get used to this humiliation. Was I used to it? Thousands of strip searches later, I simply complied. I had to. I had to adapt. Even when it went against my own best interests.

When the latest search was over, I pulled up my oversize gray pants and adjusted my underwear the best I could with my hands in cuffs. The prison uniform, all gray for the general population, came in only two sizes—too big or too small. Today, I was wearing the former, and the bottoms hung a good four inches past the length of my legs. The top half, which swallowed me, was orange and signaled to the rest of the prison population that I was a death row inmate.

"Get moving. The clock is ticking." The officer pointed to his watch.

"Yes, sir," I replied, avoiding eye contact, anything to put this behind me.

"Your turn," the officer commanded, turning his attention to Roni, the next in line, who'd been perched on the other side of the four-by-four inspection cubicle, her bleached, stringy hair draped so it covered her eyes. "Don't give me that look. We can do this the easy way or the hard way."

Don't make this harder on yourself, Roni. I counted the tiles while I walked to the guards who would escort me to my job. My pants bunched beneath my black rubber slippers. As hard as strip searches were on me, I knew they were worse on Roni. I could tell by the way she recoiled when the officers put on their latex gloves and searched her for contraband. Her body had been rummaged through before and without her permission. We were adaptable, but sometimes Roni just had to fight back.

If you'd asked me what I wanted to be when I grew up, I can guarantee you my answer wouldn't have been working at the Live or Dye Beauty Salon located within the picturesque gates of Lakeland State Penitentiary. My career path didn't go as planned, but let me fill you in on how climbing the corporate ladder works, prison-style.

My first few years of no disciplinary actions earned me the privilege of working within the unit. A coveted position that paid me seventy-two cents a day, but it gave me a productive reason to get out of bed each morning. First, I was assigned to janitorial duties, where I pushed dirt, strands of hair, and wad of paper around with a long-handled broom. I'd count, in my head as I swept, the number of days it'd take me to buy you a present, maybe a sequined prom dress or a new pair of dark denim jeans. I mopped the floors in front of each cell and soaked up the drippings from the daily overflowed toilets each day. After that was done, I scrubbed unidentifiable food and bodily substances off the cinder-block walls, earning me $14.40 a month in my commissary account. Not much, but it was enough to buy toothpaste and shampoo, which I was grateful for. Following my tenth year on the row, and since I had an impeccable behavior record, the warden allowed me to work in the beauty salon located between cell block A and death row, a five-minute handcuffed-and-shackled walk I took twice a month. I was overjoyed to have a job most inmates considered "Cadillac" (easy and enjoyable). Plus, I got to interact with the general population. The pay stayed the same, but I didn't care. Guarded by two flanking officers, I could hold scissors, cut and shampoo hair, even wax an occasional eyebrow.

Roni happened to be my first client earlier today.

She plopped down in the gray swivel chair with her hands still cuffed and her face spotted with flat red patches that started below her cheek-bones and trailed down her neck.

After a few huffs and failed attempts to get her waistband straightened on her pants, she finally spoke to me. "You remind me of my mama. You have the same-shaped mouth. Not the same smart tongue, though."

I kept an eye on the scissors while I Velcroed the black smock over Roni's orange top. I always gauged her face before I responded, the way I would test the water temperature with my toes before I stepped into a full bathtub—slowly but surely—because proceeding too quickly and without caution could get me some scorching results.

"What do you want done today?" The red blotches had faded to pale pink, so I took that as a sign it was okay to change the subject.

Roni was the newest and youngest (age twenty-three) occupant on the row. She'd spent the first few months not talking, not looking at anyone, refusing to eat, and showering only when forced. Her unoccupied eyes, disheveled peroxide-blond hair, and incoherent mumblings made her big-boned stature even more threatening. When it came right down to it, she was a shell of a person, really, with a soul that had crawled somewhere else. Scared of its own shelter, I had to guess.

I hoped she'd adjust and not go mad like some in here had been known to do. Her vacancy made some sense to me—no one taught you how to make a life for yourself in prison, but the prison staff viewed Roni's acts of withdrawal as defiant and disrespectful. Not a good way to live out your time on death row.

Lately, she'd started to come around. She would leave her cell on occasion to sit in the common dayroom that was the nucleus of the women's death row housing unit. There, we orange-shirted inmates could congregate to watch TV or make our weekly fifteen-minute phone calls. This earned social time occurred from 10 a.m. to 10 p.m. and could be withdrawn at any moment for any reason, or for no reason at all.

After six consecutive months without disciplinary action, she was allowed a haircut. I was thrilled the first time I was able to get a wide-tooth comb near her thick head of hair, which today was now black at the top and brassy only on the bottom third.

"Two inches and no more," she said today with conviction. She pointed to the back of her ponytail.

I nodded and used my index finger and thumb to confirm Roni's measurements. I rolled her over to the shampoo bowl and turned the water on, running my hands underneath until the temperature was warm enough.

I could tell by the way Roni shook her foot and stiffened her back when she spoke about her family members that their relationships were not good. I avoided asking any questions, fearing this haircut might be my last. Roni, though, with every haircut, seemed to want to tell me things, painful things that had been shoved and stomped so far down they were scraping to get out.

"You don't look like someone who would kill their kid," she said as I towel-dried her hair. She scrutinized my reflection in the plastic-coated mirror.

I knew to most people I was no more than the words stamped on my prison record, but coming from a lady convicted of hacksawing her stepfather, mother, and first cousin, and then hiding them piece by piece, duct-taped and plastic-wrapped, in a basement freezer, I viewed this veiled compliment as a smidgen judgmental.

Not that I hadn't been surprised how normal-looking the other women on death row were. Women like Carmen, with her puffed southern hair and wrinkled hands, or Jada, with her cleft chin and scent like bubble gum—both average enough to have worked beside you in a cubicle answering questions about which bed-and-breakfast you should stay at on your vacation or what was the best way to make fluffy mashed potatoes instead of the pasty ones I'd been known to make. Women who, if given the right tools—a sober mother to tuck them into bed at night, a father who kept his hands to himself—might be working at the makeup counter at the mall instead of living in a cage with all the freedom afforded to a rabid animal.

In the food chain of convicts, I'm valued alongside termites and small rodents. A child killer. Categorized as even more despicable than the group of perverts who'd molested neighborhood children waiting alone for the school bus. I was long past trying to convince others of my innocence—of the love I'd had and still had for my family, of the good mother I'd so desperately tried to be. In prison, lies, justifications, and excuses were as common as dry skin in the winter. Instead, I focused on what I could control, such as how I treated others and the kind words I spoke.

"You think I'm evil?" Roni asked me as she checked the ends of her hair to make sure they were even. She freely admitted to anyone who asked she was 100 percent guilty, deserved to die, and didn't have an ounce of remorse in her.

"My on-and-off-again stepfather screwed me every chance he could," she'd told me once, "and my mama knew it. My birthday present on the night I turned five. That bastard and my poor excuse for a mother deserved to die. My cousin was collateral damage. Saved her from another night with him, too."

I hesitated before speaking. I placed my hand on Roni's shoulder, using my back as a shield to obscure my touch from the officers. "Your stepfather did a bad thing. Your mom did worse."

I thought about you as I was doing Roni's hair. Did you share your story with the lady blow-drying your hair?

"My mom was arrested when I turned twelve. I practically raised myself."

I wondered if your words produced tears or if you'd told the story so often the sharpness had worn off.

"I'm so sorry," I imagined the faceless lady replying as she turned off the dryer and stroked your damp hair, "you had such a bad childhood."

I looked at Roni's reflection in the mirror and said with the only truth I could speak with certainty, "I see much good in you."

Her face, scarred with deep pits from anger and acne, briefly softened, and I caught a glimpse of an innocent child whose own mother never loved her.

After my last client of the day, I washed out the sink and swept the curly and straight hair into a dustpan, while the two officers bantered back and forth their predictions for the upcoming Thanksgiving bowl games. I handed the scissors back to the officer standing closest to me and watched as he locked them away in a white Formica drawer that held razors and sterilized thin black combs.

I wondered what your hair felt like, and if your honey-gold hair was still curly like your dad's or straight like mine. What did it smell like? Our home had been nothing like Roni's, but I feared your scars cut just as deep.

I returned to my cell and knew I had to write all of this down for you. My hands are weary, and my feet are cramping, but my mind is boiling over. I have no possessions to distribute, no finances to arrange, no funeral to plan, but I still have affairs to put in order. I need to stamp my place in this world even after I no longer belong to it: I am here! I matter! And most important, I need for you to know you matter.

SOPHIE

Sophie could feel the panic creeping across her face as she stared at the unopened letter. She had finally gotten to a place where she could move forward and make plans, leaving that degrading part of her life padlocked and buried with the rest of her family. Why was someone trying to take that from her?

Well, she wasn't going to let them. She was going to see Thomas before her hospital visit, as she had planned. He should be finishing with his last patient by then and maybe the two of them could grab lunch before he left to do afternoon rounds.

She folded the envelope in half and then in half again. Thomas wouldn't accidentally find the letter if she tucked it in her makeup bag, but he might if she stuffed it under last month's water bill or in an old shoe box under the bed. She couldn't take any chances, so right between her Fairly Medium powder foundation and her Perplexingly Pink lip gloss lay her secret. Her makeup, she thought, as she zipped the bag, was just as confused as the rest of her.

When she pulled her car into the physicians' parking lot at the back of Thomas's building, she realized she didn't even remember driving there. She parked next to him in the reserved area. *Perks of being a doctor's wife,* she thought every time she slid her key card through the gate.

Thomas's office was modern, to say the least, and not like other doctors' offices Sophie was used to. Gone were the standard plastic-coated waiting-room chairs, the muted tones of the previous decorating era. This waiting room had red suede sofas with square metal frames and backs with clean, shiny lines. Large plasma-screen TVs hung on the walls on the perimeter of the room. A calculated visual buffet advertised what you could have: full, pouty lips; tight, round butt; bigger breasts. The words *Cutting-Edge* and *Why Not Now?* popped up between images.

"First impressions are everything," Thomas explained to Sophie when she first toured his office. "Clients need to be thinking about potential when they walk in and perfection when they walk out." Sophie felt the need to check herself for wrinkles every time she visited.

An unfamiliar face greeted her when she approached the front desk; the usual receptionist must have been on vacation.

"May I help you?" the chipper twentysomething receptionist with perfect white teeth and a tight button-down asked.

"I'm Sophie. Sophie Logan."

"Oh, Dr. Logan's wife," the girl said, looking up. She analyzed Sophie's appearance before speaking.

"Yes. Is he finished seeing patients?"

"Last one just left before you walked in, but I think he's busy, uh, in a meeting."

"Thanks," Sophie replied, in a way that said *I'm not asking for your permission.* She opened the waiting-room door and walked down the hallway.

The door to Thomas's office was closed, so she opted to sit in a small waiting area outside a consultation room. She was bold enough to refuse orders from a temp at the front desk, but not as audacious when it came to interrupting Thomas's workday.

She checked the time on her phone. She had a little more than an hour before she had to get to the hospital. She hoped his meeting would finish soon and they'd have time to eat together.

She glanced around the room, investigating the information that lay on the brushed-metal coffee tables. Before-and-after pictures of clients documented the skills of Dr. Thomas Logan. She was most impressed with the book titled *Body Contouring After Weight Loss*, which featured picture after picture of patients once overtaken by excess skin, modeling their new sculpted bodies. Two thumbs up to them and to Thomas.

She checked her watch again. Forty-five minutes before she needed to leave. She picked up a magazine and skimmed the articles. "Redefining Gravity—There Is Hope for the Sagging Breast" or "Under-Eye Puffiness: Is It Temporary or Genetic?" Neither looked interesting, but the word *genetic* caused her insides to swerve.

Did her mom still look the same? Were the tops of her hands still soft? She shook her head and tried to make the memories stop, but they wouldn't go away.

The last time she'd visited, Sophie had tried her best to force excitement. "I received my cap and gown today." One of the happy, but not really happy, events Sophie saved up to help her mom feel better and make her seem involved.

Through the glass, she'd watched her mom lower her head.

"I wish you could be there, too." Then Sophie hung up the phone because their time was up.

"Can I get you anything?" Front Desk Girl said to Sophie after the second time she'd circled the room.

"No, I'm still fine," she replied. "Don't need a thing."

"Just checking." The girl pretended to straighten some magazines on the coffee table before leaving the room.

No sign of movement from Thomas's office, so Sophie opened her purse and dug out the folded letter from her makeup bag. Eleven years ago, she'd walked out on everyone who resided in her past and resigned from the second-rate position of making her mother happy. She wouldn't pick that job back up now.

Surely Thomas's office had a shredder. She stood and started to look around for it, but the remembrance of her mom's heartrending face stopped her. She ripped open the envelope.

Dear Mrs. Logan:

I hope this letter finds you well. I've been trying to locate you for quite some time on behalf of your mother, Mrs. Grace Bradshaw. Mrs. Bradshaw asked that I contact you and inform you of her changing status. This is a very urgent matter. Please contact me at (334) 232-2549 as soon as possible.

Regards,
Ben Taylor

The words blended on the paper and then blurred together. *Urgent matter . . . changing status.* Sophie felt nauseated.

Status? What did that even mean? She accepted the fact that her mom was still on death row, but her dad had always said a case this shaky would never survive the appeals process. "Your mom will not die in prison," he'd said, while he folded a load of once-white bath towels.

Maybe she's getting out. Sophie didn't know what to do with that possibility, either. Her necklace with an *S* monogram started to feel like it was strangling her.

Voices were coming from Thomas's office. She shoved the letter back into the envelope and crumpled them both in her purse.

"What are you doing here?" Thomas said, after emerging and doing a double take.

When she didn't answer right away, he said, "Are you okay?"

"I'm fine. I needed to pick up a donor list. For the benefit. And I wanted to see if you had time for lunch."

"Sorry, Soph. I've already eaten." His tone was apologetic as he gestured back to his door.

Eva emerged from his office, dressed in silver heels and a navy skirt. In her hands was a crinkled-up deli bag.

"Oh, hello," she said to Sophie before she turned her back and darted into the restroom.

Sophie forced herself to gather her thoughts before speaking, though she knew the look on her face must scream *appalled*. "What is she doing here?" she finally said after Thomas didn't offer any explanation.

Before he could answer, the temp girl came bolting down the hallway. "I'm going to lunch. Be sure and check your messages. Isabel Campor's family called you again."

"UM, I PICK ALEXIS," SAID MOLLY. The rest of the class snorted and giggled.

Her PE teacher ignored the taunts just like the rest of her teachers did. "Well, that just leaves you. Go and join the blue team." Sophie walked across the expansive gymnasium and through the sneers and snickers. "Maybe she'll have her mom's killer instinct," one boy mocked, before she finally found a place to sit down.

God knows she had trust issues, but right now, as she ran into St. John's Hospital for her donor meeting, she didn't know what made her want to scream more—the letter from her mom's attorney or the lacy pink bra under Eva's thin white shirt.

Her cell phone had rung at least three times. She assumed the calls were from Thomas, but she didn't look or answer. She couldn't trust the words ready to fly out of her mouth when she felt this upset.

He'd managed to give her a quick kiss on the cheek before mumbling something about Eva bringing by lunch while she dropped off some drug samples. She didn't wait for him to finish his explanation or for Eva to return from the bathroom; instead, she told him she was late for a meeting and left.

Sophie's phone rang again as she walked through the hospital lobby. The caller ID read *St. John's Hospital*, so she decided to answer.

"Thank God," Mindy said. "You have a minute?"

"Barely. I'm trying to grab someone from the hospital advisory board to see if we can finalize some donor numbers for the fund-raiser."

"I'm probably not supposed to share this information, but Max has a high fever. He's been asking for you."

MAX LOOKED SO HELPLESS when Sophie entered his room. His damp hair and flushed cheeks made her ache. His oxygen apparatus inhaled and exhaled in the background.

His frail, dependent body made her think of William. He'd lain help-less, too. Her mom praying at his bedside, her father crying, begging baby William to pull through. But he hadn't, they hadn't. Sophie had sat in the corner, trying to memorize her spelling words, willing this all to go away. *C-a-p-i-t-a-l-i-z-e.*

The back of her shoulders and her neck started to tighten. She hadn't felt this angry in a long time. Mad at all this suffering, even madder at those who inflicted it. Her mom. Max's mom. At least his mom hadn't made him sick. She'd just abandoned him when he was.

Sophie took a white terry washcloth from the stack of linens sitting on Max's bedside table and walked over to the sink to wet it. When she turned off the water she heard a little raspy voice say, "Sosie?" His frail body was working hard to speak.

"Hi, little man." She placed the wet cloth on his forehead. "I heard you're not feeling so well."

She dragged a dark-stained rocking chair from the corner of the room. The edges were jagged and chipped, revealing raw wood. A pastel patch-work quilt lay over the back of the chair, and the tag read: *Made especially for Max with love: From your friends at the Hospital Auxiliary.*

"Rock me," Max said as he held out his arms. "Read wabbit book."

Intertwined lines connected his fragile body to machines. The blood-pressure cuff squeezed his arm, leaving it white, then red. Sophie put her hand under his bed and searched for the button to release the side rail. Her actions slow, so she wouldn't disconnect anything.

"Scoot over, little man. If you can't come to Sosie, then Sosie will come to you."

Max flashed the biggest grin he could muster. Sophie maneuvered under the IV tube and over the call button and climbed in bed beside him.

"Where do we begin?" She picked up the tattered hospital copy of *The Velveteen Rabbit*.

She read to page six before realizing she was more into the book than Max was. His eyes fought hard to stay focused.

"You need to rest now, Max."

"Sosie have to go?"

"I'll lie with you until you fall asleep." She rubbed his wet head.

"Sing me song?"

Sophie wasn't sure how to handle this request. She hadn't sung a song to a child in a long time. She closed her eyes and tried to think.

Out of nowhere, the words came out slowly: "Hush little baby, don't say a word, momma's gonna buy you a mockingbird."

"That's a silly song."

"My mom used to sing to me." The memory came rushing back. Her mom holding her hair while she bent over the toilet. Her mom rocking her after her overly anxious stomach wouldn't settle. Singing that tune and those churchy lyrics to distract her so she'd feel better. *This little light of mine, I'm going to let it shine. Won't let Satan blow it out. I'm going to let it shine.* Her affection so warm and Sophie so protected. But now that night had a darker tint—what had she been sick from, really?

She won't make the mistake of being so trusting again. Blind trust belonged in her past. Nothing, she promised herself, would ever have that power over her again—especially not the veiled urgencies of this so-called important letter, or the disgusting advances by a synthetic drug rep.

She closed her eyes and continued singing as if her words could somehow bring back the mom she'd thought she knew, a mom both Max and William had deserved. "If that mockingbird don't sing, momma's going to buy you a diamond ring."

She tightened her hold on Max and hummed the rest of the forgotten lyrics until his sleepy head bobbed and landed safely on her shoulders.

GRACE

Do you remember the old wooden crate we used to pull out at Christmas? Your daddy would put that beat-up box beside the tree along with a small bale of hay. The neighbors thought we were crazy, but this tradition meant everything to me. Your grandma Pearl started it when I was a little girl, her parents before that.

Our "manger" sat empty until one of us did something love-worthy. When we were "caught," we could put a piece of hay in the manger. As a family, we were preparing Jesus's bed for his birth.

You decorated baby William's room with twenty-five paper-cutout snowflakes, diligently folded and cut each heart and triangle just to see his eyes squint when he woke from his nap. The manger became quite full that day.

Daddy threw in some hay when he came home from work and noticed that I'd run over his golf clubs with my new stick-shift station wagon. "At least you're okay," he said, as he tried to straighten the end of his putter.

You were watching in the background to see Daddy's reaction. When you saw him more concerned about me than about his golf clubs, you grabbed his hand and headed toward the manger. "Jesus's bed is going to be soft and warm this Christmas."

Over and over, I've rehearsed what I would say if I have the chance to see you again. One day, when your feelings have settled and your wounds have had a chance to heal, you will read this and see I'm not documenting my dying days in prison but recording the gifts I have been given while existing. You're one of the most precious.

I'm feeling restless tonight—I need to get out of this cell. If I stand on my tiptoes and angle my head just the right way, I can catch a glimpse of the digital clock hanging on the far wall of the dayroom. I try not to look, but for some reason, I can't stop myself. Ms. Liz, the prison chaplain, had promised to visit the dayroom this week. I hadn't seen her in a while, and wasn't sure she knew my news.

I've been thinking a lot about time lately. I guess running out of it will do that to a person. According to my mom, I used to "wish" my life away. "I can't wait to get a job and make my own money," I would tell her at least once a week. "Being a grown-up has to be so much better."

When I had you, and I didn't think I could stay awake one second longer, I begged for you to sleep through the night. When you screamed with colic, I counted the minutes until Paul would be home. Whole chunks of my life wished away because they required patience I didn't yet have.

I used to obsess about the time when I was first locked up. Did you know there are only 914 Saturdays from the time a child is born until they leave for college?

Did you go to college?

If I couldn't find a clock I would ask the officer, "Can you tell me the time, please?" Some would answer. Others would taunt me: "Have someplace you need to be, Bradshaw?"

My name still made the evening news back then, and I could tell from the one-word answers you gave me during our weekly phone call that sixth grade was not going well for you. Paul had written down your class schedule for me. At 11:55, if I could find a clock, I closed my eyes and prayed. Don't let Sophie sit alone at lunch, dear God, please don't let her sit alone . . .

At 6:15 p.m., I wondered what Paul was making for dinner. Did he have enough energy to help you with your homework?

After a while, I had to let those things go. My prayers still would go up, but the day-to-day worrying became too exhausting. Details of our family's lives I would never know because they were too many to recount in the fifteen minutes we were allowed on the phone. For sanity's sake, it was better not to try.

All I have to do is look around me to know time doesn't heal all wounds. If it did, maybe this place would have some happier hearts or some empty beds. And perhaps you'd be visiting me, pressing pictures on the glass and sharing with me the moments that made you smile or caused you to cry.

Passing time does nothing to heal our brokenness. It's the work we put into our mending that makes us well.

We shared 659 Saturdays together before I left our home. Only 26 of those included William. I want one more Saturday. I need time to fix us.

I'm going to ask Ms. Liz if she can bring in a manger. Any old box will do. I feel the need to do something love-worthy. I hope your bed is warm and soft tonight.

SOPHIE

"I'm looking forward to some cornbread stuffing and pecan pie," Thomas said, pulling into the passing lane.

Sophie pulled out the earbuds she'd put on an hour into the four-hour drive to Charleston, where Thomas's parents lived. The last few lines of Miranda Lambert's "Over You" trailed off faintly in her lap.

"Me, too." But after thinking about pencil-thin Eva, she decided she'd eat only turkey and a deviled egg.

They hadn't talked at all about her quick day-before exit or anything else of magnitude since Thomas had come home late last night. They'd both been tired and still had to pack. And weren't some secrets better off left unsaid?

"You okay, baby?" Thomas asked after they had been in the car more than an hour. His eyes met hers, and his question seemed sincere. "You're not saying much."

"I'm fine." She looked away, not giving him the chance to explore her silence any further. She couldn't remember the last time "fine" described her.

The mature part of Sophie knew she should in turn ask him how he was doing, how he felt since his patient died. Had he figured anything out? However, in this moment, the hold-a-grudge fraction of her took over and she remained silent. She put the earbuds in her ears and scrolled through her playlists.

Maybe she was being paranoid about Eva? She considered the possibility, then considered her state of mind. Her pink Prada purse, tucked between her feet, still hid the letter from her mother's lawyer.

She hadn't exactly been thinking clearly when Eva stepped out of Thomas's office. Drug reps visit doctors. That's what they do. And Eva, no matter how much Sophie despised her, was a drug rep. All five-foot-ten thin inches of her.

Sophie closed her eyes and attempted to "rise above" and "kill her with kindness," all the things her dad tried to instill in her after he became her moral compass. But even the thought of Eva irritated her.

"I'm still a little crazy about what happened at the hospital. You know, the little girl. I've never lost a patient before."

Sophie could hear him, but she wasn't sure he knew that. She chose to think about Max, praying his fever had broke.

Thomas stared straight ahead with both hands gripped tightly around the bottom of the steering wheel.

"Do you know what happened?" she asked, letting go of her punishment and, for the moment, her grudge.

"I'm not sure." He took one hand off the wheel and ran it through his hair. "I'm not. The hospital is going to review the case pending her autopsy. I brought my notes and whatever hospital records I could copy without looking suspicious. I thought maybe Dad and Carter could give me some advice."

Sophie nodded. Thomas's dad was a prominent cardiac surgeon who flew across the country and gave lectures to physicians on when to use a synthetic heart valve. Something he invented. Sophie wasn't sure exactly what it was, but Thomas said it paid a whole lot better than nose jobs. Carter, Thomas's older brother, worked as a prosecutor in the district attorney's office.

"Are you sure you want to talk to your dad?" A valid question, since Thomas always seemed to be on the defensive when he was around him.

"I don't want to talk to anybody," he said, "but I don't have a choice."

Sophie took her earbuds out, wrapped them in a ball, and tossed the coconspirator of her passive-aggressiveness in the glove compartment.

"She was being bullied." Thomas tightened his grip on the steering wheel, his neck held stiff. "She wanted her burn scars to go away because she was being teased at school."

"That's awful."

"I *feel* awful. You know I don't like to treat kids, but something about this little girl tugged at me."

"Why, do you think?"

"Scary," Thomas lamented, and his neck and shoulders softened downward. "The kids at school ran from her because they said she looked scary."

Sophie could completely relate to that poor little girl.

Sophie studied her husband's defenseless face. She didn't witness his vulnerability very often, but when she did, it made her ask the question: *Would he empathize with me?*

"Sweetheart," Sophie said, her words slow and forced, "I have something I want to tell you." She pulled her purse from between her feet and set it on her lap.

Thomas turned to look at her—very briefly, though, because traffic had started to back up. The stop-and-go of holiday travel made this moment less than ideal.

"What is it, baby?" he asked her, while beeping his horn at a teenage driver texting in the next lane.

Sophie unlatched her purse and pulled out the letter.

"Pay attention to the road," Thomas pointed and mouthed as he passed the texting teenager.

Sophie halted her disclosure when the girl honked back and threw up her middle finger.

"Nice," Thomas yelled through Sophie's cracked window. "Classy."

"You finished?" Sophie asked, before pushing the button to close her window.

"I'm done," Thomas replied. He cracked his knuckles against the steering wheel. "What were we talking about?"

"I just wanted to tell you I'm sorry." She slipped the letter back into her purse and then tugged on his sleeve. "I'm sorry you lost your patient."

MRS. LOGAN (CALL ME MARGARET, DEAR) had done everything to open her arms to Sophie, including phoning her every year at the beginning of November to ask if she "wanted anything special on the menu," a gesture Sophie knew went far beyond adding pumpkin pie and sweet-potato casserole. It was his mom's way of making her feel as if she belonged.

There were questions at first after Thomas called his mother and repeated the exact lie Sophie had told him. "No, Mom, she doesn't have a family." His voice lowered when he realized Sophie was in the next room. "I don't know all the details." He paused. "I've asked, but she doesn't like to talk about it."

She could tell his mother was pressing for more, trying to understand the precedent of the poor orphan girl who would soon become her daughter-in-law. Sophie still remembered the sympathy in their eyes the first time they met her and the recognition she felt in their tight hugs. Their constant tone of sympathy was sometimes hard to take, but Sophie worried that if they knew the truth, that sympathy would be replaced by disgust, which she feared much more.

"Was your mother a good cook?" Margaret asked her their first holiday together. The abrupt question startled Sophie and caused her to nick her thumb with the potato peeler. She composed her answers while Margaret left to get a Band-Aid.

"My mom loved to cook," Sophie said as Margaret squeezed Betadine over Sophie's bleeding finger. She knew Thomas's mom didn't really care about the taste of her mom's fried chicken, but it was a small way to bust through Sophie's barricade and bond with her.

"She made wedding cakes for people." Both statements were true, and somehow the sprinkling of honesty made the "already dead" part of her deceit seem like a smaller infraction.

All of their efforts did make her feel at home, and Sophie genuinely enjoyed her holidays spent with the Logan family. Everything from the blue Willow–patterned china to the bacon-wrapped scallop appetizers served promptly at 5:30 p.m., and the dinner that followed at 6 p.m. on the button.

This Thanksgiving, like all holidays, Dr. Logan sat at the head of the long dark-stained table. Margaret still made place cards even though everyone sat at the same spot every time they gathered for a meal: Carter and his family on one side, Thomas and Sophie on the other. Margaret took the end closest to the kitchen. All the chairs had high carved backs and didn't scoot very well. It took at least three moves before you could escape—that was what Sophie had been thinking the first time she joined them for a formal meal.

After Dr. Logan blessed the food, he scooped up a big helping of mashed potatoes. As he passed the bowl to Thomas, he said, "You have a birthday coming up. Turning thirty, I hear." He didn't make much small talk, but when he did, Sophie listened. His deep, commanding voice intimidated her.

"Unfortunately, you heard correct," she replied as Thomas passed her the seven-layer salad. She took a small spoonful and handed the salad to her mother-in-law.

Dr. Logan poured some gravy on his mashed potatoes and directed his next question to Thomas. "Don't you think it's time for you two to give this old man some grandbabies?" The word *babies* sounded much louder.

Sophie swallowed three times to get down a bacon bit while waiting for Thomas to answer a question that felt more like an order.

He handed her a glass of water and said, "We've been practicing, but not quite ready for the big leagues."

His father laughed loudly, seeming satisfied. She and Thomas did want to have kids, but with the demands of his job, Thomas decided it'd be best to put it off a little longer. Sophie didn't argue, especially with her gene pool. Motherhood was best kept in the distant future.

Margaret changed the subject and asked Vivianne, Carter and Caroline's only child, if she wanted some cranberry sauce.

"No, thank you, Grandma Margaret," the five-year-old said with impeccable manners. "Aunt Sophie, will you color with me later?"

After the last couple days, Sophie couldn't wait to pick up a crayon. "There's nothing in the world I would rather do."

AFTER DINNER, the men retired to the TV room while Caroline, Margaret, and Sophie cleared the table and talked about the after-Thanksgiving sales. Vivianne sat cross-legged on the floor, waiting patiently for them to finish.

Sophie tried to pay attention to Caroline's ponderings about how all the "top designers" were cheapening their names by bringing their lines into discount department stores such as Kohl's and Target, and threw in an occasional comment like, "I love Vera's Lavender Label flats," but something about her was off. She felt susceptible and out of place.

"Aunt Sophie, are you almost done?" The excitement in Vivi's voice reminded her of Max. Max, all alone, eating his creamed peas and processed turkey slices.

"Almost done, Vivianne."

Maybe it was the letter looming in her purse with words warning her of a past that hasn't gone away. And a mother who, no matter what she had done, still sat alone on Thanksgiving in a place no one would choose to be.

"You feel okay, Sophie? You look kind of pale," Caroline asked.

"A little queasy," Sophie replied as she excused herself and headed to the restroom. She closed the door and slid down the wall to sit on the floor.

Relax, snap out of this funk, forget about the letter—but nothing she told herself helped. She closed her eyes and shook her head, but old memories crept in and refused to go away. Pushing themselves into her presence, not allowing her to fight back.

Thanksgiving Day when she was ten years old popped into her mind. Sophie in her twin bed, in her pink room, under her purple polka–dotted comforter. Protected and safe. Her puppy asleep beside her. She could hear her mom in the kitchen, opening and shutting the oven door, the smell of homemade sweet bread all around her. The mixer made a rhythmic clank as it hit the sides of a pan while she whipped the potatoes and added "just a smidgen" of cream cheese.

Sophie heard a marching band on TV right before her dad yelled, "Wake up, sleeping beauty, the parade is about to start." She could hear his footsteps moving closer to her door. He stopped long enough to taste the baked macaroni and cheese. "Creamy enough?" her mom asked.

She saw them all sitting around their small, oval breakfast table eating on disposable plates decorated with giant brown turkeys (less cleanup, more time together, her mother told her), holding hands while her father said grace. "Thank you, Lord, for all we have. Our chairs are full and our hearts are grateful." William slapped the tray of his high chair while their mom fed him small bites of applesauce. This was one of the rare days when he giggled like a normal baby, one that didn't throw up all his food and spend his days being shuttled between medical appointments. Sophie wished she had more memories like that.

Sophie took some deep breaths and tried to count to ten. How long had it been since she allowed herself to revisit these moments she could never get back?

"LET'S GRAB THE PAPER from your husband," Margaret said to Caroline as Sophie walked back into the kitchen. "I want to see if Macy's is putting their Coach bags on sale."

As they followed her into the living room, Carter saw them and put down the first section. "He deserves to fry," Carter said, referring to the headline on the front page. Sophie read the bold print over his shoulder: "Walter Mayberry to Be Executed at Lakeland Penitentiary."

That's the prison my mom is in.

Something lodged in her chest.

"Eye for an eye," Carter continued, as though he was giving closing arguments in front of a jury. "The man killed young girls as a recreational activity. Murdered in his spare time. The world is better off without this scumbag." Margaret covered Vivianne's ears.

"Calm down, Johnnie Cochran, this is your day off," teased Caroline as she tried to grab the sales flyers from him.

"Wrong side of the courtroom," Carter served back. "I don't defend people, sweet pea. I lock them up and throw away the key." He tossed a pretend key over his shoulder and swiped his hands together, his imaginary victory won.

"Baby-killer next on the chopping block," Sophie heard him say just before her world turned black and her head hit the floor.

GRACE

My cell door unlocked right on time. All the doors on the cell block did except Roni's. I'm not sure what she did this time to lose privileges, but it must have been something. I could hear Jada counting her steps in her cell. "One, two, three, four, turn. One, two, three, four, turn."

"You coming?" I said to her as I walked past.

She ignored me, so I took a seat at the metal picnic table and started shuffling through the stack of magazines. Ms. Liz collected old publications from her women's group at church and brought them to us once a month. All different kinds, from crossword puzzles to *Consumer Reports*, had one thing in common—the one-by-three-inch rectangle cut out of the bottom right corner of each front cover.

Ms. Liz was my spiritual adviser, and we usually met at least once a week, but it had been a while. I wasn't sure why she hadn't been there, but I missed her and I needed advising now more than ever.

"Ms. Liz coming today?" I asked Officer Jones, who was dialing the telephone from her desk in the dayroom. "Haven't seen her," she replied without looking up.

"This is Jones"—her voice serious. She paused and then said, "So it's a go?"

I glanced up. So did she, and then she lowered her voice. "First one in several years; this place is going to be a circus."

The voice on the other end must have agreed with her. Lakeland State Penitentiary was the largest maximum-security prison in the state and had both a men's and a women's death row. The new governor had promised he would be tough on crime and even tougher on criminals. "Too much of your hard-earned money is going to support those who have broken the law. Those who have been sentenced to death are sitting year after year in our prisons while their appeals draw out and cost you, the taxpayer, more money." He'd shouted the words as if he was promising a refund. "I promise to expedite this lengthy process and let their punishments be carried out." The crowd cheered through the newscast.

Officer Jones finished her call in private. Or I tuned her out; I'm not sure which. It was obvious someone in this place would be going before me. I didn't know whom.

Carmen came out of her cell about twenty minutes after I did. Even on death row, she made her appearances fashionably late.

Forgoing a greeting, she picked up last month's *Travel + Leisure* and said, "I bet the person who donated this has never traveled out of the state." Her long nails clicked on the metal table. "Her husband's probably a cheap-ass."

She continued to flip through the pages, not appearing to care if I agreed or not.

"I bet they travel all the time," I said after a few minutes. I didn't want to start a fight with Carmen, but I was trying to be love-worthy, after all, and this subscriber had been kind enough to donate the magazine. "She probably pays for her kids to get their hair weaved every time they go to the beach."

Carmen grunted and continued flipping the pages. She had been here the longest and was the toughest one for me to figure out. Roni I can understand. Burn marks from a hot iron framed her world. I'm not sure she ever felt the excitement of riding a bike for the first time without the training wheels, or experienced the joy that bubbles in your chest when someone said "I like your smile" or "You look pretty in that dress."

The same can't be said for Carmen. She grew up in a house with a cook and a driver and had a story about every vacation destination mentioned in each donated issue. The way she cocked her head when she examined her slice of thin bologna or the green Jell-O served in a plastic cup told all of us this place was beneath her. Her shiny black hair, twisted tight in a French knot, framed sharp, high cheekbones and thin lips.

"She looks like a praying mantis," Jada had said once, when she thought Carmen was sleeping. "Damn, a gray hair or wrinkle is even too scared to live on that bitch."

"I'll show you a praying mantis," Carmen had screamed, rushing full-speed out of her cell, with her hand raised in the air. An officer intervened before Carmen had a chance to attack. She spent three days in isolation after that.

Carmen tossed the magazine onto the pile and started browsing through *National Geographic*. "Venice is way overrated," she said. "Stan wants to go, but I'd rather go someplace else." Her eyes stared off and she didn't continue.

Stan was her fourth husband. They'd married seven years ago, after Carmen had been on the row for almost a decade. Ms. Liz conducted the simple ceremony; Carmen and Stan said their vows separated by glass. "Probably the safest husband she's ever had," one of the officers joked.

Carmen was known to many as the Candy Bar Killer for adding various toxic concoctions to the baked goods of husbands one through three. We'd never talked about her convictions or her motivations, but one time while flipping through *Taste of Home*, Carmen said, "I made this crunchy layered caramel cake once for my second husband."

I looked for the November issue of *Woman's Day*. I saved the calendars out of the back of each issue from the section called Month of Menus.

Some housewives, I supposed, used this section and its handy shopping guide to plan meals for their families. I could picture them whipping up the Brown Sugar Meatloaf and mashed potatoes while their children fought over who licked the mixing spoons.

I had a much simpler use for the Month of Menus. I used it to mark off my remaining days.

SOPHIE

"He's hurting my ears," Sophie cried, her glittery purple fingernails pressed hard against the sides of her head. "Make him stop crying!" Her mom tried to console William, jiggle him up and down, but nothing she did seemed to work. Baby William's body didn't look squishy anymore. He looked hard and unbending, like her Sabrina baby doll with the blue shiny eyes that didn't move.

"Uncle Thomas, she's still saying funny things!" Vivianne yelled. The screech in the little girl's voice startled Sophie.

She opened her eyes but had no idea where she was. The dark room gave her few clues, although the sage-green chenille curtains looked familiar. She tried to lift her head and look around, but it felt heavy and sore.

Sophie blinked her eyes and tried to focus. She could see Vivianne sitting crossed-legged at the end of her bed, drawing chubby hearts up and down each of her tiny thighs with a strawberry-scented marker.

"Use your coloring book," Thomas told her as he walked back into the bedroom.

Thanksgiving. The Logan family. It was all coming back to her. Sophie sat up on the side of the bed and tried to stand, but the moving room caused her to almost tip over.

"Slow down." Thomas grabbed her arm to steady her.

"What happened to me?"

"You fainted," Thomas said, his wide clinical eyes examining hers. Sophie pictured him putting on his lab coat, stethoscope around his neck, and asking her how long she'd been experiencing these strange symptoms. She knew as soon as he cupped her face he was not looking at his wife but for symmetry in the pupils of a normally healthy twenty-nine-year-old female.

"Thought of a good sale made you that excited, huh?"

Sophie grimaced and removed his scrutinizing hand from her chin. She reached around and felt the large egg on the back of her head.

"Quite a bump." He helped her lie back down. He tucked the comforter in all around her and sat down beside her. "How are you feeling?"

"Uncoordinated," Sophie joked. Her attempt at humor made her head throb even more.

"You've been out for a while." He brushed the hair away from her eyes and kissed her on the forehead. The concerned look in his eyes told her he was her husband once again. "I was getting worried."

"I don't remember passing out."

"Caroline said you told her you didn't feel well. Nauseated?"

Sophie started to remember. Her mom and dad, their last Thanksgiving together, William in his high chair. Carter. The newspaper.

The room and her stomach started to move again. She closed her eyes and prayed she wouldn't throw up. *Is my mom going to die?*

"Are you okay, Aunt Sophie?" Vivi mimicked Thomas and used her scented marker to look into Sophie's eyes.

For a moment, right after the nausea passed, Sophie considered answering that question honestly, blurting out to the both of them she couldn't remember the last time she felt okay and her "excitement" had nothing to do with the after-Thanksgiving sales and that no matter how many navy suede pumps and Prada purses she owned, nothing would fill the empty cavern that had burrowed itself deep inside her the day her mother was dragged away from her in handcuffs. That her fainting had everything to do with his brother's callous declaration of a man's execution as if everything in his perfect world of right and wrong, cut and dry, fit neatly into a little box without emotion or backstory— devoid of any requirement for empathy. And the mother who'd bobby-pinned her hair away from her face and singsonged, "100 percent failure rate if you don't try" might be next.

She thought about asking Vivianne to leave the room and then grabbing Thomas and shaking him until he understood why he needed to make her feel better. Anything to help her get rid of the sharp pain that filled her every time she allowed herself to remember something good about her mother. The mom who sat beside her in bed just like Thomas was doing now, promising nothing bad would ever happen to her. Did she promise that to William, too?

"Sophie, are you okay?"

Sophie opened her eyes and looked at Thomas, searching for safety, gauging if now was the time or place to tell him the truth.

"You were having a scary dream," Vivianne declared before Sophie could speak. "Some baby wouldn't stop crying." She dug out a black marker that smelled like licorice from her plastic tote underneath the bed.

"Who were you dreaming about? Do you remember?" Thomas rubbed Sophie's forearm. "Who is William?"

Sophie's face felt cold and hot at the same time. *What did I say?* She replayed her dream over in her head. Her brother, that awful night, one of the last times her family was together in her home.

"Max," she said quickly, her competency at lying startling her. "I'm sure I said Max. It makes me sad when he has to spend the holidays alone."

Thomas seemed to believe this latest lie just like he believed all the ones before. Sophie licked her dry lips with her even drier tongue. Each white lie, no matter how justifiable, seemed to rip something from her, from them. Pretty soon, she feared, she'd have nothing left to shred.

Sophie felt better when she woke up the next morning, although she wasn't sure she could make it through the rest of the weekend at the Logans'. The incessant questions—"How are you feeling, dear?" or "Are you sure I can't make you something else to eat?"—were driving her insane. She knew Thomas's family meant well, but her problems couldn't be fixed with vegetable soup and a Tylenol. Her problems probably couldn't be fixed at all.

Time alone was what she really wanted. Time to think, to figure out what she needed to do. After much persuasion, Sophie finally convinced her mother-in-law and sister-in-law to go shopping without her. "I'll be fine, I promise. I have two doctors plopped in the living room, watching football."

"That's what I'm afraid of," Margaret said. "Unless you come out dressed like a Dallas Cowboys cheerleader, they might forget you exist."

Sophie laughed and then pretended she was shaking some pom-poms. The Logan men did like their football. "You girls go on. I will not stand in the way of a good sale." She raised her right hand as if she was a Girl Scout taking an oath. Caroline and Margaret nodded in agreement. Vivianne, in her hot-pink sequined sunglasses, camped out by the front door. "Let's go, Mommy!" she squealed.

"I'm going to read and then take a nap. Don't worry about me. I've got a dance move or two up my sleeve if I need to get someone's attention."

Thomas yelled from the other room, "Looking forward to seeing that later."

After they finally left, Sophie told Thomas she was going to lie down. Instead, she locked herself in the bedroom, squatted down in the closet, and read the newspaper article Carter had been yelling about.

"Governor Makes Good on Promises—Refuses to Intervene with Court's Rulings" headlined page three of the *Charleston Daily News*. "Governor Whitaker pledged swift justice for victims' families and a speedy appeals process for those convicted," the newspaper article stated. "'We are failing to carry out the will of our justice system when we keep these inmates on death row and prolong the already lengthy appeals process. Let the courts do their job and let their death sentences be overturned or carried out.'"

Sophie scanned through the rest of the article. The last sentence said the same thing Carter had so eloquently blurted out: "A woman convicted of murdering her infant son is the next in line to face execution."

Sophie wadded up the newspaper and checked her cell phone to see how many bars she had. She had to dial the number two times before she did it right, then her uncooperative hands barely held the phone steady enough for her to hear. When the call finally went through, a recorded message on the other end said: "You have reached the law offices of Benjamin Taylor and Associates. Our office is closed for the Thanksgiving holiday. Please leave a brief message and we will return your call as soon as possible."

Sophie considered leaving a message but didn't know exactly how to sum up her inquiries in a few short seconds. *Is my mom next in line to be executed?* A legal secretary with a sticky note might find that message somewhat disturbing.

She ended the call and decided her message would best be delivered in person.

"I HAVE TO MEET WITH some prospective chefs for the fund-raiser," she explained to Thomas after they returned home on Sunday. "I forgot my calendar and this completely slipped my mind. I should've told you earlier, but a group of them are participating in an exhibit close to Charlotte, so I can see most of my options in one place. It will save me a lot of time if I do it this way."

"You want to leave tomorrow? Are you sure you're feeling okay?" Thomas frowned. "You slept the entire drive home, and the trip to Charlotte's an even longer drive. I don't know if this is a good idea."

"I'm fine, really. I feel like myself today."

He stopped filtering through the stack of mail Sophie had placed on the counter, reached over, and felt the back of her head. "You still have a pretty good bump."

"Stop!" Sophie removed his arm. "I'm *fine*." Her words came out harsher than she'd intended them to.

Thomas studied her face for a while, as if he were looking at someone he wasn't sure he really knew. "I love you, I'm worried about you. That's all."

She stared down at her wedding ring, twisting it around on her finger. Anything not to look into his eyes.

"Go, if you think you need to, but be careful. Fainting isn't normal. Please promise me you'll at least make an appointment to see your doctor as soon as you get back."

SOPHIE ROLLED IN AND OUT of bed a half-dozen times, each time mumbling another excuse to Thomas as to why she couldn't sleep. "I have so much to do before I leave tomorrow" was what she said the final time her restlessness woke him up. He took his pillow and left to sleep on the sofa.

Every fib made her feel like she was digging a hole for herself that would someday bury her. She questioned her decision to leave at least twenty times. *Forget about that part of your life. It's over, keep your clean (jagged, at best) break, and stop all the second-guessing.*

Maybe she was reading too much into the newspaper article. It hadn't given a name—certainly the prison had more than one person who'd killed a baby, a thought that disturbed her on many levels. And possibly the letter meant something else. Papers she needed to sign? There must be many reasons for a lawyer to contact a client's family.

Sophie was halfway to Charlotte before she convinced herself Ben Taylor only wanted to be paid. The strong words in his letter were his way of getting her attention. Her mother had no money left after the legal fees from her trial. "I know I'm behind on the mortgage," a thirteen-year-old Sophie overheard her dad whisper in the phone. "Please give me some more time."

She started to call Ben Taylor's bluff, to turn her car around and go home, but the thought of making up another lie to Thomas stopped her. She couldn't turn back—not now, anyway.

GRACE

I hope Sophie was distracted today. Maybe out buying some lipstick or sledding, wearing her red mittens somewhere. Anything that kept her occupied and away from a newspaper. I can't comfort her and I couldn't bear the thought of her—alone—hearing the news about someone being executed.

Officer Jones was right. This place was crazy. I tried not to look out my window, but the honking horns and chants drew me in. I was surprised, I guess, by the interest. The man being put to death hadn't had a visitor in years. I hope he had one today.

I couldn't stop myself from wondering: *Is he scared? Does he have an appetite? Has he thought about his last words?*

I knew I was going to have to answer those questions, sooner than I'd like to, but to be quite honest I was having a hard time lumping myself in his category. That guy did some pretty bad stuff.

I attempted to keep busy. Tried to force myself to stop thinking about what was happening on the other side of the prison, but even the air felt different in here. Electric, but heavy at the same time.

We were on lockdown until further notice, which means we can't leave our cells for any reason. My radio works only part-time. The antenna is broken and has to be propped at just the right angle, and even then it can get only a few stations. I usually hear about every third word.

I cleaned when I needed to pass the time, determined to rid every indentation in my crème-colored cinder-block walls of filth. No matter how many times I scrubbed, I still thought I saw residue from somebody else's excrement. After my arms wore out, I stopped and did some sit-ups. My abs, I have to say, looked pretty good.

Before I was in here, I never exercised. I'd make up a thousand different reasons as to why I couldn't walk on the treadmill or run in my neighborhood. "I'm exhausted," or "Paul needs his church clothes washed." Now, when physical activity was considered an earned privilege, I'd give up days of sleep just to do jumping jacks in a rainstorm.

"Tray coming through," Officer Mackey shouted through the door. He had a thick accent, from someplace north of here, like New York or New Jersey. He's nice enough, but when he talked fast my mouth felt like sandpaper.

My dinner tray popped through the door and transported a cold, shriveled-up hot dog and watery applesauce. I was starving, so I was grateful the bun, at least, wasn't soggy.

"Stand for count," he ordered, after I'd had my tray for fifteen minutes. I took a quick drink of my water.

I stood up and faced front. He stared at me for a second through the window and then wrote something in red ink on his paper.

"Stand for count," he yelled into Roni's cell.

In a few seconds, he repeated himself again. *Stand for count, Roni.* I'd seen her have to be dragged out of her cell before, and that wasn't pleasant for anyone.

I didn't hear him say anything else, so I guessed this time she listened.

"Count all clear," he said, presumably to Officer Jones. She'd said she was working this evening.

"The doors will open in ten minutes, ladies. You can go to the dayroom or stay in your cells. The choice is yours."

I put my tray in the slot, thankful my cell door would finally be opened. The truth was, though, I didn't feel like talking to anyone. I cared only about writing to Sophie. Jada and Carmen must feel the same way. I haven't heard a word from either one of them all night.

"You coming out?" Roni asked after our doors unlocked. Inmates weren't allowed to congregate in any area other than the dayroom. She kept moving down the hallway as she talked. "I was hoping we could write." She waved a few letters at me in the air.

"Be there in a minute," I answered. Something love-worthy will do us both good.

Roni received mail several times a week. When her first letter arrived, we were sitting together. I watched her stare at the envelope, taking in the front and then the back. She even put it up to her nose and smelled it.

"Who's your letter from?" I had asked her after several minutes of this strange behavior.

She'd looked up with her tight eyes fixed squarely on me. I wished I could take back my question.

"Sorry. None of my business." I put my hands up in surrender and scooted my chair over.

She still didn't answer or look away.

I'd done it this time. I sprung up, praying she wouldn't follow me, but she grabbed my arm and pulled me back down.

"I'm sorry, Roni." My eyes stuck on her this time, begging her not to slam me against the concrete floor. "I won't ask again."

She took her arm off me. "I don't know who it's from." She threw the letter in my lap. "You look."

I rubbed my arm for a few seconds before picking up the letter, which was now lying faceup on the floor.

Roni can't read, I figured out, since the name was written plain and clear.

"It's from a Carl Cooper," I told her, trying to gauge her reaction before I said any more. When she didn't respond, I said, "He lives in Alabama."

She still didn't say a word. After a few long minutes, she snatched the envelope from my hand and tore it in half.

A few weeks later another letter came. She asked me to read it to her when we were eating lunch together in the dayroom. I wasn't sure why she'd changed her mind, but I removed the paper from the open slit in the top of the envelope.

"Dear Roni," it started, *"I didn't hear back from you. Did you get my last letter?"*

She stared at her sweet tea, stirring it with her plastic spoon. I continued: *"I heard what happened to you. I'm so very sorry."*

She took her spoon out and put it beside her drink. Her head slumped over the table.

"I know I haven't been a part of your life"—I glanced up from the page to see if I should go on reading—*"but I'd like to change that."*

Roni lifted her head up and stiffened her back against the chair. She pushed her half-eaten egg salad sandwich to the center of the table.

"I'd like to meet you."

She cocked her rigid head and fixed her gaze, staring at something or someplace I couldn't see. Red lines formed in the corners of her eyes. She took the letter from me before I had a chance to finish.

I opened my mouth before I thought better. "Who's the letter from?"

She answered this time, but her voice sounded brittle. "My father. My biological father."

She didn't say another word and I didn't, either. The letters continued to stack up until one day when Carmen was in the infirmary and Jada paced in her cell, Roni asked me if I would help her write him back.

So tonight, like many times before, she and I sat together as I helped her write a reply to his latest question. Some parts of her face, for the first time I'd seen, anyway, moved effortlessly. The pencil she held tightly in her hand copied the last sentence I'd written for her. "Yes, you can visit over Christmas."

Roni's countenance had changed, and it was a milestone worth documenting, a photo a mother should have placed in her scrapbook. A picture I'd happily taken of Sophie.

If I had some hay, I'd place it in a manger, because this day was love-worthy. If I can't see my daughter this December, maybe I can help Carl Cooper see his.

SOPHIE

The drive to Brookfield took longer than Sophie anticipated. So long, in fact, she prayed she would make it to the attorney's office before they closed for the evening. Sophie checked the time on the dashboard of her car. Four-forty-five. *Please, Mr. Taylor, be in your office.* She couldn't stand spending any more time than necessary in her hometown.

Her car rounded the last long, winding curve before entering Brook-field—population 1,451. The green *Welcome to Brookfield* sign hadn't changed since she left eleven years ago. *Hasn't anyone had a baby in this town or died of old age?* She knew of at least four people who no longer could be counted as residents in the census. Didn't the Bradshaw family account for anything?

She drove past the sign and bitterly entered her past. *I will not let this place get to me, I will not let this place get to me.* She chanted her tune of immunity as she tried to remember where his office was located. Down-town (or maybe uptown in a place this small) by the courthouse and across from the 40th Street Café. Another five minutes, one flashing stoplight, and two right turns, and she should be there.

About the time Sophie started to exhale, she heard sirens. She checked her rearview mirror, supposing it would be too much to ask if the black-and-white police car riding her bumper was after someone else. *Great, a town with one police officer and he happens to clock me.*

She flicked on her right turn signal and pulled her SUV over into the gravel parking lot in front of the IGA grocery store. The faded gray-and-white vertical-striped siding still looked exactly the same as it had a decade ago. The lightbulb in the oversize red *A* still flickered, still not fully illuminated—begging for someone, for anyone, to recognize it needed attention.

The policeman followed close behind her, keeping his sirens on even after both cars came to a complete stop. *All right, already,* Sophie thought to herself. *Can't believe the speed limit is still twenty-five miles per hour through this part of town. Zero traffic and you still have to drive slow as hell.*

A cop in his early sixties emerged from the police car. His thick black belt, armed with a holster, handcuffs, and a billy club, underlined his draping belly. "Ma'am, good evening. Are you in a hurry to get someplace?"

"I'm sorry," Sophie said, deciding to play ignorant, hoping her speedometer was as dishonest as she was. "Was I going too fast?"

"I have you clocked at forty-nine miles per hour. By my calculations, that is twenty-four miles over the speed limit." His overenunciated words took the southern draw to a new level.

"Oh no!" Sophie said, trying to decide if ignorance or an apology would get her on her way faster. "I'm so sorry," she decided. "I'm not feeling well. I guess I'm a little distracted."

"Can I see your license and registration, please?" His voice sounded vaguely familiar. Sophie pulled her license out of the slot in her billfold and then reached over and retrieved her registration from the console between her front seats. She handed them both to the officer.

"Well, Mrs. Logan," the officer said, looking at her driver's license, then back at her, "what brings you in such a hurry to the lovely town of Brookfield?"

"In town on family business," Sophie told him. "I used to live here."

The officer looked at her license once again, and then looked back at Sophie, studying her ring finger and her face before he spoke. "What's your maiden name?"

Sophie pressed her lips together and contemplated the possible implications of engaging him in a high-speed chase.

The officer asked her again. "Ma'am, your maiden name?"

Flashes of O.J. and the white-Bronco debacle sped through her mind. "Bradshaw. My name used to be Sophie Bradshaw."

He once again studied the picture on her license and then looked back at her, squinting. "Are you Grace Bradshaw's daughter?"

They both put the pieces of their last interaction together at about the same time. He'd been one of the officers outside her brother's hospital room. *Grace Bradshaw, you are under arrest for the murder of your infant son, William Joseph Bradshaw.*

He looked at her with the same pitiable look he had on the day he'd witnessed her sobbing in her father's arms. *Don't take my mommy. Leave my mommy alone.*

The officer handed Sophie back her license and registration, as if this act of goodwill might somehow make up for the pain he inflicted all those years ago.

"Hope you feel better, Mrs. Logan. I'll let you go with a warning this time. Slow down and drive safe."

"MAY I HELP YOU?"

"I need to see Ben Taylor," Sophie said to the woman pulling her key from the arched knotty-walnut front door. A bronze fleur-de-lis door knocker hung beside a scratched gold-plated sign that read *The Law Offices of Benjamin R. Taylor.* "Is he here?"

"Our office is closed for the day, Ms. Colby. You should've checked your calendar." Her hair didn't move as she bobbled her head. "Your appointment was yesterday."

"I'm not Ms. Colby," Sophie said. "I need to see Mr. Taylor."

The woman dropped the keys in her embroidered clutch before finally glancing in Sophie's direction. "Oh! Sorry about that. I just assumed. Just to let you know, Mr. Taylor is too busy to handle any more child-custody cases or bad marriages that are contemplating divorce." She sized up Sophie to see if she might fit into either one of those categories.

Sophie sized her up, too, thinking she had a lot of confidence for a woman whose bouffant and pale blue dress screamed Alice from *The Brady Bunch*.

"I'm not here for that," Sophie replied, wiping underneath her eyes with the tips of her fingers. She didn't need another person in this town feeling sorry for her, but this was her own fault. She should've checked her reflection after a long day of driving. Black smudge marks now transferred themselves to the tips of her right hand as she dabbed at her smudged makeup. "I received a letter in the mail. He asked to see me."

The woman grabbed the scrolled handrail and moved rather quickly down the stairs. "Be here around one p.m. tomorrow and I'll see if I can squeeze you in."

SOPHIE SAT IN HER CAR for such a long time that people leaving the café began to look inside to make sure she was still breathing. Should she wait until tomorrow afternoon and hope she could see Ben Taylor? Or should she drive back home and hope Thomas was asleep and didn't ask her any questions?

Her cell phone rang before she could decide.

"Hello."

"Hey, baby, checking on you to see if you made it to Charlotte okay."

For a moment Sophie struggled to remember the last lie she'd told Thomas. Charlotte—oh, yes, meeting with chefs for the fund-raiser.

"I did make it here fine. Problem is"—she paused again, trying to fabricate a dilemma—"I didn't get to meet with everyone I wanted to."

"That's a problem," Thomas said. He sounded distracted but interested. "What are you going to do?"

"I'm not sure. Maybe stay tonight. Long way to come if I don't get the information I need." Half-truths were becoming her specialty.

"Are you still there?" she asked after he didn't respond.

"Sorry, still here. Have a lot going on. Why don't you spend the night? I'm going to be at my office for a while."

"I think I will," Sophie replied, thankful for the easy interaction. "What's going on with you?"

"I'm going over some notes from the hospital. You remember the little girl who died?"

"Of course I remember. You sound concerned. Anything going on?"

"An attorney's office called requesting my records. You know that can't be good. I'm going over things, trying to figure out what possibly could've gone wrong." She heard him shuffle some pages as he talked.

She could picture him, the Sherlock Holmes of the surgery department, sitting behind his polished dark cherry desk, the drawers detailed with elegant filigree. One hand running through his hair, the other scanning every single lab value and vital sign in the child's record. Journals stacked in front of him, one on top of the other, in alphabetical order and color-coded by procedure. Framed diplomas, lining the wall behind him, declaring his multiple accolades. *Summa Cum Laude. Chief Resident with Highest Honors. Distinguished Fellow in Plastics and Reconstructive Surgery.* Thomas did not miss details.

"I'm sure you did everything right. You're a great doctor."

"I don't think I made a mistake, but Carter and my dad said to protect myself and protect the practice. Don't want to do anything to jeopardize my run for chief of surgery."

He said "chief of surgery" sarcastically, making Sophie think his family wanted it way more than Thomas did.

"A lawsuit," Thomas continued in a more reverent voice, "involving a child almost never comes out in the doctor's favor, whether they did something wrong or not."

"In other words—avoid a scandal?"

"Avoid a scandal," Thomas repeated—empathically, but once again sarcastically. "You know my family—wouldn't want to tarnish the family name. To quote my dad: 'Sometimes it is better to make things go away than to let the whole world see your indignity.'" Sophie felt that comment right between the eyes.

On the edge of Thomas's desk, posing behind a fragile piece of glass, sat two newlyweds. A seemingly happy couple, impeccably dressed, donning paper-white smiles. "You two have the world at your fingertips," the photographer told them when they viewed their prints.

"I'm looking at our picture," Thomas said, after Sophie had been silent for a little too long. "We might need to get it reframed. There's a tiny crack in the glass."

GRACE

*Six minutes ago, Walter Mayberry died. I know the exact time of
his death because Officer Jones turned on the TV in the dayroom
and let those of us who wanted to watch the media coverage do so.
No one did. Carmen clicked her overgrown nails on the metal table,
complaining to Jada that the lack of vitamins in her "meal plan"
was making her cuticles split. Roni riffled through an old Sports
Illustrated and grunted ever so dramatically, as though the bite-
fight between Holyfield and Tyson just happened.*

*At first I didn't want to watch, either. I worried you were
watching, and I didn't want you to see what was about to happen.
What was about to happen to me. But then curiosity, mixed with a
good bit of anxiety, set in and I couldn't take my eyes off the screen.*

*This is the first execution in South Carolina in many years. I
guess that's why there's so much media attention, so much debate.
The TV cameras panned the crowd. One man was holding a sign
that read "Forget Injections, Use a Pickax." Drops of painted red
blood trailed from the last word. Others were standing in a circle,
holding candles—praying his life would be spared, I guess.*

*I didn't know Walter, but Officer Jones did. She had worked in
the men's unit before transferring to the women's section of the
prison. I'd heard about Walter, though—the Graveside Strangler.
What terrible things he did to those innocent girls.*

The TV station flashed their pictures throughout the coverage. I tried not to look, but I couldn't help myself. School photos, I'm sure. One girl had braids tied with tiny black-and-white bows. She had a gap between her top two teeth. The other had long, wavy auburn hair, parted on the side and clipped with a gold barrette. She wore a forest-green cardigan.

Then a picture of thirty-four-year-old Walter Mayberry popped up on the screen. His face was dominated by cumbersome black, thick-rimmed glasses, the kind that covered your eyebrows and ended at the bottom of your nose—probably prison-issued, or all he could afford. Underneath the lenses, his gray eyes looked lost.

Walter told Officer Jones he wasn't sure when the urges first started. His uncontrollable impulses to harm young girls who happened to be standing on their tiptoes, putting change into the vending machine while waiting at his dad's garage.

He hated himself afterward, but the urges wouldn't leave, no matter how hard he fought. His despicable acts played over and over in his mind; sometimes the thoughts excited him, but mainly they tortured him. His only relief came after he came to death row. His court-appointed psychiatrist fought to get him treatment.

Officer Jones said it was a new drug approved to treat paraphiliacs, or people who can't control their sexual urges. After he received weekly injections for a couple months, his high levels of testosterone went down and his obsessive thoughts moved away. His tumultuous mind turned calm and peaceful.

I kept seeing the images of those girls in my mind. What horror their parents must be going through. They deserved justice, and I prayed they received peace.

The other part of me felt sorry for him. He was a victim, too. In no way did that make him innocent or make his crimes less horrendous. It did, though, help me to understand him better.

*He had to live with a monster every day, and it resided inside
his head.*

*The television flickered on and off, but stayed on. The reporters
were talking about how he'd spent his last day. The fried eggs he ate
for breakfast and the grilled cheese he didn't eat for lunch. His final
meal, by choice, happened to be the same thing the rest of the
inmates ate for dinner: beef stew with diced potatoes and carrots,
cornbread, and an eight-ounce glass of watered-down sweet tea.*

*It was nights (or early mornings) like these that make me look
around in a panic. How did I end up in here? I wasn't mentally ill.
I hadn't harmed anyone. I had two parents who were crazy
about me. When I walked into the room, my mom's and dad's faces
lit up. I hope you saw the pleasure on my face when I looked at you.*

*Somewhere there's a picture of me holding you right after you
were born. It used to be framed on the table beside my bed. You had
just opened your eyes and were giving me the once-over. I wasn't sure
if you were going to smile or cry, but then you reached up and
wrapped your fingers around my finger as if to say, "Hey, you're
okay." It was in that moment I knew I was meant to be your mom.*

*The row was unusually quiet tonight. Carmen was humming our
Sunday-morning chapel song Ms. Liz had taught her when she first
was incarcerated here:* Softly and tenderly Jesus is calling, calling
for you and for me. See, on the portals, He's waiting and
watching. Calling, O sinner, come home. *The rest of the row,
like me, was probably praying tonight our dreams would be peaceful.
I prayed you slept in perfect peace.*

A few people remained, now kneeling in a circle with their candles lit.
Would these same people be here to protest against me?

A long black hearse pulled out of the prison yard, followed by two
police cars. Inside was the body of Walter Mayberry on the way to be

buried in the prison cemetery, hidden down a gravel road behind a large covering of magnolia trees. According to the news, none of his family or his victims' families attended his execution.

I returned to my room to write all of this to Sophie, and then I turned on my radio. I needed to listen to some music before I fell asleep. The station was full of static, and before I could turn if off I heard a man in a somber voice say, "The next scheduled execution in the state of South Carolina will take place on February fifteenth. Grace Bradshaw, you might remember, is the woman who murdered her infant son by repeatedly putting windshield-wiper fluid into his bottle."

SOPHIE

Sophie didn't sleep more than a half-hour at a time all night. Thomas's words saturated her every thought and tainted her every perception. *Avoid a scandal. Make it go away. Avoid a scandal.* No matter how many times she spun the conversation with Thomas in her mind, a mother on death row always came out sounding scandalous.

The only bed and breakfast in town had five rooms, and they all smelled like cat litter. Mrs. Neiland, the owner, gave Sophie her pick of the place, since she was the first (and only, by the looks of things) guest to check in that night.

Eager to do something other than socialize with Mrs. Neiland, Sophie woke the next morning before daylight, put on her running clothes, and escaped out the side door. A jog could clear her head and give her an excuse to miss breakfast, which smelled like it wasn't going to be any better quality than the rooms.

Thomas didn't like Sophie running so early in the mornings. "You never know who's roaming the streets before the crack of dawn," he'd warn, when her insomnia led her to lace up her sneakers before the sun came up. She knew he wouldn't approve of this early-morning run, but the crime rate in Brookfield had to be nonexistent.

As far as she knew, the only violent crime committed in Brookfield had occurred in her own house. "Try and protect me from that, Thomas." She smirked as she spoke the words out loud.

For the longest time, Sophie had actually believed her mom was innocent. Her dad told her time and again: "This is all a mistake. Your mom loved William. She never would have hurt him. Someday the truth will come out."

He promised to save her mom and get her out of that horrible, scary place. A pledge he repeated to his wife and daughter every time they visited the prison. "I will find out what happened. Don't give up, Gracie, please don't give up"—his hands touching hers through the glass window separating them. "We will be at home soon, together, as a family." Every word sounding less and less convincing as the years dragged by.

Sophie had believed her dad. After the dishes were washed and put away and her dad checked her homework, they both sifted through newspaper articles and court transcripts, organizing file folders that read *Expert Defense Witnesses* and *New People to Interview*. Each folder stuffed with regret and dollar signs. "It takes money to mount a good defense," her dad told her as he looked through the old court cases, labs tests, and profiles of expert witnesses that he could never actually afford to hire.

"We can't give up, Sophie. We can never give up," he said to her as he lay in the hospital bed after his first round of chest pains led to open-heart surgery. Sophie, who was then a junior in high school, squeezed her dad's hand and promised him she would continue to fight even if he was too weak to help her.

A few months later, the battle became hers. Around Sophie's eighteenth birthday, she came home to find her father slumped over at the kitchen table, his heart finally stopped.

After his death, Sophie's friends, especially Jillian, tried to get Sophie to "be a normal teenager" and go to the mall or at least to a drive-through. Every night after school, when other kids were applying to college or searching for prom dresses, Sophie was either visiting her mom in prison or searching for ways to get her out.

Close to Christmas of her senior year, Jillian gave Sophie a ride home after school. "I'm worried about you," she said as she got out of the car and invited herself into Sophie's living room. "You are so obsessed with getting your mom free, you've made yourself a prisoner." She'd pointed to the dishes piled in the sink and the overflowing trash cans. "Locked up in this house, doing God knows what."

"I'm trying to get my mom out of prison," Sophie cried. Her voice escalated to a volume that startled even her.

"It's Christmas. You're here alone." Jillian spoke softly, trying to calm her. "No tree, no lights. Nothing. Please come stay at my house."

"Why, so you can lecture me? I get the 'normal kid' speech from neighbors when they feel well enough to check in on me."

Jillian, who shared third lunch and always ordered the mean girls to scoot over so Sophie could sit by her, started to apologize. "I'm sorry. I have no idea what it's like to have a mother in prison. Or, for that matter, to have a father who's passed away, but Sophie"—she paused as if to weigh the consequences of what she was about to say—"someone has to tell you the truth."

"The truth? I know the truth." Her words hissed as they came out. "What are you talking about?"

Jillian pulled the coffee table close to the sofa and sat across from Sophie, their bare knees touching. "Your mom is sick. Sick in the head. She made William sick. She made him die." Jillian tugged on her French braid, refusing to sugarcoat the truth any longer. "Everyone knows that but you."

Sophie was speechless, deflated, like all the hope her dad had filled her with had run off with the words of a friend she assumed believed in her mother like she did.

"How can you say that? You *know* my mother. You went shopping with her. You saw all the times my mom took William to the doctor. You saw how much he cried. You of all people should know she wasn't capable of hurting anyone."

"Well, apparently she was. She hurt your brother. You heard the prosecutors. She had Munchausen." Jillian's once responsive eyes hardened.

Sophie clutched her stomach and turned away. "Can you please go? I need to be alone."

"Fine, I'll leave you alone," Jillian replied. "But think about it—the description for Munchausen fits."

SOPHIE RAN FASTER AND FASTER through the streets of Brookfield, but with every turn another bad memory or unwelcome thought invaded her. Her high school, out of session for the holidays, only reminded her of graduation. Alone.

While other seniors had thrown their hats and celebrated, Sophie kept her head down and her goals clear (*Get my diploma and get out of here*), but no matter how much she avoided others, she still couldn't escape the stares and whispers, even from her teachers. *That poor Bradshaw girl. What is she going to do now?*

William would have been eighteen this year. A senior, graduating with his class in this exact place. Sophie wondered what he would have looked like, what he would have become.

The high school was within walking distance of her childhood home. The house she'd packed up and pushed away, vowing never to return and never look back. Her dad's Ford Explorer weighed down by everything she could possibly fit into a college dorm room. Her clothes, a few linens, a bicycle, and William's baby blanket—a faded blue-and-pink-and-yellow crocheted blanket now hidden in a JCPenney bag underneath the box preserving her wedding dress back at her house in West Lake.

Family pictures, dishes, and all her mom's case files still resided at 365

North Prairie Street. At least, she assumed it was all still there, although she'd never been back. A few days after Jillian confronted her, she'd finally had the courage to power up her dad's computer to take a closer look at all of the court documents.

She knew he always kept his password on a yellow sticky note locked in his desk drawer. When she couldn't find the drawer key anywhere, she'd taken a hammer to the lock and beat it until the latch disassembled and dangled from the inside of the small drawer. Her heart had beat faster than it ever had as she entered the password, john832, into the box on the computer screen. A Bible verse, Sophie later figured out, which read: *And you will know the truth, and the truth will set you free.*

On that day, the truth did set her free. Instead of unwrapping presents on Christmas Day, she opened documents from Brookfield's chief medical examiner: *Cause of death: ethylene glycol poisoning.* Police reports: *bottle of windshield wiper fluid found in the Bradshaws' garage.* Toxicology reports: *traces of ethylene glycol in bottle Grace Bradshaw last fed William with at the hospital.* Notes from a court-appointed psychiatrist: *mother who fits profile of someone suffering from Munchausen by proxy. Depressed mother who seeks attention from medical personnel by repeatedly making child sick.*

Seeing these without her father there to immediately translate what she was reading, she realized that Jillian had been right. They were all right. The mean kids in the hallway who snickered at her when she passed—"Why didn't your mom poison you?"—to the janitor after school who'd told her, "It doesn't matter who you come from, you control your destiny."

How could she have been so stupid? How could her dad have been so naïve? Her mom was guilty. Guilty of lying, of poisoning and killing her only son. Sophie's brother. Had her mother wished she could kill her, too?

Sophie had turned off the computer, devastated. Furious at her dad for manipulating the facts, for dying, but most of all for making her believe.

SOPHIE THOUGHT ABOUT TURNING AROUND, or at least not looking at her old house when she ran by the church located at the corner of her street and not too far from her high school. But something inside her felt otherwise, and before she could stop herself, she turned and found herself standing in front of her childhood.

It looked exactly as she remembered, a modest Victorian-style two-story home with a cracked wraparound lattice-framed porch still needing a paint job. Chipped pieces of yellow paint hung for dear life to rotted wood, praying the next gust of wind would not send them on their way. Weeds and dandelions covered the sidewalk in front of the house and forcefully pushed their way through the broken concrete.

Sophie hadn't set foot in the house since she locked the doors the summer before her freshman year of college. The city, she guessed, had been maintaining the lawn. She'd stopped paying those bills when she married Thomas and failed to leave a forwarding address.

I'm not sure I can do this, she thought to herself as she stood in the driveway of the property she once called home. The swing on the front porch was still in the same place, empty and unoccupied, as if waiting for its family. She pictured her mom sitting there, swinging, with a fresh glass of lemonade, watching for her to turn the corner on her way home from school. *How was your day, sweetie? Any homework?*

Her mom would be so sad to see the house run-down like this, she thought, as she contemplated whether or not to search for the spare key that used to be taped behind the wrought-iron mailbox that hung on the wall outside the front door.

A car horn dazed her before she could look for the key. "I'm glad I found you here, Mrs. Logan," the woman from the law office shouted through her open car window. "I didn't put two and two together until I was brushing my teeth this morning. Mr. Taylor would never forgive me if I let you get away."

GRACE

This week has been hard. I'm not going to pretend to be strong—I don't think I have the energy. There were times I felt like my last breaths couldn't get here fast enough. I realize that sounds morbid, especially coming from me, but these past few days have been almost unbearable. Walter's execution made everything around here feel heavy. My spine even fought me when I tried to stand up straight. I hate to be negative, especially in my journal to you, but I have to be honest.

Even in prison, holidays are days of note, but not this Thanksgiving. My last Thanksgiving, and I contemplated staying in bed all day. Sleeping through like it never happened. The thing that stopped me was this strange sense of obligation I felt to Jada and Roni, like I needed to make sure they didn't feel alone this holiday season. Everyone deserves a nice holiday, don't you think?

Carmen's husband came to visit, so she spent the morning teasing her hair, trying to get some "height" at her crown so her face didn't look so long. I tried to be polite when she asked me for the third time if her face looked younger if she parted her hair on the right or on the left side. "Your husband will like it either way," I finally said, in the most encouraging voice I could muster.

Around 11:47 a.m., the food trays came out. Late, but at least the processed turkey slices weren't cold. Roni, Jada, and I joined one another at the metal round table in the dayroom. No one said "Happy Thanksgiving" on this otherwise ordinary day, but we made a point to sit together. An unspoken survival tip to help us manage the mundane.

"Serena should be getting her driver's license this week," Jada boasted, swirling the congealed brown gravy into her mashed potatoes. "Daryl said his daughter wouldn't be driving a piece-of-crap car to school like he had to. He'd get her something nice to drive."

The only time Jada spoke with such animation was when she was talking about her family. I suspect she'd say the same thing about me.

"Daryl didn't want his kids to do without. He bought Robbie one of those camouflaged Jeep trucks on his fourth birthday. Paid three hundred and some dollars for it. He rode that thing up and down the driveway until the wheels fell off."

She laughed, and I did, too. Roni grunted. She had her head tilted to the side and her thumbnail was busy picking dried macaroni off the corner of her tray. I tried to ignore this disgusting evidence appearing on our sanitized food trays more often than not. It was hard enough to eat the food in here the first time around.

"They're probably going to eat at his mom's around one. They do every year."

"That sounds nice," I said to Jada. She reminded me of the Mrs. Beasley doll I had as a child. When you pulled her string, she repeated the same few phrases over and over.

I'd heard the prison doctor had tried to bring her back to reality. "Your family is gone." His words had met only an empty stare. "Your husband and two kids died in a house fire, remember?"

I'm not sure Jada has ever acknowledged that fact. She still talks about them in the present tense, even though she's been sitting here without them for the past nine times we've been served pumpkin pie.

The judge called her a pathological liar with no maternal instincts when he sentenced her for three counts of premeditated murder. Empty gasoline cans and three sixteen-day-old life-insurance policies were found in Jada's car the night of the blaze. She was the only one who made it out alive.

I made it my mission not to judge Jada, or the other ladies who now shared my holidays. I chose instead to love the people I knew they were meant to become if they had made different choices or had been given different skill sets. As terrible as their crimes were, I made it a point not to define them by their worst mistakes made so many years ago.

Were you alone today?

We had twelve Thanksgivings together before I left you. Another five with you sitting across the glass from me, sneaking glances at your watch, forcing yourself to fake happy so I'd believe everything was all right. I didn't know the seventeenth Thursday we spent celebrating would be our last.

Who are you with?

Did you think about me?

Did you tell them about our cinnamon rolls, how late we stayed up rolling the dough and sticking our fingers in the powdered-sugar icing, laughing, and licking it off until we made ourselves sick?

I cherish those memories, but when I think about it, I don't care if you told them about our homemade desserts, or about my philosophy on setting a simple table—I hope you just said, "It was my home, and I loved being there."

I've spent a lot of time in my life not knowing. Not knowing if it will rain when I've planned our after-church picnic, or not

*remembering the friend of a friend's name I've met several times.
These things don't bother me too much because I know there are
solutions out there somewhere. Like factual responses, answered by
watching the Weather Channel or apologetically asking your
friend's friend his name once again.*

*The big unknowns are what keep me from my peace. Taunting
me, like a snotty girl at recess: "Where's your daughter?" "What
really happened to your son?"*

*I replay, without will, the months before William's death. The
endless hours trying to get him to eat, the helplessness when he
continued to lose weight and the horrifying moments when his body
would inexplicably stiffen. And then, finally, the time it never
ended and I realized once I left him at the hospital that he was gone
forever.*

*Our day before was perfect. You walked Teddy through the
park while I pushed William in his new stroller. Do you
remember the one that had the paisley canopy so he wouldn't get
too much sun? Every so often we'd stop and Paul would sing to
William.*

*"The wheels on the bus go round and round, round and round,
round and round." William had just learned to clap his hands.*

*After we walked home, I fixed William a bottle while you tried
to teach Teddy how to shake for a treat. "Shake," you'd say to him
over and over while you held a Milk-Bone above his head.*

*Paul prepared his sermon in the study while I fed William.
At first he acted hungry, sucking so hard formula drooled out
of his mouth, pooling in the folds underneath his chin.*

"Need another bib," I yelled to you from the living room.

*"Hungry, hungry hippo." You poked his belly as you handed
me a burp rag.*

I'll never forget what I saw next. What you saw next.

William was no longer William. His pudgy face became hard and the thick formula leaking out of his mouth started to bubble.

"Get Daddy," I shouted. "Get Daddy fast."

By the time Paul ran into the living room, William's blue eyes had stopped moving, but his eyelids hadn't. They blinked—over, and over, and over again—until they didn't anymore.

When the paramedics took William away, I never imagined he wouldn't be returning.

That I wouldn't be returning.

My last perfect day, and the final day in our home I'd spend with you.

xoxoxo

After the meal, and after I had put in my self-imposed social time, I returned to my cell. I didn't want to watch my last bowl game on TV, or glance at the sales in the newspaper advertising Christmas presents I'd never buy. I just wanted to pull that gray, scratchy blanket over my head and go to sleep.

But I didn't. I couldn't. I had only a few more months to write to Sophie. For that reason and for that reason alone, I needed to keep breathing. I keep remembering things I need to teach her.

SOPHIE

Ben Taylor, in Sophie's mind, had slicked-back, jet-black hair; his face would be ruddy and intense, his voice fast and boisterous. Instead, when his secretary escorted Sophie into his office, she found him to be quite the opposite, a fatherly type. Strong, capable, good-natured, keeping his children from taking that first puff on a cigarette because they would just know it was wrong.

"Sophie, I'm so glad to finally meet you." His hand extended as he met her at the door to his office, his welcome warm and his tone disarming. His hair had just enough silver to look distinguished and his face enough lines to seem wise.

"Mr. Taylor, I'm sorry I've not been in contact with you earlier. I hope you can understand I've tried to move on, put this part of my life behind me." Her words rushed to keep up with her defenses. "So if you wouldn't mind, please tell me how much my mother owes you and I'll pay the balance. I have a long drive back home."

"Have a seat, please." He motioned to a charcoal leather tufted sofa against the office wall. Sophie abided and took a seat as he walked over to his desk and grabbed some papers, presumably containing her mother's account information. She could only imagine what the invoices would read: *Consultation with Grace Bradshaw—still on death row—$1,500.00. Another consultation with Grace Bradshaw—conviction stands, still on death row—$1,500.00.*

Her cynicism was on full speed today. Underneath it all, she was trying to figure out how to hide this bill from Thomas.

Ben sat down on the couch beside her. "I apologize if I've given you the impression the letter was my attempt to get paid. Your father's church provided him with quite a substantial life-insurance policy. It paid your mother's legal fees, and with your mother's instructions, I've used the surplus to keep up the house. The balance is dwindling, but there's some money you're entitled to, if you'd like."

"I don't need the money, Mr. Taylor." Sophie's two-carat emerald-cut diamond ring showed him that. "And I'm sure my mother could still use your services."

"You were a hard one to track down," he said, smiling and seemingly pleased he'd found her. "I've been trying to get in touch with you for the last five years. Your mother for longer than that. She misses you."

Sophie didn't smile back. "Mr. Taylor, as I said to you when I walked in, I have put this part of my life behind me. I wasted my middle and high school years loving someone who was supposed to love me back, love my brother back." She dug through her purse for her car keys and started to stand. "I was so stupid. Stupid to believe her, all while the whole town knew she was guilty."

"I can't imagine the pain you've endured." He put his hand on her shoulder with just enough pressure to prompt her to sit back down.

"You have no idea." She bit her lower lip. "I lost my brother and my father, all because of her. My entire life has been altered because of my mother. Pain doesn't begin to describe what I have endured."

It had been eleven years since Sophie had had a real conversation about her mother, one that acknowledged her existence and conveyed her hurt. Part of her liked the release; the other part of her felt like she was perched at the top of a large roller coaster, then plummeting down fast without the bar secured.

Ben paused, giving her a minute to regroup. "Sophie," he said, "I'm not trying to stir up old wounds."

"Then what are you trying to do?"

"I wanted . . . well, your mother wanted to contact you and let you know what is going on with her case."

Sophie put her hand on the arm of the sofa. She didn't want to know. She didn't want him to confirm what Carter had said at Thanksgiving. She wanted to believe her mom and her past were both still locked securely behind iron bars, where they belonged.

"I took your mother's case about five years ago. It seemed her state-appointed attorneys weren't doing much and had basically stopped pursuing anything of relevance to the case after her conviction. Before your father died, he made two provisions: one was for you and your education, and the other was for your mom to secure a different legal team if she so desired." He watched for her to acknowledge this.

"Okay," she said. "What does this have to do with me?"

"I took on your mother's case after I received her letter. I drove to Lakeland and visited with her. She's not at all what I expected." He shook his head and smiled.

"No," she said, "you wouldn't think someone with Betty Crocker hands and a Martha Stewart smile could do such a thing."

Ben's smile disappeared. "The thing is, Sophie, I don't believe she did."

A tap on the door. "The clerk at the courthouse called. Judge wants you in his office ASAP," said Louise, who today was wearing a black belted pantsuit. She sneezed, then wiped her nose with a lavender handkerchief.

"I was afraid that would happen," Ben said, glancing at his watch, then at Sophie. "How long are you in town?"

"As soon as I leave here and check out of my room, I'm on my way."

"My meeting with the judge shouldn't take more than an hour and a half or so. Meet me at the café, say around one-thirty, and I'll buy you lunch. You need to hear what I have to say."

"I'll think about it." Sophie pushed a piece of string lying on the shiny hardwood floor around with her tennis shoe.

"Louise," Ben yelled—unnecessarily, since she was still listening at the door. "Wash your hands and then give Sophie that envelope—you know, the one from her mother."

SOPHIE LEFT THE ATTORNEY'S OFFICE still in her jogging suit. Her plan was to go to the B-and-B, shower, check out, and then be on her way. She had bantered back and forth in her mind all the reasons she wasn't obligated to stay. After all, her father had paid the bill, and she certainly didn't owe her mother anything. She'd made her clean break years ago, and even if her mom was going to be executed, what could she do about it? Her mother—the mother she'd known—had died a long time ago, along with the rest of the Bradshaws.

Ben Taylor could go on believing her mother was innocent all he wanted to; after all, that was his job. *My responsibilities are to Thomas, myself, and the family we may (but probably shouldn't) someday create.* She thought about Max sitting alone in his hospital bed, his mother out living her life without a care in the world. Abandoning him just like her mother had abandoned her. If she left now and moved forward, that at least would be justice, not only for her, but for William and Max. She congratulated herself for a decision well made.

When she got back to the B-and-B, her room had already been cleaned, her bed had been made, and new towels had been placed in a wicker basket by the sink in the bathroom. The curtains covering the sliding glass window had been pulled open and spider plants were in full view. Sophie tossed her keys and her purse on the bed. The manila envelope Louise had handed her was still sealed. The contents, Sophie suspected, were things the prison needed to get rid of. Probably her mom's wedding ring, driver's license, things of that sort. Items usually given to a next of kin.

She decided to shower first, and then pack her clothes. She'd wait until later to open the envelope—much later, after she did the only other thing she needed to do before she left the tiny town of Brookfield.

THE CEMETERY LAY ON THE eastern part of Brookfield and bordered the only highway leading into town. A twenty-five-acre piece of land covered with towering oak trees and untold stories of lives cut too short.

On Saturday mornings during high school, Sophie would dump out her composition notebooks from her backpack and fill the front pocket with items her mom needed, like underwear and cotton socks. In the other pocket she'd put items she needed for the stop she made on the way home. Little Golden Books to read to her brother when she visited him at the cemetery.

After she left for college and stopped visiting her mother, the trips to see William and her father at the cemetery subsided. She placated her con-science with every-other-week floral deliveries she placed using her one and only pre-Thomas credit card.

The last floral arrangement stopped after she married Thomas and he questioned the bill. "Who are you sending flowers to?" he had asked one day, after getting the mail before she did.

"My parents' grave site," she'd answered, without thinking her re-sponse through. "I can't bear the thought of it looking lonely since I can't visit."

"That's sweet," Thomas said, kissing her on the cheek before moving on to the next piece of mail.

The subject never came up again. Thomas didn't object and money certainly wasn't an issue, but Sophie decided moving on meant letting go, releasing the burden she had placed on herself to look after her dad and brother. It wasn't as though flower arrangements could change their destinies or make their final resting place more comfortable.

She parked her car near the front of the cemetery. If she remembered correctly, her dad was buried ten rows back from the first row of stones and seventeen markers over.

Sophie began to count out loud just like she had as a kid: "One, two . . ." If she kept her head down and concentrated, she wouldn't have to think about the fact she was the only one present aboveground.

"Ten. Now sixteen over. One, two, three . . ."

Number seventeen, exactly as Sophie remembered.

WITH LOVE WE REMEMBER
PAUL WILLIAM BRADSHAW

The inscription wasn't very creative, but Sophie hadn't known what else to write at age eighteen. The wings of an angel adorned the top of the stone.

Right beside him lay William, his marker much smaller.

WILLIAM JOSEPH BRADSHAW
GOD'S GREATEST GIFT RETURNED TO HIM.
ABSENT FROM OUR LIVES BUT FOREVER IN OUR HEARTS.

Sophie bent down and traced William's name with her finger.

"Hey, baby boy," she said. The cold grass around his headstone crunched as she sat down. "I'm sorry I haven't been here in a while to see you. I've missed you."

Weeds had grown in around the sides, making the date of his birthday disappear.

She tried to pull some of them away, but the deep roots held firm.

"I'm married now. I wish you could meet him. His name is Thomas."

The wind started to blow. Dried leaves blew and covered his grave-stone. Sophie wiped them off as fast as she could. She then used both hands to jerk every unwelcomed weed from the firm ground until her cold fingers bled.

"Please forgive me for not saving you," she said to him, as she laid her head down on top of his.

GRACE

"What do you want done today?" I asked Roni. It was three and a half weeks since I'd been allowed to work in the salon. My hands were a little shaky. Several women had put in requests for haircuts, so today was going to be busy. I was glad for the distraction and thankful for the work.

Death row inmates took the first appointments of the morning so the officers could minimize the interactions they had with the general population. Kinda strange, I thought, since I was the one holding the scissors, but rules were rules.

"I want something different," Roni replied, her face branded with resolve. Her disposition had changed since she started corresponding with her father. One might even describe her as chipper these days.

"Give me some layers." She handed me a picture she'd torn out of *People* magazine. Jodie Foster was standing on the red carpet in a shimmering beaded gown.

"My dad said he loved her in *Silence of the Lambs*."

I took the picture and studied it. I was all for a good makeover, but I wasn't a miracle worker. Roni's hair was short on the sides and long in the back, and vaguely reminded me of a serial shoplifter I'd once seen on *The Jerry Springer Show*.

"You realize I'm going to have to cut your length and let the top grow out some before your hair can look exactly like Jodie Foster's?" I emphasized the word *exactly* so she didn't lose the newly found glow in her cheeks.

Roni looked at her reflection in the plastic-coated mirror in front of her swivel chair. With a heavy sigh, she grabbed Jodie out of my hands and said, "Damn it, Grace. Just give me the usual."

After a few minutes of reverent negotiations, I was able to talk her into taking a few inches off the length and softening the long gap between her bangs and the middle of her back. She also allowed me to cut in a few soft angles around her face.

Roni seemed pleased when she left. "Do you want a tip?" she asked me. An off-center grin started to emerge.

"Sure," I replied. "Think this will be a first."

"Get a different job."

She was still chuckling at her own joke when the officer handcuffed her and led her out of the beauty salon and back to her cell.

I was on my twelfth haircut of the day when the officer interrupted and said, "Last haircut, Bradshaw. The warden wants to see you."

This was my seventeenth year in Lakeland and I can say I'd seen Warden Richards only a handful of times. I heard him announce things over the loudspeaker and saw his name at the bottom of memos . . .

ALL INMATES FROM THIS POINT FORWARD ARE ONLY ALLOWED TO USE THREE-INCH TOOTHBRUSHES. NORMAL-SIZE TOOTHBRUSHES ARE AGAINST POLICY AND ARE CONSIDERED CONTRABAND. THREE-INCH TOOTHBRUSHES WILL BE ISSUED IMMEDIATELY.

WARDEN ELROD RICHARDS

It was weird to think I would *never, ever* use a normal-size toothbrush again, but hey, we all had to adjust.

I closed the salon as instructed. The two officers put my hands and feet back in shackles and I shuffled, sandwiched between them, to the waiting area outside the warden's office.

"Take 'em off," the female officer said to me. I dragged my feet behind the curtained area and forced myself to think about the taste of roasted marshmallows smothered between chocolate and graham crackers while the officers inspected me. They handed me a different uniform when they finished. This new waistband pinched my skin.

"Prisoner 44607 on deck," the male officer yelled as he opened the door into the warden's office.

Warden Richards was sitting behind a scratched metal desk. Ms. Liz sat across from him in a folding chair. Neither looked at me when I entered. I asked them if something awful had happened to Sophie.

"Please take a seat," the warden said, motioning to the seat beside Ms. Liz.

He didn't believe in pleasantries, nor did he look like he could be in charge of a maximum-security prison. His total weight with firearms couldn't have exceeded 130 pounds.

He slid a paper across the desk to me. Ms. Liz didn't say anything to me. Her eyes were closed. I think she was praying.

I bent over the desk to read the paper. I needed my reading glasses, but I could clearly see at the top of the page the paper read: DEATH WARRANT.

I took a deep breath and sat back in my chair. My vision blurred and I needed a minute to think.

Ms. Liz finally spoke: "Grace, the warden told me your final appeal had been denied. You are aware of that, right?" Her words were quiet and thin.

"My attorney told me. I met with him a few weeks ago."

"I know this is difficult for you to do, but the warden needs you to read the paper. You have to be aware of what is going to happen."

I bent over the paper again. The small print moved around.

Ms. Liz took the paper from in front of me. "Do I have your permission to read this out loud to her?"

"This has to get done some way," the warden replied. A framed picture of him shaking the governor's hand sat on the bookshelf behind him.

Ms. Liz inhaled slowly and started to read. "The South Carolina Department of Criminal Justice has ordered that on February 15—" Her voice cracked and she stopped reading long enough to take a drink from her bottled water. "That on February 15, Grace Margaret Bradshaw be placed in a room arranged for execution—" She stopped reading again.

"For God's sake. Give me the paper," the warden ordered. He pushed his silver-rimmed glasses up on his nose.

"That on February 15, Grace Margaret Bradshaw be placed in a room arranged for execution and be injected with a substance or substances in lethal quantity sufficient enough to cause death and to continue with injection until such time until the said Grace Margaret Bradshaw is dead."

He read the words without stopping. "Do you understand the order as it has been given?"

I answered yes. And that was the last thing I remembered.

SOPHIE

Ben Taylor sat at the back booth in the corner of the 40th Street Café. He seemed to be involved in something significant, because his eyes didn't look up from his laptop even when the bells jingled as Sophie opened the front door.

"Welcome to the Fortieth Street," said the waitress, juggling a turkey club platter in one hand and a coffeepot in another. "Sit down anywhere you'd like."

The waitress didn't recognize the grown-up Bradshaw daughter, but Sophie couldn't forget her familiar face. Sophie's dad, too tired from work and too depressed to eat another meal at their once-full family table, often took her to the café for dinner. Their once-a-week treat turned into three to four times. She always ordered the grilled cheese on sourdough, her dad whatever special Lucy suggested.

"You need some meat on those bones, Paul," Lucy said, with a wink at first, then a slight brush of her arm against his when she scooted by with menus and waters. Her long nails changed color every time they ate there: sometimes they were deep red, other times clear, with rhinestones outlining the top.

Sophie knew Lucy desired more from her dad than weight gain. Her father, oblivious to anyone's affection, would read the newspaper and ask Sophie the same questions day after day: "How was math today?" or "Everyone at school being nice?"

One day, between serving him his chicken-fried steak with fried okra and rhubarb pie, Lucy worked up the nerve to ask him on a date.

"Paul, you know I do a lot of the cooking around here and you do a whole lot of the eating," she said, as her voice and gaping neckline lowered. "Why don't you let me come over and make you a home-cooked meal."

Sophie stopped gulping her milk long enough to blurt out, "My mom is gone, not dead."

Her dad, whose face now resembled the color of Twizzlers, gave Sophie "the look." She didn't get that look often, but when she did, she knew he meant business.

"You are a great cook, Lucy, one of the best, but Sophie and I are doing just fine. I'll continue to enjoy your creamed corn from right here, if you don't mind."

"You know where to find me if you change your mind." She touched his hand as she refilled his water. When he left a ten-dollar tip instead of his usual five, Sophie knew he'd felt bad about hurting her feelings.

Sophie stood at the end of Ben Taylor's booth, waiting for him to look up. "Hello," she finally said, after he still hadn't noticed her.

"Hello. Glad you came." He slid out of the booth and stood while she sat down. "Are you hungry?"

Sophie realized suddenly that she hadn't eaten since she entered Brookfield. "Yes, a little bit."

Ben handed her a menu, but Sophie declined. When Lucy came to take their order, she wanted the usual—a grilled cheese sandwich on sourdough.

Sophie and Ben made small talk throughout lunch. He asked about her life, her husband, and if she worked. Her answers were polite but brief, since she didn't want her mother to know anything about her, especially since she was using her lawyer as a go-between. To deflect his questions, she asked questions back to him. Two grown children, one a lawyer just like him, and the other a girls' volleyball coach at a small D-I college outside Chicago. Both boys.

"How long have you been married?" Sophie noticed Ben didn't mention his wife one time during their discussion.

"Twenty-three years," Ben answered. "My wife passed away a year after we moved to Brookfield." He pulled out his billfold to show her an old family photo.

"She was beautiful," Sophie said as she took the photo out of the plastic covering. "How did she die, if you don't mind me asking?"

"A brain aneurysm. It was very sudden." He took the photo back and looked at it for several seconds before he slipped it into his wallet. "I took the time I had with her for granted. My biggest regret."

"I'm sorry for your loss."

"And I'm sorry for yours."

Both remained silent for a moment before Ben brought up the conversation they were here to discuss.

"As I told you earlier, I've been your mother's attorney for the last several years. The first case I took since moving here, actually. The public defender she had did a horrible job. She didn't interview witnesses she should have and put people on the stand who were not well prepared. They were eaten alive by the prosecutor." He rolled a straw between his stiffened hands.

"My dad wasn't thrilled with them, either, but I saw the evidence. We didn't have a lot of money and they didn't have a lot to work with. The ethylene glycol in my brother's bottle, the windshield-wiper fluid hidden in our house . . . it didn't look good." Her voice sounded cold as she spoke those old words.

"I know the evidence and their accusations quite well. The prosecutors drilled into the defense that your mother had Munchausen—"

"That my mom purposefully made my brother sick so she could take him to the doctor." Words she regurgitated out loud, but had said many times before to herself. "She craved attention."

"Refill?" Lucy grabbed their water glasses before they could decline.

"Yes, that's what they said," he repeated after Lucy left, agreeing with the definition but not the charge. "She doesn't fit the profile."

"My brother is dead. He became sick only when he was around her. Profile or no profile, the evidence convinced me."

"You and every appeals board," Ben responded matter-of-factly. "Your mom's case keeps me awake at night. The pieces just don't fit."

Sophie chewed the last bite of her grilled cheese.

"Why didn't your mom make you sick?" Ben asked. He spoke softly, because Lucy was wiping down the still-empty booth behind them for the third time.

Sophie swallowed twice, but the cheese from her sandwich didn't go down. She picked up her water and took a long sip. After swallowing again, she said, "Maybe she did."

"What do you mean?" Ben asked, not disguising his surprise.

"I don't know what I mean. I'm second-guessing everything that happened in my childhood now. Every time I threw up, every stomachache—did she cause that, too?"

Ben took his napkin off his lap and put it on the table. "Do you think she would do that?"

"I really don't know." *Why not me? Why William?*

Ben didn't say anything for a few seconds. Sophie felt like he was giving her a chance to reconsider, to say something that would help him help her mother. When she didn't, he finally said, "I have done everything I could think of to get the courts to retry her case, but unfortunately your mother's last appeal has been denied." He stopped, giving her time to absorb what was coming next, but before he could continue, Lucy rushed over with the coffeepot.

"Sophie Bradshaw, I should have known it was you when you ordered that grilled cheese. I haven't seen you in ages." She plunked the coffeepot down on the table and moved in for a side hug. With her arm squeezing Sophie's, she said, "I hope this lawyer here can help your mom before she's executed."

BEN PAID THE BILL, helped Sophie put on her jacket, and escorted her across the street to his office. Lucy's exaggerated greeting had stirred the café, and the subsequent stares of the people sitting along the counter were too much for Sophie to handle.

"I hate this place," she said as she followed Ben into his office. "I couldn't wait to leave. I can't believe I'm here now."

The old feelings of being the center of unwanted attention over-whelmed her. She didn't know whether to sit down or run.

"You didn't deserve this, but I don't believe your mom deserves this, either. I need you to understand me. Your mother's appeals are gone, and her execution date has been set. If the governor doesn't intervene, your mother will die by lethal injection on February fifteenth."

SOPHIE CRIED MOST OF THE way home. What did Ben Taylor expect her to say? That all of a sudden she believed her mom was innocent? She didn't. But did she really want her to die?

Going back to Brookfield, dredging up mud she'd shaken off long ago, had been a huge mistake, she decided. "I'm going to seek clemency from the governor," Ben had said, "but it's a long, if not impossible, shot. Please consider visiting your mother one last time, before it's too late."

Sophie had left his office without committing either way. She did agree to give him her cell-phone number, and asked him to call only if absolutely necessary. She didn't know in this situation what exactly constituted an emergency.

She took his number as well, promising to call if she decided to visit. "My husband and his family know nothing about my past, and I'd like to keep it that way."

He'd nodded, but his downturned gaze said he didn't understand. "I believe in Grace," he'd said, walking her to his office door. "Help me figure out what we are missing."

At every red light, when Sophie had time to pause, she pictured her mom being strapped to a gurney. Long needles being pushed into her veins. Her voice quivering as she said her last words. Her mother dying all alone.

It was almost 7 p.m. when Sophie swiped her card and pulled into the parking lot outside Thomas's office, thinking he'd be working late again and not yet at home. She checked her cell phone as soon as she parked. It was surprising that Thomas hadn't called since the day before, but then again, she hadn't felt like calling him. No communication until she returned home felt better than making up more lies.

She riffled through her purse for her makeup bag. Eye concealer didn't do a thing to cover her dark circles. Lack of sleep and puffy eyes had clearly won this battle.

She ran her fingers through her hair and applied Thomas's favorite shade of lipstick. On this night she couldn't care less about sexy, but understanding and forgiveness she would take. She had to tell him the truth and she had to do it now, before she lost her nerve. Thomas had to understand why she lied to him and why she hadn't told him before now. She needed him to help her decide what to do.

Sophie walked to the back of the building and tried the outside door. It was locked, so she walked around to the other side and tried another entrance. Had everyone left for the day?

She scanned the lot. Thomas's car was parked in the usual spot, and another car she didn't recognize was parked behind the dumpsters. A white van with the logo VERY MERRY MAIDS was parked by the side door.

Other than the cleaning crew, everyone seemed to be gone. Sophie tapped on the side door to get someone's attention. A vacuum hummed in the background, telling Sophie her pleas for entry might take a while.

She pulled her cell phone out and texted Thomas: *R u busy?* She sat down on the sidewalk curb to check her e-mail when he didn't answer right away.

Extremely, Thomas replied a few minutes later. She could see little dots on her message screen indicating he was typing. *At hospital. Late surgery. Call u later.*

She walked back to the parking lot to make sure it was his car she'd seen. A WEST LAKE HOMEOWNER sticker proved she wasn't crazy. *Did he ride from his office to the hospital with one of his partners?*

Sophie braced herself on the hood of his car.

A lady carrying a vacuum and a bucket of water opened the side door.

"Hold the door," Sophie yelled to her. "Everybody gone for the day?" she asked as she walked in.

"Everybody but the young doctor." The maid winked. "Think he's back there with his pretty wife, by the sound of things."

"Dr. Logan?" Sophie asked.

"I don't know. The cute one," the cleaning lady said while picking up a piece of lint off the floor. "The one with the dark wavy hair."

Sophie didn't know if she was going to throw up or pass out, but decided neither would help her find out what was going on with Thomas. Her lighted cell phone helped her find her way down the dark hallway.

The maid was mistaken, Sophie reassured herself. *He's gotten rides to the hospital with his partners before, especially if they were in the OR together.* A few weeks ago, Thomas's partner had left his car in the office lot and Thomas had driven him home. A long call night could make a short car drive home seem like an eternity.

By the time Sophie reached the end of the hallway, she had convinced herself she was being foolish and the maid was being nosy. She rubbed her hand against the wall to find a light switch.

As soon as she flipped the switch, her worst fears were confirmed. On the chair outside Thomas's office lay Eva's Coach purse and her red sling-back high-heeled shoes.

GRACE

Beep. Beep. Beep. Something tight was squeezing my arm. I tried to take it off, but I couldn't reach it.

"Don't try and move. I'll be over there in a minute."

I had no idea who was speaking to me or where I was, but the bright lights made my eyes sting. The side of my head felt wet and crusty at the same time. I tried to sit up, but I couldn't because my arms and legs were in restraints. I started to gag.

A heavyset lady with a bun and a blue cardigan turned my head to the side and shoved an emesis basin under my mouth. "Hold on. Let me get the head of your bed up."

She pushed a button and the top of my mattress started to rise. Nothing came out of my stomach, despite my repeated attempts.

"Dry heaves," she said. "Nothing left in there." She removed the blood-pressure cuff from my arm. The loud Velcro rip pierced my ears and I shut my eyes again. "I can give you something for nausea now that you're awake." She grabbed a syringe off a tray and injected something in the bottle hanging beside my bed. "Do you know where you are?"

Was it time for me to die?

"Infirmary. You fainted in the warden's office. Smacked your head on the corner of his desk. Been out of it since last night."

February 15. Now I remembered. *Then I thought of Sophie.*

"May I have something to drink?" My tongue stuck to my lips.

"I'll get you some ice chips to start." The soles of her shoes squished on the floor as she walked away.

"Up for a visitor?" I heard a soothing voice ask. I opened one eye to see Ms. Liz place a warm washcloth on my head. "I didn't know if you were ever going to wake up."

I didn't know I had a choice.

The nurse returned and handed Ms. Liz my ice chips. She put some in a spoon and then up to my lips. Her fingers were bony and bent.

"What can I do to help you through this?" she asked after I'd had a few spoonfuls of ice. She rubbed the thick joints on her right hand.

"Turn back time," I said. I tried to smile, but it wasn't a happy smile.

"Any luck finding your daughter?" I knew she knew the answer before she asked.

We used to talk about Sophie all the time during our sessions, but I didn't have any new stories to tell. So I'd stopped talking. *Tomorrow is Sophie's birthday*, I wanted to tell her. *She's turning thirty.*

"My lawyer said he won't give up." I tilted my head to the side because my eyes burned. "I'm not sure I want him to find her."

"Oh, Grace," Ms. Liz said. "You're not thinking clearly. Of course you want to see her before . . ." She stopped, but I could finish her sentence.

"She's moved forward." It's not about what I want, I wanted to tell her. My life will soon be over and I want Sophie's to go on. I have caused her enough pain. What if Ben finds her—and we have to say good-bye? "I hope she has a new family that loves her now."

"I will pray for that, too." She bent her head down and rubbed the back of her neck. "I've been in this prison for a long time, and I've met people whose very presence made my soul take cover. Born wicked, I really believe. Then I've met killers who donated the money in their commissary account, all of it, to buy school supplies for another inmate's kid. Prison makes some people worse and it makes some people better, but you . . ." She stopped. I had no idea where she was going with this. "You have stayed the same. You came in selfless and you're leaving selfless. You haven't changed a bit."

I knew all of that wasn't true. I'd not become bitter, but I wasn't much to look at. I had a dream (or maybe a nightmare) about seeing Sophie face-to-face again, after all these years, and my sunken face was the one she didn't recognize. *I'm looking for my mom. Has anyone seen my mom?*

"You have a daughter, right?" I asked Ms. Liz.

"Yes, I do. My oldest is married and has two kids. My middle daughter, Hildie, works for a lawn-and-garden store in San Diego. My baby, Olive, is still trying to figure herself out."

"Can I ask you a question, then?"

"Sure."

"What is one thing you'd make sure your daughters knew before you died?"

Dear Sophie,

I had an accident today, but the prison doc said I should feel fine in a couple days. Ordered me to stay off my feet for the next forty-eight hours. I could have stayed in the infirmary, but I begged them to let me go back to my cell. "What's the worst thing that could happen?" I heard the doctor say rhetorically to the nurse.

Twenty-three stitches now extend from my eyebrow to my ear on the right side of my head. I guess I can be thankful—I won't have to live with that scar for long.

One of the other inmates, Roni, has a scar. It's a thick curved gash starting at the nape of her neck and winding down, tapering right before the small in her back. I saw it when she lifted up her orange shirt to be strip-searched. "Roni," I shouted, before I could stop myself. "What in the world happened to you?"

She thrust up her chin and with an icy smile said, "Wires from my bed frame. My stepdad's way of reminding me never to hide from him again."

I love what my friend Kimberly had to say about scars. You remember her, right? The one who had breast cancer. She'd bring Tessa over to play with you on the Slip'N Slide when her blood counts allowed her to get out of the house. Really, she said it about bald heads, but the same applies here.

Kimberly made a whole list of things after her chemo stopped working titled "Things to Bury." Sometimes she called it her "I don't have to be socially acceptable because I'm dying" list. A mantra, of sorts, for those who chose to do what they wanted to do in the first place.

I can't recall everything she had written down except for the one that impacted me the most. BURY MY INSECURITIES. She took her bandana off her head when I asked her to explain that one to me.

"I used to be afraid of the stares."

"The stares?" I asked her, like I didn't already know what she meant. I fiddled with a navy-blue thread dangling from a button on my blouse.

"You can stare at my bald head." Kimberly grabbed my hand to stop my fiddling and looked me square in the eyes. "I'm okay with it now."

She did something twirly with her eyes, which made us both laugh.

"Losing my hair made me almost as scared as my diagnosis did." She opened the patio door to make sure you and Tessa were still sliding before she continued. "Then one night Charlie was working, and I had to run to the grocery store. I saw another person who was wearing a bandana, and we connected."

"You connected?"

"Well, our bald heads connected," she said with a slight laugh. "My bald head helped me empathize with someone else's bald head. It was in that moment I realized bald heads need other bald heads to heal."

Bald heads heal bald heads, and scars heal scars.

I'm making it the goal of my scar to help Roni heal hers.

I can't remember the rest of Kimberly's list, but this one you might find funny: BURY MY GIRDLE. (Do women still wear those awful things?) We burned eight pairs of constricting Lycra over a lighted grill in our backyard. "Your muffin top should never ever be mistreated," she said to you and Tessa as she poked the black body shaper with a stick.

Dying makes some people smarter and much more comfortable in their own skin, don't you think?

SOPHIE

Sophie stood frozen in the hallway outside an empty doctor's office. She knew her next move needed to be well planned out. Her first, second, and third reactions were to barrel through the door and dissect Eva's cheating heart with a scalpel. Surely Thomas had one around here somewhere.

Then after a few moments of reasoning, intermixed with intense gum chewing, she realized Thomas should be the one to blame. Her anger should be directed toward him. First for his lies, then for his poor choice in women to cheat with. She could see the headlines now: "Doctor's Wife Kills Husband's Mistress with Own Scalpel."

Neither option was rational or productive, since the paper would then read "Daughter Shares Cell with Mother on Death Row," but the longer Sophie stood outside Thomas's door, the madder she became. Hearing Eva giggle and Thomas laugh . . .

What were they doing in there? It didn't sound like sex, but it didn't sound work-related, either.

Sophie started to knock, to confront them both, but just the thought of seeing Eva straightening her silk blouse with that "he wants me more than you" look made her want to hit something. The safest thing for her to do was leave before someone other than her got hurt.

WHY *WOULDN'T* THOMAS CHEAT ON HER? Deep down in the places Sophie tried so hard to cover up, to reconstruct, to move past, there remained an orphan whom nobody ever wanted. No Elizabeth Arden lipstick or Chanel satin scarves would make her worthy of a life she didn't deserve to live. She couldn't believe it had taken Thomas this long to stray.

Sophie wasn't going home, but she was tired of driving. So after an hour of dissecting herself and fantasizing about dismembering Eva, her car ended up in the parking lot of St. John's Hospital.

Visiting hours for non–family members were over at eight, but Sophie hoped her status had progressed to more than that, considering she spent so much time with Max. If it hadn't, maybe Mindy was on and could let her at least read him a story before he fell asleep.

Mindy was pushing the medicine cart when Sophie walked through the door into the pediatric wing. The first thing in her horrible day that had gone right.

"Are you okay?" Mindy asked her. "You look like hell."

Her brutal honesty made Sophie laugh, since Mindy was normally very careful to word her comments gently.

"Tell me what you really think," Sophie said. She caught a glimpse of her reflection in the stainless-steel linen cart in the hallway. "This mascara is supposed to be waterproof." She scrambled through her purse for a Kleenex.

Mindy handed her a wet wipe from the top of the medicine cart. "Want to talk about it?"

"Actually, I do," she said, before her internal guards stopped her. "But now's not the time. You're working, and besides, I need to see my little man."

Mindy nodded. "You better hurry. His big eyes were drooping just a minute ago."

Sophie stopped by the restroom before going into Max's room. The last thing she wanted to do was scare the poor boy before he fell asleep. The black smudges underneath her swollen eyelids startled even her.

Her cell phone beeped as she was wiping the black tracks from above her cheekbones.

Finding her phone buried deep in her purse took more energy than she wanted to expend, but the repeated alerts made ignoring the message impossible. When she found the phone, a message from Thomas read *Leaving work now. I miss you.*

Sophie thought about tossing the phone against the wall or into the toilet, but she remembered her mother's attorney had her number. Not that she wanted to hear from him or any other man in her life, but some gnawing sense of obligation won her over.

Ignore Thomas, she told herself. *Deal with him later.* First of all, she didn't know what she would say or how she would say it. If you call someone a cheater with a southern accent, does that make it sound any better?

She shut off her phone and threw it in her purse. The only person she felt sure about was waiting for her across the hall.

Max's back was turned to Sophie when she entered his room. Buzz Lightyear and his companions all stood across from one another around the perimeter of his bed. In formation for an upcoming battle, no doubt, thwarted by a little boy's sleepy eyes and worn-out body. His *Toy Story* blanket had fallen out of his crib and was lying on the floor.

Sophie bent down and picked it up. She placed the trim close to his face, just the way he liked it. Her heart weighed with the thought of it falling out and Max crying for it with no one to hear or come to pick it up. Did he cry for long? Or did he never start, knowing his tears were futile because no one was around to wipe them away?

It wasn't that the nursing staff was inattentive—quite the opposite. Max got all his physical needs met. Vitals every four hours, a nurses' aide to pour milk on his Cap'n Crunch, and an occupational therapist to give him wagon rides and teach him to tie his shoes. The secret trips to McDonald's and hiding under the covers with his mommy were what he was missing.

Who comforted him when he woke up in the middle of the night scared of a bump forming in the hospital curtains or the creaking noise coming from under his bed? Who told him everything was going to be okay when his lungs filled up with fluid and his body shook from shaking chills from one more high fever? Who would be his tooth fairy when his front incisor fell out? All those milestones would go uncelebrated in the history of this little boy.

Sophie leaned over the side rail and brushed the long waves away from his face. He needed a haircut, she thought, making a mental note to ask Mindy how that worked in the hospital. Max's arms stirred and he looked like he was about to wake up.

"Max?"

She realized waking him was selfish, but she knew he could always use some love, no matter what time of night. When he didn't move, she bent over and kissed his plump cheek. Her lips lingered a little too long, still hoping he would wake up and show her his toothy smile. Or sit up and be so glad to see her she'd have a reason to stay. A place to stay. She could sleep right beside him in the recliner.

When he didn't wake up, she pulled the chair by his bed and watched his tiny chest move up and down. The corners of his mouth twitched as if he was dreaming of somewhere or something sweet. For the first time, she thought about scooping him up and taking him home with her. Making all the wrongs that had been done to him all better with one gigantic act of right. She could love him and take care of him, since his mother wouldn't. At least then he'd have a fighting chance.

Thomas had lost his right to an opinion. If she stayed with him, and that was a big if, he'd have to get over the fact that having a child, a special-needs child, would be challenging and time-consuming. She could hear his arguments now. *Max needs a full-time caregiver. Are you prepared to do that?*

She didn't care what he thought. For once, she didn't care what Thomas needed. She cared only about Max and what was best for him. It was the first definitive decision she'd made in a long time. And this decision felt right.

SOPHIE WOKE TO SOMEONE RUBBING her shoulder. "You going to stay here all night?" Mindy said in a voice just above a whisper. "Thomas must be worried sick about you."

"What time is it?" Sophie replied, trying to find her cell phone.

"Five-fifteen in the morning."

"Oh my gosh, I can't believe I fell asleep!" She turned on her phone and quickly became distracted by the multiple alerts: 9:17 p.m.—*where r u? Call me.* 9:45 p.m.—*worried, call me.* Five missed calls, five voice-mails, all from Thomas. The last one saying if she didn't call him soon he was calling the police.

"Better take care of this." She showed Mindy her phone, then pushed the recliner back against the wall and kissed Max one final time before leaving. "Let's talk soon?" she said to Mindy. "I want to know how you're doing with Stephen being gone."

"Anytime," Mindy told her. Sophie held her arms out and gave Mindy a much-needed hug.

"Hey, isn't today your birthday?" Mindy asked her, after their longer-than-ever embrace.

"Oh, I guess it is." The large whiteboard in Max's room displayed to-day's date.

"Well, happy birthday! Call me later and we will celebrate."

"Will do," Sophie told her, as she left a sleeping Max and dialed her husband's cell number.

THOMAS ANSWERED THE PHONE on the first ring. "Thank God. Are you okay?"

"I'm fine. I didn't mean to scare you. You said you were going to be late, so I went to visit Max. I fell asleep." There were several things she purposefully left unsaid in that sentence.

"I thought something happened to you. I called every hospital between here and Charlotte. The police were no help. They told me to call back today if you didn't show up." Sophie could tell he was frustrated. Relieved, but frustrated.

"I'm sorry. I didn't mean to worry you." She couldn't believe she was the one apologizing. "We need to talk. I'm walking out of the hospital. I need to go through Starbucks first and get something to drink. Want anything?" Had she really just asked him if he wanted Starbucks? She was as crazy as her mom.

"I want you to be at home, that's what I want—" His frustration was now turning into irritation.

"I said I was sorry," she snapped back.

"I'm glad you're okay," Thomas said, regrouping his tone and his choice of words. "Every noise I heard I prayed it was the garage door opening. I need to leave for an early surgery. Fifth cup of coffee, I guess I'm a little on edge."

"We both are." Sophie did not want to wait any longer to confront him about his late-night affairs, but she didn't want to do it on her phone in the hospital corridor, either.

"Remember we have the Heart Ball tonight?" he asked before she could make it to someplace more private. "My whole office is going. It'll be a good chance for you to hit some of them up for donations."

The Heart Ball. She had completely forgotten. Her birthday—she guessed he didn't care.

Thirty years old today, and the only present she wanted she'd just left, asleep in his bed all by himself.

GRACE

I haven't written Sophie in a few days. My eyesight's been a bit fuzzy since the fall. I've tried to nap two or three times this afternoon, but the sound of cursing, toilets flushing, and opposing radio stations kept waking me up. Carmen was listening to twang (she calls it Grand Ole Opry music), and Roni had on a NASCAR race. I contemplated taking out my own stitches so my head wouldn't explode.

My pillow had just gotten comfortable when the officer yelled, "Stand for count."

Flashing dots obstructed my vision, so I couldn't see who was shouting at me through the window as I tried to stand. I braced my leg against the side of my cot so I didn't lose my balance.

"Bradshaw, the chaplain is here to see you."

"Sir?" I replied. He had to know the doctor gave instructions for me to stay in bed.

"Move it along. Put your hands through."

I held on to the side of the wall and tried to move as fast as I was being ordered to, but the room started to fade. My choices were obey and fall on the concrete floor or disobey and fall on my bed. I chose the bed.

"Bradshaw, if you ever want to see the light of day again, stand up and give me your hands." His words faded and I didn't hear what he said next. He continued shouting as he opened the door to my cell.

"When I give you an order," he bellowed close to my face, "you follow it."

I'd never seen this guy before. He grabbed my arm and forced me to stand up. The metal on his belt buckle caught the side of my forehead on my way up. I felt one of my stitches pop.

"You can make your last days pleasant or unpleasant. The choice is yours," he barked as he shoved me against the wall. The cold of the cinder blocks felt good against my face.

He cuffed me and I followed him the best I could to the dayroom.

Live life with a counterintuitive love. I could hear Paul whispering one of his sermons in my ringing ear. *Let your enemies bring out the best in you, not the worst.*

"She's bleeding," Ms. Liz said as we approached the table she was sitting at.

"She doesn't follow orders," the officer replied, stretching out the word *she*. He pulled out a chair and pushed me down in it. "Fifteen minutes," he said, and walked away.

"I asked for permission to see you *in your cell*," Ms. Liz said. She made sure the officer's back was turned before stroking my forearm. She pulled a tissue from her bag and blotted the blood dripping down the side of my face.

"Do you want to go to the infirmary?" she whispered.

"No." I wanted Paul.

"Can you get me a drink of water?" The inside of my mouth felt sunburned.

She did, and a minute or two later I felt okay again.

"I have an answer to your question." She unfolded a piece of notebook paper from her small black Bible.

"What question is that?" I asked her.

"The question you asked me a few days ago. I've thought a lot about it."

She placed the paper on her lap and straightened it with her arthritic hands. "You asked me what's the one thing I'd want my daughters to know before I died."

I had remembered, but I didn't think she would. When she left my bedside that day, I knew I'd crossed a line. In prison, relationships were one-sided. I was supposed to listen and obey. No questions asked. I'd let Ms. Liz into my life when I shared with her stories about my family. I hadn't expected her to let me into hers.

"The obvious answer to your question is that I would want my girls to know I love them."

I could tell this conversation meant something to her, too, by the way she looked deep into my eyes.

"I think they know that, though," she continued. "I also want them to know that every time I look at them, I'm swollen with pride. I still can't believe I"—she put her curled fingers to her chest—"got to play a small part in their creation." She looked back down at her paper. "I hope they know that."

I started to tear up and then I sniffled. She handed me another tissue. I leaned toward her because I didn't want to miss a word of what she had to say.

Ms. Liz opened her Bible. Notes written in black pen covered the margins. A dark purple velvet ribbon marked her place.

I thought she was about to read me Scripture, but she didn't. Instead she took a long sip of her bottled water.

"This isn't a standard conversation I have with inmates." She put down her bottled water and hesitated, like she was making sure her seat belt was fastened or the stove was turned off. "But as I told you before, you're different. I feel I can trust you."

I haven't heard those words in well over seventeen years.

"I haven't always been a great mother." She lifted her Bible off her lap and then looked at me for my reaction.

"No judgment here." I held up my handcuffed hands and we both laughed.

"Let's just say my youngest daughter and I have not always seen eye to eye on things. I believed proper parenting meant I had to have a list of rules for my girls to follow. I wanted to raise good girls who waited until they were married to have sex, and didn't drink a sip of alcohol unless it was presented to them at the Communion table in the Lord's house."

She brushed her hand over the cover of the Bible. "Olive always rebelled. If I said curfew was at midnight she'd come in at two. If I said she could date when she turned sixteen, she'd come in with a hickey at fifteen and a half just to spite me."

Ms. Liz picked up the Bible and placed it on her chest. "I turned this book into a set of rules."

"Five minutes," the officer yelled.

"To make a long story short, Olive wouldn't award me Mother of the Year.

"She got into some trouble with a boy in high school, and she didn't feel like she could come to me." Her voice cracked. I wanted to touch her hand or hug her.

"I would have helped her with the baby, but I guess she didn't trust that."

I nodded like I knew how Ms. Liz was feeling.

"I didn't find out she had the abortion until months later. I overheard her on the phone with a friend."

"How is Olive doing now?"

"She is doing fine, I think, but our relationship is strained. I can see it when she looks at me. Always wondering if I'm disappointed in her."

Ms. Liz looked over at the officer. He started to walk our way. Our time today was almost over.

"So to answer your question—"

"Time's up."

Ms. Liz slipped a folded-up piece of paper from her Bible into my hands before the officer noticed. I squeezed it tight, feeling almost normal as he escorted me back to my cell.

SOPHIE

Sophie hadn't seen or talked to Thomas all day. He'd left a note for her on the Keurig machine that morning that read *Got paged to OR, call you later,* but he didn't. No "I'm sorry I'm cheating" text or "I hope you're having a great birthday" long-stemmed roses awaiting her by the front door.

So after hours of analyzing her next move, interspersed with imagining various painful ways to remove Eva's gel-filled claws from Thomas's back, Sophie decided to do something for herself. She dug out her measuring tape from the linen closet and began designing a bedroom. A little boy's room, with trains and LEGOs and walls painted bright blue.

The doorbell rang around 7:30 p.m., right as she was Googling "most secure way to install an indoor tire swing." She contemplated not answering, pretending to be gone, but the lights in the foyer had already given her away.

The bell rang again before she could open the front door. She expected to see Joey, the neighbor's impatient kid, dressed in full Boy Scout uniform, selling popcorn. A big tin full of caramel corn dipped in chocolate didn't sound like a bad idea. A birthday present to herself. She'd pop in a movie and eat herself into a more acceptable place.

When Sophie answered, she found Thomas waiting under the outside lights, wearing his black tux. "Your chariot awaits," he said, motioning to the limo parked in their circle drive. His arm dropped once he noticed her torn denim jeans and UNC T-shirt.

"The Heart Ball," Sophie said, now recalling his earlier reminder. "I got distracted and totally forgot."

"I can see that," he said. When she stared back at him and said nothing, he looked at his watch and said, "It's okay, baby. Hurry up and get ready. We still have time."

"I'm not going to the stupid Heart Ball. You and I, we need to talk."

"Sophie, what is going on with you?" Thomas put one finger in the air to signal to the driver they'd be a minute. "You've been acting strange for days."

"Are you kidding me?" she shrieked. "You seem to be the one who's acting. You and—"

Thomas cut her off before she could elaborate. "Whatever is going on with you—you need to calm down." He turned to make sure the driver wasn't watching them. He was, so Thomas waved and held up his "one minute" finger again. "We can talk, but now's not the time. I've got a car waiting for us. My partners are waiting on us. I've told them all about your fund-raiser. You have to go."

Sophie didn't have any more energy to argue or the will to object. In this moment, she hated Thomas, but not enough to damage everything he'd worked for—everything she'd worked for. She could pretend she was happy and devoted to Thomas for at least one more night.

"Please, go get ready," Thomas begged her, and his eyes rounded. "This is important to me."

Sophie finally relented, but not calmly. She slammed her bedroom door before jumping into the shower. *At least I know the chefs. I pray they're serving good wine and tons of shrimp.* She could drink, eat, and force herself to make small talk for a few hours if she had to.

But when she toweled off from her shower and stood before the full-length mirror, the mottled skin covering her cheekbones clashing with the dark circles under her eyes didn't make her feel any better about turning thirty.

"Oh, Sophie," she could hear the synthetics say as she chose between the mint-green sequined dress with the low-cut neckline and the deep purple gown with the keyhole opening down the back, "you look fabulous in that dress." But as soon as she turned around, she feared one of them would whisper, "If her husband was a carpenter, why wouldn't she get new shelves?" She pulled the Victoria's Secret satin strapless push-up from her lingerie drawer.

There's always going to be someone prettier, someone uglier, someone skinnier or who has bigger boobs, her mom told her before she left to go to prison. *Define yourself by the size of your heart, not the size of your jeans. You're exactly how you are supposed to be.*

THE DRIVER WAITED OUTSIDE THE CAR with the back door open. "Quite an elaborate ride you've secured for us tonight," Sophie said, trying to fake nice as Thomas walked her to the limo. "Car in the shop?"

Thomas smiled, seemingly glad she was finally ready and in a better mood. She slid in the backseat and he scooted in beside her. "I missed you," he said as he kissed her cheek and put his hand on her thigh.

She wanted to believe him, kiss him back, cuddle up beside him and hear him say, "I love only you," but she couldn't. Too many things had happened in the past few days, not the least of which was Ben's words: "If the governor doesn't intervene, your mother will die by lethal injection on February fifteenth."

For all of her adult life, Sophie had prided herself on making it alone. Not needing to rely on anyone, because everyone will let you down. Thomas was her husband, her soul mate, her best friend, but she let him get only so close. Was that why he'd turned to Eva?

She scolded herself for going to his office, for thinking about telling him the truth about her family. Confessing her betrayals and begging for his comfort and forgiveness.

She didn't deserve his loyalty, but she wanted it more than anything. As his cologne filled the limo and his shoulder touched hers, she had to stop herself from laying her head on his shoulder and begging him for the truth. "Do you really love me," she wanted to scream, "or have we fallen apart, too?"

"Are you okay?" Thomas asked when she took his hand off her leg.

"I'm just tired." She hoped he'd let it go at that.

"How are you feeling? Any more nausea?"

"I'm all better," Sophie replied. "Actually, I'm kind of hungry."

"I hope you're not upset," Thomas said carefully, "but I ran in to Dr. Chemales in the hospital."

"Please tell me you didn't make me an appointment."

"Don't be mad. He said he could see you tomorrow around ten o'clock."

"I could've made that myself," she said in a less-than-grateful tone.

"I'm sorry," Thomas said, defending himself against more than he knew. "He was rounding at the hospital. I was worried about you."

"Next time, ask me first." She attempted to moderate her sharp pitch. "I'm not sure I need to go now."

"I think you do. It's not normal to faint for no reason. Please keep the appointment—if not for you, do it for me."

Before she responded, Sophie pondered the word *normal*. Was it customary to suspect your husband was fooling around? Or for little boys like Max to be abandoned in a hospital to become someone else's concern? Was it standard Thanksgiving banter to hear your brother-in-law casually announce your mother's execution after reading about it in the newspaper?

"Sophie, I can cancel the appointment if you don't want to go."

"No, I'll go." She didn't want to argue. About this or about Eva. She decided to let both go for tonight. But only for tonight.

"Thank you for taking care of me." *My health, anyway,* she thought to herself as she turned away from him and stared out the limousine window.

SOPHIE BEGAN TO SUSPECT SOMETHING else might be going on other than the Heart Ball when the limousine pulled up in front of the Ritz-Carlton and she saw Mindy quickly dart through the revolving doors. The Heart Ball wasn't Mindy's thing, especially since she and her husband had recently separated. She had never attended before, and Sophie couldn't imagine her being here now.

Her suspicions were confirmed when the driver opened her door, winked, and told her she didn't look at day over twenty-one. Sophie wasn't fond of surprises, but a significant part of her was relieved Thomas hadn't forgotten her birthday. From the looks of things, he'd remembered quite well.

She checked her reflection in the limo's black-tinted windows. Thomas must've noticed, because he gently touched the side of her cheek and whispered, "You look amazing."

As they entered the hotel, Thomas did what he always did when they were together in public. He placed his hand on the small of her back and led her in like she was the most important girl in the room.

THE THREE-PIECE ORCHESTRA played "Happy Birthday" on cue as all the synthetics rushed over to greet Sophie. Kate squeezed her arm first. "You look gorgeous."

Sophie didn't enjoy being the center of something she hadn't planned on and hated even more being left alone in a group of people who were clearly more Thomas's friends than hers. Several doctors from his practice waved hello as they made their way over.

After the formalities were completed, Mindy snuck up beside her and whispered in her ear, "You look great. Feeling better?"

"You want the truth?" Sophie tried to mask her words by saying them through gritted teeth.

Before Mindy could answer, Eva bounced up wearing a bloodred strapless gown dripping with small iridescent beads. "Happy birthday, Sophie," she screeched, raising her drink glass for a toast. Not the first glass, evidently, since half of her wine spewed over the sides, christening everyone in the near vicinity. Mindy's champagne-colored dress took the brunt of the waterfall.

"I'm so sorry," Eva said, trying to find someone to take her glass while she seized cocktail napkins to wipe off the trail of wine cascading down Mindy's breast. Her rubbing only made the stain worse.

"For God's sake, Eva, let me do it." Sophie snatched the soaked cocktail napkins out of her hand. "Let's go get some club soda."

"Thomas, dance with me," Eva said, smearing her words while pulling him onto the dance floor. Sophie turned to watch as Eva, who could not walk in a straight line, pressed herself against Thomas.

"Slow down, Eva. The first dance goes to my wife." Thomas detached her sticky arms from around his neck. "Where's your husband?"

"He couldn't make it." Her slurring made her statement sound like one long word. "I want you to dance with me." She fought to get her arms back around his neck.

Kate injected herself into the situation just as Sophie was about to.

"Let's go get you some coffee," Kate said, grabbing Eva hard enough to get her attention. "You're making a fool of yourself."

"I'm just trying to have a good time. Isn't that what you're supposed to do at parties?" She glared at Thomas, then directed her comments to Sophie. "Stop being so frigid all the time and dance with your husband."

Sophie took a step forward before Thomas stopped her. "Not here. Not in front of everyone," he said. "My partners are here." He looked around to see if anyone was watching while he pretended to adjust the clasp on Sophie's pearl necklace. "Please don't make a scene."

Sophie nodded, but not before giving one last long and threatening stare at Eva.

"Let me refill your drink glass," she said to her, sweetly enough for those eavesdropping to overhear. She went in for a hug to make sure everyone around thought the two of them were okay. Sophie wrapped her arms around her synthetic friend. She moved Eva's twisted updo away from her ear so she wouldn't miss a word. "Go home, Eva, before I do something that will make you incredibly uncomfortable."

GRACE

Nobody in life gets exactly what they think they are going to get. I tried to remind myself of that as Officer Mackey shouted at me from outside my door.

"Bradshaw, time to go to the infirmary."

It was dark outside and infirmary visits happened only during the day.

I looked out the slit in my door and tried to see if he was alone.

He stared back at me. "The infirmary called," he said. "Put your hands through."

I did as I was told.

After the door opened, I said to him, "I feel fine. Stitches come out after the tenth day. Do you know what this is about?"

"Nope. I'm just following orders." His words sounded hollow.

Carmen had had a nighttime appointment a few months ago. I had peeked out my window when I heard her being escorted out of her cell. I heard her crying when she came back. When I asked her about it the next day, she told me to shut up and that it didn't concern me.

I was beginning to wonder if she'd answer my question now. My mind told me I should trust Officer Mackey—he'd never harmed me before—but my pulse didn't. Flight or fight was kicking in, and neither one of those was a viable option.

Officer Mackey put his thumb up to the scanner outside of the infirmary. At first the scanner lit up red. "Damn technology," he said under his breath. A series of green lights appeared after he wiped his thumb off for the third time.

When the door slid open, I could see barely anything. Total darkness except for a small dim light located within the locked medicine cabinet. Six unoccupied gurneys lay eerily empty, waiting for their next patients.

"Sit down," Officer Mackey said. He attached shackles to the legs of the chair closest to the infirmary door.

Was this where Carmen sat before? Sweat dripped through my stitches; the wound started to feel like a bee sting. I bent my head down to wipe the sweat off, but I couldn't reach.

I closed my eyes and did the only thing that calmed me when I couldn't stand this place anymore. I pictured Sophie at nine, chocolate frosting all over the tips of her fingers and smeared across the corners of her mouth. "I couldn't wait until my party, Mommy. Are you mad?"

After an eternity of sitting in the dark, the door to the infirmary opened. Warden Richards entered flanked by two male correctional officers. None of them spoke or looked in my direction. The officer on the right flipped on a light.

"Do you have the paperwork?" The warden flickered his fingers in the direction of the closest officer. He had a shaved head and looked as though he might have been in the military.

"Yes, sir." He handed the warden a manila envelope from off the counter.

I heard the scanner outside beep and the prison physician entered the room.

"Glad you could join us," the warden said, without looking up. He licked his thumb to separate the papers from the envelope.

"I apologize, sir. I was almost home when your secretary called."

The warden stopped shuffling and squinted at the doctor. "We need to get this one right." He then squinted at me.

"Yes, sir," the doctor replied. "Mayberry's veins collapsed. I'll make sure this one"—he angled his head in my direction—"is well hydrated."

"Bring her here," the warden snapped, motioning to a chair tucked under a table. "I want to get home at some point tonight." An officer unshackled me and escorted me over.

"You have quite a cut on your head." The warden pulled his eyeglasses from his front pocket and put them on before examining the side of my head. "I thought we'd do this next go-around in the infirmary. Might save us a step." He chuckled at his own humor.

I did not.

"Ms. Bradshaw, do you remember me reading the death warrant?"

I nod. I barely did, but I could summarize.

"We have strict protocols to follow when we put an inmate to death. Lots of paperwork to fill out, you know." He rubbed the back of his neck at the enormity of it all. "We usually wait until the execution date is within forty-five days to fill all this out, but you know, with the holidays upon us, I'd like to get this started."

He pulled out several forms and lined them up on the table. I struggled to read the fine print.

"Turn on another light," the warden barked. Someone flipped one on.

I didn't understand the legal jargon. The light didn't help.

"Do I need to read all of these now?" The first full sentence I'd said since arrival.

"Are you refusing to read the documents?"

"No, sir. I wanted to know if I could go over these with my attorney before I signed?" I made sure the tail end of my sentence sounded like a question.

"Document that prisoner number 44607 refused to sign." The metal legs on his chair scuffed against the floor as he stood to leave.

"Can I take the papers to my cell and read them over?" I asked respectfully.

He stared at me for a second, glancing first at my stitches, then directly into my eyes, assessing, presumably, the request of a mother he thought wicked enough to murder her own baby.

"You have forty-eight hours," he said to me. To the doctor he said, before he walked out the door, "Check her veins. This needs to go off without a hitch."

When I returned to my cell, I reread the note Ms. Liz had shared with me. The one thing she wanted her daughters to know before she died.

Handwritten on the slip of paper were her words:

Trust your struggles. You don't have all the pieces yet.

SOPHIE

Sophie's head was in a fog when she woke up the next morning. Eva. Thomas. The party. Her mom. She didn't know which situation to try to process first.

"You believe me about Eva, don't you?" Thomas said as he came back into the bedroom from taking a shower.

"I don't know what to believe." Sophie pulled the comforter over her shoulders and tucked it under her chin. "I know what I saw." She wanted him to say more or at least repeat the explanation he'd given her last night: "I only want to be with you."

Thomas threw his towel on the floor and sat beside her on the bed. "Look at me."

When she didn't, he kneeled down in front of her. "I've never lied to you. What you saw at my office and heard at the party was all Eva. Eva being Eva. My mistake was asking her to help plan your party. I didn't realize she'd read more into it than that."

Sophie started to pull away, but the more she looked into Thomas's eyes, the more she believed him. He hadn't lied to her before. That was her thing, not his.

She studied the shape of his mouth when he talked, the curves in his brow. She scrutinized every feature as she would if she were studying a suspected perpetrator in a series of police photos. All while looking for any discrepancy in his story, anything to indicate he'd been unfaithful.

"I'm trying to believe you're telling me the truth. I should've asked you about it weeks ago, after I saw her at your office the first time. I didn't want you to think I was insecure or suspicious."

Thomas kissed her softly on the lips. "You are a little insecure and suspicious," he replied, picking up his towel and tossing it at her. Sophie didn't catch it or laugh.

"Too soon?" Thomas said.

"Way too soon!"

Thomas pulled on his scrubs and then checked for messages on his cell phone and pager. Sophie watched his every move from their bed, gauging how empty her life would be if he wasn't in it.

He noticed her staring and sat down on the bed beside her. "When are you going to get it through that thick skull of yours," Thomas said with a smile that made her feel good all over, "you're all that matters to me?"

SOPHIE ARRIVED AT STARBUCKS EARLY to clear her head before she talked to Mindy. A breakfast, they'd both decided last night, was needed. Sophie wanted a closer friend, but she needed a confidant. While ordering her coffee she contemplated how much to let Mindy in.

"A low-fat Salted Caramel Macchiato, no whip," she said to the barista behind the counter. Sophie wondered what this girl's story was. *Working her way through college like I did, or taking a gap year to figure herself out?* Sophie studied her as she put the lid on the paper cup. Her name badge had a yellow smiley face on it partly covering up the last of the letters in S-T-A-C. Was it with a *y* or an *ie*? Somebody had given the smiley face a mustache.

"Here you go," the girl said, handing the warm drink to Sophie. Sophie decided she looked more like an *ie*.

She grabbed a table in the corner and pulled out her phone to check her calendar. Something about being organized and in control helped calm her nerves. Doctor's appointment at ten. She'd almost forgotten. Too much to do. She thought about canceling it, then thought about Thomas ("I'm worried about you. It isn't normal."). She decided she'd better go.

As she continued to idly scroll through her calendar, she realized she didn't have much time before the fund-raiser. *We're coming down to the wire,* she thought as she counted the days on her calendar. It was only eight and a half weeks away.

And the next day, she realized, as she scrolled through the month of February, *is the day my mother will be executed.*

"YOU OKAY?" MINDY SAID. She pulled a chair from the table next to theirs and took a seat beside Sophie. "You look like you're deep in thought."

"Oh, hi," Sophie said as she tucked her phone into her purse and slid it off the middle of the table. She hadn't seen Mindy come in or order. "A little tired from last night."

"That was quite a party." Mindy picked up her coffee and took a sip. "Eva sure knows how to liven things up. I've never seen anyone so skilled at becoming the center of attention."

"She certainly wants to be Thomas's center of attention."

Mindy poofed out her lips, imitating Eva. "That may be true," she said, puckering and panting, "but Thomas woves you." Her lips returned to normal. "He planned your surprise party for weeks, making sure I'd be there, asking my opinion on your gift."

Sophie held up the blue topaz ring occupying most of her right hand's ring finger. *Your birthstone. And a symbol of love and fidelity.* Thomas's words as he gave the ring to her once they'd returned home from the party.

"Thomas does know how to buy a gift," Sophie said as they both admired her ring.

"Thanks for meeting me here," she said after a minute. "I'm glad we finally have some time to catch up. I really want to know how you're doing with Stephen being gone."

"I'm not going to lie—this has been the hardest thing I've ever had to go through. It's devastating for the twins." Mindy's face turned pale and Sophie thought she was about to cry. "Some days, I'm not sure I can make it."

This question-and-answer felt foreign to her, but she forced herself to maintain eye contact. "Is there . . . is there any chance for you two?"

"I don't think he's coming back." Mindy scratched at her empty ring finger. "Stephen hasn't been happy in a long time. Not happy with me, the way I look, the words I say. He says we've grown apart."

"If it matters, I think Stephen has lost his mind." Clearly something one friend says to another when she doesn't have a clue what's actually going on, but it was all she could come up with.

Mindy fiddled with a straw wrapper that had fallen underneath their table.

"I want to be there for you." Sophie scooted her chair back, reached over, and put her hand on Mindy's arm. "I'm not very good at giving advice, but I am a good listener. I'd love to be a closer friend."

Mindy put her hand on top of hers, closed her eyes, and nodded.

"Enough about me," Mindy said, patting Sophie's hand in gratitude before reaching for her coffee. She crossed and then uncrossed her legs before asking, "What, besides Evil Eva, is going on with you? You looked quite upset the night I saw you at the hospital." Mindy picked off a piece of her cranberry cookie.

All the tables around them were getting filled, making intimate conversation more difficult. A mother with her hair in a banana clip sat in the last open seat closest to them and started feeding her toddler small pieces of her lemon scone. "More, Mamma, more!" Sophie tried to decide how much of herself she was going to reveal.

"I just had a bad day all around," she said, choosing to test the waters with the less traumatic of her choices first. "I thought Thomas was cheating."

"With whom?" Mindy tried to ask before completely swallowing her sip of coffee.

"You know with whom." Sophie handed her a napkin to wipe away the liquid trailing down the side of her mouth. Mindy wiped and then laughed.

"Don't mean to make light of your concern, but I know for a fact that is not true. I've seen Thomas around her when she 'happens to stop' at the hospital while he's doing rounds. Strictly business."

"I believe that now—I think—but when he asked her to help plan my surprise, she took the invitation to mean more than talking to the orchestra about playing me the birthday song."

"If it makes you feel any better, Thomas asked me to help him, too, although I'm afraid I wasn't much help. There were two meetings at his office: one I was late for, and the other I got called in to work."

"The meeting he had at his office last week with her—when I came to the hospital crying?"

"Yes, that's the one. It sucks, keeping secrets from you."

Sophie's heart instantly lightened. She'd done her best to believe Thomas, but nothing felt as good as having confirmation. "He's been so busy lately." She moved her chair closer to the table because the noisy room made it difficult to hear. "Kind of distant."

"I know he's been sick about that little girl's death. Questioning what he did or didn't do. He talked to me about it last night." Mindy exhaled and put her fisted hands in her lap. "I have, too. I've lost a lot of sleep over this one. The hospital bigwigs have summoned the charts. I think the family is going to sue."

"Oh, no!" It was Thomas's nightmare.

"Not that I should be talking about any of this with you," Mindy said, side-glancing to see if the banana-clip lady was listening. "The board has been meeting with each of us, asking us what we did, what happened, things along those lines."

"What did you tell them?" Sophie wished she could take the question back the moment she saw Mindy's face. "I mean, do you think Thomas did anything wrong?"

"I don't know." Mindy sucked in her cheeks, then blew out. She put the rest of her cookie back in its bag. "I don't."

"The girl was being bullied. She wanted the surgery. Her parents insisted."

Sophie didn't actually know how insistent her parents had been. Thomas had felt sorry for her, but they'd had to sign a consent for surgery, hadn't they?

"The autopsy showed the girl died of malignant hyperthermia."

"What's that?"

"It's a severe reaction to anesthesia. Rare, but when it does happen it's usually in the OR, not post-op, like it was in this case."

"Wouldn't the anesthesiologist be at fault, then?"

"Maybe, but Legal is asking questions to all of us. How long did you monitor the child in the OR? What was her pressure in recovery? Every person who cared for her will be questioned."

"Thomas doesn't miss details like that," Sophie said, feeling the need to defend her husband from something he may or may not have done from someone who wasn't the one accusing. "Does he?"

"I don't think anyone did anything wrong." Mindy lowered her voice to a barely audible whisper. "The anesthesiologist, the surgical post-op nurse; I even examined the patient. This reaction just presented in a way that no one could've expected."

Sophie slid back in her chair while trying to process what Mindy was saying. "Maybe the nurse should've called Thomas earlier, or maybe he should've stayed at the hospital longer." She stopped talking and picked up a napkin. She started rolling it between her index finger and thumb. "We can all second-guess ourselves to death."

GRACE

I didn't sleep well last night. Every time I'd doze off, I'd hear the warden say, "We need to get this one right." Then I'd feel cold hands roll up my sleeves while examining my forearm. "This one here looks like the best vein."

When the sun rose, I decided to get up. I hadn't looked at the papers they gave me, but I couldn't forget about them, either. The manila envelope bullied me—three feet away and perched to suffocate me at any moment.

I took a deep breath and turned on the lamp. The *Woman's Day* calendar recommended making shrimp-and-broccoli stir-fry for dinner tonight. If I closed my eyes, I could smell the shrimp sizzling in the hot wok as I threw them in. Paul loved stir-fry.

I picked up the November calendar and used my index finger to count back—it had been three weeks since I'd seen my attorney. I needed to call him when we got to use the phone this week to see if he could help with the forms. I picked up the envelope and poured out the contents.

Sophie's report cards used to come in a similar envelope. *Pleasure to have in class. All A's, honor roll. Great class participation in English.* Paul and I treated her to a root beer float. William scrunched up his nose when Sophie swiped her finger through the whipped cream and into his mouth. "If you get good grades, you can have more of this," she whispered in his tiny ear.

A year after my incarceration, Paul visited without her. He did that sometimes when we needed to talk. He held Sophie's report card up to the glass. *Seems withdrawn. Poor participation. Missing work. Suggest counseling to deal with isolation and angry outburst.*

"I'm doing the best I can," Paul said, his skin blotchy around his eyes and mouth. "She won't talk to me. I'm losing her." He stooped over and put his elbows on the ledge as he held the phone.

"She loves you, Paul." I tried to encourage him, but I felt helpless. I closed my eyes for a second so I could feel his scruffy face against mine. "One second at a time. She'll come around."

"I'll get her to talk," he said, reassuring himself as well as me.

I knew my legal bills had wiped out our bank account. We couldn't afford to pay for a counselor for Sophie.

"Don't worry about us." He rubbed his chest with the palm of his hand. He was heartbroken, and I think the rest of him was now broken, too.

I shook my head, willing away the painful memories. I couldn't think about the pain I'd caused them. I had to get this paperwork done. The thought of being reunited with William and Paul didn't make leaving Sophie more bearable.

I pulled out the five sheets of paper and laid them side by side on my bed.

The first was headlined LAST MEAL REQUEST. *Food allowance can not exceed $15.00 and must be purchased locally. Requests for alcohol will be denied.*

The TV announcer's words played in my ears: *"Walter Mayberry chose to forgo his McDonald's options and instead ate what the rest of the inmate populations dined on . . . beef stew with diced potatoes and carrots, cornbread, and an eight-ounce glass of sweet tea."*

I slid that paper underneath the rest. I wasn't ready to hear what the reporter had to say about me just yet. I picked up the next sheet.

EXECUTION WITNESS LIST.

My mom, the only grandparent still living at the time of Sophie's birth, had traveled four hours to be in the delivery room. She kept asking the nurse questions as I started to push. "Is she in much pain? Can't you do anything about her pain?" Paul held my hand with one arm and steadied her back with the other as we witnessed the first of our two miracles.

I didn't expect another. If Sophie did show up, I'd never let her see me be put to death. I checked the box that said *No Request for Witnesses* and signed my name. My going-away party would be small, but my home-coming celebration would be grand. I wondered if William was still a baby in heaven or if he was now full-grown.

APPLICATION FOR EXECUTIVE CLEMENCY.

I needed to talk to Ben about that one. Should I continue fighting? Only if it would buy Ben more time to find Sophie, I decided. That paper went to the back of the pile.

DISPOSAL OF PROPERTY AND DISPOSAL OF REMAINS.
Name and address of family member designated to coordinate remains:

_____ .

I'd always thought I'd be buried next to Paul and William. Didn't think I'd have to provide my own transportation there. Maybe Ben could arrange this?

LAST WILL & TESTAMENT.

Ben had all of that on file. Everything went to Sophie. I'd make sure he knew to give a copy of my will to the warden.

This was all too much to think about when I'd gotten so little sleep. I stared at the papers again. The bold-print letters made my heart pound.

What sounds good to eat before the needle goes in? Who'd you invite to watch you die? The cinder-block walls moved in closer.

I gathered all the papers together as quickly as I could and shoved them back in the envelope, pushing through and spreading the bronze clasp forcefully to shut up their words before they could taunt me further.

Deep breaths, I reminded myself. An exercise Ms. Liz practiced with me when my anxiety got the best of me. "Count to ten," she told me. "Now take yourself away from here."

I did what I did when I couldn't stand this place any longer. I closed my eyes and pictured Paul kneeling in front of me. His wavy cinnamon-colored hair curled around his forehead and he smelled like cut grass. "I cannot take another breath without you." He opened a red velvet box he'd hidden in the side pocket of his black trousers. I thought he might cry. "You are home to me. Please say you'll be my wife."

SOPHIE

Was it Thomas's fault? Sophie couldn't help but speculate. Mindy, although she hadn't come right out and said so, didn't go out of her way to imply otherwise. Thomas may have partially been responsible, and this mess had changed someone else's family forever.

"Mrs. Logan," a stout nurse dressed in scrubs called from the waiting-room door. "Come on back."

Sophie stood and followed her to the nurses' station.

"One-ten over sixty-four, that's good. Temp normal. Let's weigh you and get you into a room."

Sophie stepped on the scale. The nurse moved the weighted measure over to the hundred-pound mark and then slid the small weight over to the right. "Looks like you've lost weight since your last visit. Eight pounds." She scrolled through the electronic chart. "Better eat over the holidays or you're going to blow away."

"I've not had much of an appetite," Sophie said, looking down at her hands and twirling her wedding ring around on her finger.

The nurse escorted Sophie into another room, handed her a paper gown, and sat down on a stool across from the exam table. "Is weight loss what brings you here today?"

Sophie sat down on the exam table and crossed her legs. "My husband is what made me come today." The paper gown still in her hands. She didn't know if she was supposed to put it on now or wait. "He apparently thinks a person fainting on Thanksgiving is an abnormal occurrence."

The nurse typed something into the chart. "I'd have to agree with your husband on that one."

Just then, Dr. Chemales opened the door.

"Good morning, Sophie, good to see you again." Dr. Chemales held his hand out to shake hers. "It has been a while."

"It has." Sophie couldn't remember the last time she'd seen him. Maybe only once or twice since she and Thomas moved here. Dr. Chemales had lost some hair since then, but he still had the same genuine bedside manner. "There's really no need to see me today, but Thomas insisted."

"I know how those doctors can be with their wives," he said with a grin. "Why don't you tell me what's going on? Thomas mentioned something about you fainting."

"I did faint, but only once. I'm feeling better now."

Dr. Chemales sat down on the stool and put his chart on the table. He pointed and clicked, and then asked, "Both parents deceased?"

"Yes," Sophie said, having forgotten for a minute that she had even lied on her medical records.

"Dad died of heart disease?" he said while still looking at the chart. "Age fifty-two?"

"Yes." Did a shattered heart fall into the disease category?

"That's young." Dr. Chemales looked up at Sophie.

"Very," Sophie replied.

"And your mom?" His eyes returned to the chart for information. "What medical issues did your mom have?"

Her fabricated stories were getting more and more difficult to tell and harder to cover up. Coming clean seemed too overwhelming. "She died of breast cancer when I was twelve."

"I'm sorry." His medical questions were more empathetic than clinical.

"Are you seeing your gynecologist for mammograms? Breast cancer is hereditary, you know."

"I do and I am," she replied quickly, hoping this visit would be over soon.

Dr. Chemales prodded and poked, then finally said, "Well, everything looks fine to me. You probably were a little dehydrated. Let's get some blood work and a urine sample to make sure nothing else is going on."

"I told Thomas I was fine," Sophie said, glad to be right about something.

"You are fine, but fainting is certainly something you should get checked out. Thomas was right to have you come in."

"Better safe than sorry, I know," Sophie said, repeating the phrase her dad always told her when he asked her to do anything from wear a bike helmet long before the law required it to turning on the outside lights before she walked down the stairs.

"The nurse will take you to the lab. I'll call you if there's anything to cause you concern."

JUST AS SOPHIE PULLED HER CAR into an open parking space in front of Barnes & Noble, her phone rang.

"Mrs. Logan?"

"This is she."

"This is the nurse from Dr. Chemales's office. He wanted me to call and tell you we don't have to wait to get the results of the rest of your tests to find out why you fainted."

"What?" Sophie asked. "He said I was dehydrated."

"Wait one moment, Mrs. Logan."

"Sophie, this is Dr. Chemales. Congratulations. You and Thomas are going to have a baby."

GRACE

I rushed out of my cell as soon as the doors clanked open. Ms. Liz should have left the December *Woman's Day*, and I wanted to grab the calendar before someone else did. Officer Jones smiled when she saw me. She waved the magazine in the air to let me know she had my back—in this area, anyway.

"Thank you," I mouthed to her.

"Got another one," Roni said from behind me. She shoved a letter in front of me before I could make my way over to claim my calendar.

"Your dad must write a letter a day!"

"Read it to me," she said.

"Sit down." I directed her over to the table. "We'll read it together."

She tore open the envelope, careful not to rip through the red hearts drawn all over the backside. Carl had written *DAD* on one heart with an arrow going straight over to the other hearts. *Missing you* was written over top of that.

Ten days, the first line started. I asked Roni to sound it out. "Ta-ta-ten." I nudged her.

After a few tries, she grew frustrated. "Is he coming or not?" she yelled, sweat beads mounting on her forehead as she started to stand up.

"Ten days until I see you face-to-face," I responded back fast. "I'm just trying to help you learn."

Her foot started tapping, quickly at first, then she stopped. Her nostrils flared out as she inhaled. "I'm tired of feeling stupid. Will you please just tell me what he wants?"

I scanned through the rest of the letter. "He says the only thing he wants for Christmas is to meet you."

Roni took the letter from me. She grunted something I didn't quite make out before she jolted up and walked back to her cell.

Carmen and Jada were sitting with the prison's recreational therapist. She was allowed to visit us in a group twice a month if we had no write-ups. We usually saw her four or five times a year.

Jada didn't look up when I sat down. "My kids are going to like this ornament," she said as she sprinkled red glitter all over the glue-soaked pinecone.

Carmen rolled her eyes at me and then rolled me a pinecone. "Take your mind off your troubles." We hadn't talked about my upcoming date—or discussed the fact she was probably next.

I picked up the Elmer's glue and started to squirt. This would be the seventeenth Christmas ornament I'd made on the inside. My tree, if they allowed us to have one, would be decorated with a variety of Christmas cheer fabricated with Popsicle sticks and white paper snowflakes. On the back in red Sharpie I always wrote *To Sophie, Love Mom*.

I turned the pinecone around and looked at all sides, not sure where I'd write that this year.

Carmen read my mind and slid over a tag made out of gingerbread-embossed scrapbook paper. "Here," she said. "Write to your daughter on this."

I give her a faint smile. Carmen wasn't usually insightful or compassionate. Her records, according to her, diagnosed her with narcissistic personality disorder. I looked it up one time when the rolling book cart had a medical dictionary. The fat royal-blue book said she was incapable of recognizing feelings in others and pursued mainly selfish goals.

I couldn't help but see what the fat blue book had to say about me.

I flipped the pages in the *Diagnostic and Statistical Manual of Mental Disorders*.

Munchausen by proxy: a psychiatric disorder in which someone inflicts harm to someone in their care to garner sympathy and attention.

"Here, use the white glitter," Carmen offered. "It'll remind Sophie of snow."

I picked up the tag Carmen had slid my way, thankful that just for today her diagnosis (and mine) was more than a little off.

SOPHIE

Sophie found herself sitting on the exam table, cold and shivering, waiting for the obstetrician to walk into the room. One of the perks of being a doctor's wife is knowing other doctors' wives. A quick phone call to Kate, and Sophie became the first patient on Jack's packed December 23 morning schedule.

Of course, Sophie didn't tell Kate the real reason she needed to see her husband. And it wasn't any of Kate's business she'd fainted, so she made up another plausible excuse, "feeling tired, probably anemic" and needed "energy quick" to finish the preparations for the Secret Chef fund-raiser. A weird phone call at best, asking Kate to pull some strings so her husband could examine her hidden parts. Low iron seemed believable and important and didn't require Kate to picture Sophie undressed from the waist down with her legs spread wide open and resting in stirrups.

Normally, she saw Dr. Johnson, a female partner in the practice, but she was lecturing at the medical school and couldn't fit Sophie in until the week after Christmas. She couldn't wait, and no matter how weird it was being examined by a neighbor, she needed additional confirmation that the three sticks she peed on last night were telling the truth as soon as possible. Dr. Chemales was an internist, not an obstetrician. Couldn't he be mistaken?

Sophie didn't tell Thomas about her visit beforehand. Not that he would have heard her anyway. As soon as he walked through the door, he kissed her on the top of her head, went for a run, and made a phone call to his dad. He closed the study door, but Sophie could hear him say things like "I think I need to settle this" and "I don't know what the ramifications will be."

The last thing she wanted to tell Thomas was that she was pregnant. She didn't believe it herself. She wasn't ready for a baby. She wanted Max.

Sophie picked up her iPhone and started to search "conditions causing a false pregnancy test," when the doctor tapped on the door.

"Well, I guess congratulations are in order." He held his hand out to hers after she dropped her phone into her purse.

Sophie forced her mouth to turn upward, a gratitude of sorts for him working her into his schedule and for liking her enough to be excited for what he presumed to be good news.

"Are you sure?" she asked, giving him one more chance to change his story. "I haven't missed a period."

"Positive. Your hCG levels are quite high." He checked her chart again before he spoke. "I take it this was unplanned?"

Unplanned. Unprepared for. Take your pick.

"Having any symptoms? Morning sickness, tenderness in your breasts, overly tired?"

"My stomach has been a little queasy, but I've always had a weird stomach. I fainted, but just one time. Incredibly light-headed."

"Your blood sugar may have gotten a little low or you may be anemic."

Sophie welcomed the anemia. At least her white lie to Kate would be partially true.

"I'll check your iron when we draw your blood. I know you see Dr. Johnson, but I feel like we should do an initial prenatal workup today, if your schedule allows."

"Uh . . ." Sophie stammered, and reached for her phone to check the time. When she didn't give him an answer, Jack asked again.

"I can't have my neighbor leaving here and passing out. Kate would never forgive me. Can we at least do some blood work and an ultrasound, find out how far along you are?"

Sophie nodded, still trying to believe she had a tiny human growing inside of her. She put her hands over her stomach and tried to make herself feel like she'd imagined a good mother would. Ecstatic? Frantically texting all her contacts: *I've waited my whole life for this.*

Jack opened the door and called for his nurse. "I'm going to let Dr. Johnson do Mrs. Logan's cervical and breast exam on her next visit. Get her started on the paperwork, and tell Betsy to bring the ultrasound machine in here so we can find out when this baby is due."

"This baby's a good thing," Jack said before he left the exam room. "It'll take Thomas's mind off everything else."

Everything else? Sophie started to ask, when the nurse wheeled in the ultrasound.

A few minutes later, Sophie found herself staring at a TV monitor.

"Here is the yolk sac," the technician said, making little cross marks over the screen. She alternated moving the wand and typing. "Yes, this is exactly what we want to see." She stopped probing and pointed to a small flicker in the middle of the screen. "That is your baby's beating heart."

Sophie concentrated on the movement as the tech moved the wand and continued to mark.

"Looks good. Strong heartbeat." She murmured some other things about fluid and sac width, but to Sophie it all ran together. One more thing in her life fluttering out of her control.

"FILL OUT THESE FORMS," Jack's nurse said to Sophie after she dressed. Sophie's eyes glazed over. The nurse handed her the paperwork and put her hand over the top of Sophie's. "This is a lot to take in. Was this baby a surprise?"

"A big one," Sophie replied, trying to muster some response that didn't make her sound like a terrible mother right from the start. Baby photos plastered the walls of the hallway where she stood. Huge, round, judgmental eyes stared at her.

"I mean, it's not like we don't want to have a family; the timing, I guess, is just a little off."

"I've had four babies. All grown now, but I can tell you I felt the same way with every pregnancy. Overwhelmed and underprepared." The nurse pointed to the waiting room outside the lab and escorted Sophie there. "You should talk to your mom. I bet she felt the same way."

"My mom and I don't talk," Sophie blurted out before she could filter her story.

"Oh, I am so sorry. I always open my big mouth, assuming everybody's families are like mine. I talk to my girls several times a day."

"It's okay," Sophie said when the nurse kept rattling on about a disagreement she had with her middle daughter over Thanksgiving: "We didn't speak for days. Over sweet-potato casserole. Something that silly." The nurse rolled her eyes.

"Our problems are a little bigger." A fight over a Thanksgiving Day side dish sounded like heaven. Sophie wanted so desperately to have petty adult fights with her mother instead of not speaking or never seeing her alive again.

When she didn't say anything, the nurse did. "I hope this baby will somehow bring you two back together. I'll let you get to this paperwork."

Sophie knew she'd said enough, too much, so she chose not to respond. How could she tell someone her mother would never meet this baby, her first grandchild? She would be dead and buried by then.

She sat down in the chair most isolated from the other "excited" expectant mothers. Three pages of medical forms plagued her. How could she possibly care full-time for a baby? She suspected she hadn't fully thought through adopting Max if filling in her name, Social Security number, and insurance information created this much panic.

Concentrate, she tried to tell herself. *Take the emotions out of this and focus.* She didn't have any health problems. An occasional migraine around her period. No allergies, diabetes, high blood pressure, or kidney failure. First page flew by quickly.

Age of first menstruation? She couldn't remember if it was twelve or thirteen, but she did recall what grade she was in and who she'd had to tell. She'd started during December of her eighth-grade year. That month she was cast as Suzy Shopper in the school's holiday play. A role requiring her to stand onstage through most of the two-hour performance and either sing in the chorus or dance around, pretending her purse was stuffed and too heavy to carry.

Her cramps prevented her from doing her spins during the dress rehearsal, so the chorus teacher had her sit out when the other kids were twisting and jumping. Before the evening performance, Sophie ran to the bathroom and discovered her red-and-green plaid skirt was soaked with blood. Her mom had been incarcerated long before she'd had a chance to discuss puberty with Sophie, and her dad's idea of discussing pubic hair and breast buds was sliding a book titled *So You're Becoming a Woman* under her door on her twelfth birthday.

The chorus teacher happened to be in the bathroom spraying on deodorant and heard Sophie sniffling. "Sweetie, are you okay? We're about to perform."

Sophie opened the stall door and showed her the stains on her skirt. One look into Sophie's terrified eyes and the teacher must have known this was her first period.

"We'll get you fixed right up." She pulled a quarter out of her bag and slid it into the white rectangular box on the wall. A brown box labeled *Kotex* slid out, and she handed it to Sophie. "You wait right here and I'll be back with some fresh underwear and a new skirt."

The chorus teacher must've made a call to Sophie's dad, because after she walked home a big blue box of Always with wings was sitting on her bed. Sophie wanted so much to call her mom and ask questions like "Why do I need wings?" and "Should I use a pad or a tampon?" but her mom's telephone privileges once again had been denied. When she and her dad drove to visit her the next month, Sophie couldn't whisper the questions without her dad hearing. After the visit, she snuck into her bedroom and pulled out the book from under her bed. She read chapter three: "The Ups and Downs of Your Menstrual Cycle."

Sophie skimmed the rest of the questions. *Family history of depression?* She'd heard her parents whispering something when they thought Sophie was asleep in the back of the car. "If you need to get back on medicine, please tell me, Grace." Sophie filled in that blank with a question mark.

Are any of your siblings deceased? If so, state age at death and cause: William, eight months. She could not bring herself to write the word *murdered* next to his name. Why would that matter, anyway? She left the second part of the question blank and prayed Thomas would never see this.

"Mrs. Logan, ready to get your blood drawn?" a young man in a white lab coat asked. Sophie signed her name at the bottom of the page and then walked into the lab.

After several attempts and three filled vials, he put a Band-Aid on her arm and escorted her to a chair in Jack's private office. A picture of Jack and Kate with sun visors on while holding fishing poles decorated his desk.

"The sonogram looks good. The baby looks healthy," he said to her as soon as she sat down.

"How far along am I?" Sophie asked, realizing this was the first time she had acknowledged the baby out loud. It was becoming real.

"The baby is measuring at about eleven weeks, which means your due date is somewhere around"—he consulted the chart—"June twenty-fifth." Thomas had been born in June. She could already hear Margaret on the phone with the party planner: "We'll need two cakes: a three-tiered vanilla-frosted one for my son Thomas, and a smaller chocolate one with lots of sprinkles for my grandbaby. You have to get your hands and face messy on your first birthday—it's a Logan family tradition."

"The blood work should be back later this afternoon. I had them run yours stat, since you've been feeling faint. I want you to start on these prenatal vitamins, and I'm presuming you're anemic due to your symptoms, so I'm starting you on these iron pills." He handed her both bottles. "If you're not, we can discontinue those, but keep them because chances are you'll need them at some point during your pregnancy."

Jack asked her for the forms. "Okay, so no red flags with your medical history. Your dad died of heart disease, and your mom, is she still living?"

"Yes." Sophie hesitated, but she couldn't lie. Now her baby was involved.

"Healthy?" he asked.

"As far as I know." Jack looked up but didn't ask anything further.

"You had one sibling, I see here. Died in infancy?" When she didn't say anything, he said, "Do you know your brother's cause of death?"

For years Sophie had mastered the art of avoiding this conversation, but not anymore. She knew technically Jack wasn't allowed to tell Kate, but she wasn't naïve enough to think that didn't mean he might. Didn't Thomas deserve to hear this first?

She couldn't worry about that now. She could worry only about her baby and taking care of the baby's needs. For the first time, she felt like a mother.

"William was sick most of his infancy. My mom, um, had trouble feeding him. Took him to the doctor all the time. He never wanted to take a bottle, and when he did, he threw up." She paused to look at Jack to see if it was safe to go on. He was taking notes, not looking at her, so she continued. "He seemed drowsy and didn't like to hold his head up. The day he died, he had a seizure."

Jack paused his writing just as Sophie was about to tell him the whole story. Before she could, he asked, "Did your brother have a metabolic disorder?"

GRACE

The will to do, The soul to dare.

—SIR WALTER SCOTT

Sophie, I did something I thought I'd never do. I can twist, turn, and justify it a million different ways, but in the end, I am responsible because I chose not to be brave. Instead, I opted for the easier choice. I made the choice to do nothing.

Earlier this evening, Carmen stood with her back to all of us, whispering into the phone—the same ritual practiced every week when she made her collect call home. She knew the phone calls were being recorded, but that didn't stop her from engaging in some pretty lewd conversations with husband number four. Some days she spoke in a soft, sultry voice; other days she moaned and groaned so loud the officer cut her off midsentence.

She twirled her hair and swayed back and forth like a girl getting asked to the prom. I tried not to stare, but Roni, who was next in line, kept looking at the clock and then glaring at Carmen. Three minutes left, according to my timekeeping, and I thought Roni might explode.

The last letter Roni wrote to her father (I wrote—she dictated) said she'd call him on December 23.

Please be waiting by the phone, *she had me write*, because one try is all I get and I want to hear what your voice sounds like. *I added the* please.

"Hurry up, Carmen," *she growled, while pacing back and forth.*

Carmen ignored her, but belted out a few seismic sounds in her direction.

Roni's dad worked the night shift at the gas station he owned. The call would not happen if she didn't reach him soon.

"One minute left," *the officer shouted unnecessarily—done or not, the line automatically cuts off when your time is up.*

Roni pulled a small piece of paper out of the top of her pants and unfolded it. She studied the numbers while slowing her steps.

"Until next time," *Carmen said in the lowest pitch possible. She clinked the phone down loudly and then spun around to see who was watching.*

"About damn time," *Roni said, her face inches from Carmen's. She brushed her unintentionally with her right shoulder as she reached to dial.*

"Ouch!" *Carmen screamed. The officer stood up from behind his desk and ran over.* "She hit me."

Before Roni had a chance to protest, the officer pushed her up against the wall.

"You just can't stay out of trouble, can you?"

Carmen put her hand over her left shoulder and cried, "I think it's dislocated."

Roni looked over her shoulder to find me. When her gaze met mine, I looked away. I LOOKED AWAY.

The officer pushed her face back against the wall and cuffed her hands. As he escorted her back to the cell, she pleaded, "Tell him, Grace. You saw what happened. Tell him."

I started to open my mouth, but the words refused to come out.

They're stuck inside me, reminding me of the last time I snitched.
I needed to call Ben, and I knew no good deed was without
consequence in prison. Three inmates had taught me the "code" with
the melted end of a toothbrush after I witnessed a new lifer being
harassed in her first few weeks at Lakeland. The officers stood by
and did nothing. Don't be nosy and never rat on another inmate.
Three months of not being able to sit down when you urinate is
enough of a reminder that in prison one's moral compass doesn't
always point you in the right direction.

The officer pushed Roni back into her cell. "How many write-ups
does this make for you?"

She didn't answer, but I could have. None, in the last few
months, anyway. Since her dad wrote her, Roni had done everything
by the book, even asking Jada to turn down her music because
Officer Jones rubbed her head like she had a headache.

None of that mattered. Roni would be on restriction. No hearing
her dad say "I'm glad I found you" on the phone or examining his
features to see if they looked like hers when he tried to visit on
Christmas Day.

"Bradshaw, do you want your call or not?" the officer said
after he locked Roni's cell.

My chin started to quiver as I made my way over to the phone.
I didn't know if I could hate myself any more. Or any more
than I hated Carmen.

"Ben Taylor's office." I thought it was Louise, his secretary, who answered the phone after the fifth ring, but I couldn't quite tell.

"Collect call from Lakeland State Penitentiary. Will you accept charges?"

"Prisoner's name?" She cleared her throat and coughed. Louise.

"State your name," the operator said.

"It's me, Louise. Grace Bradshaw."

"Well, why didn't you say so?" Louise replied. "Of course I will."

The phone line clicked and then an automated voice said, "Four minutes remaining."

How was that possible? I started to argue but realized it was a moot point, so I spoke fast. "Can I talk to Mr. Taylor?"

"Grace, I'm so glad you called." Louise stopped to cough. "He needs to talk to you."

"Is he there?" I said, even faster.

Louise coughed again. "Damn frog caught in my throat."

"The warden gave me papers and I'm scared to sign them without talking to Ben first." Three minutes left.

"Don't do it. You can't trust that weasely warden." She put something in her mouth. I heard her sucking. "Ben's in court today, but he's dying to talk to you." She paused for a second, and then her voice climbed higher. "Oh my, that came out wrong. Please forgive me."

"No need," I said. "About my case or about Sophie?"

Louise cleared her throat and coughed again. "I'm not sure I should be the one who tells you."

I started to beg, but I heard her other line ring.

"Hold on. Ben's on the other line."

She placed me on hold. "Jolene" by Dolly Parton belted in my ear and my stomach started to churn. *Jolene, Jolene, Jolene, Joooolene. Please, God, let him tell me he's found Sophie.*

"Grace, this is Ben."

"Hi, Ben. Please tell me you have good news."

And that was the last thing I said before the line went dead.

SOPHIE

Sophie didn't know whom to talk to first. But when she returned to her car and took out her phone, it was Ben Taylor's cell number she dialed. "Please pick up. Please pick up." After the fourth ring, his voicemail came on: *"This is Ben Taylor and I am unable to take your call at this time . . ."* Sophie tapped her foot on the floorboard and waited for his greeting to end.

"Ben, this is Sophie Logan. Please call me right away. It's urgent I talk to you."

This whole day had been a blur. So much information swelled in her mind, she couldn't decide what to think about first. Could it be true? Could her baby brother have been ill like Jack suggested? Sophie hadn't told him about her mother's conviction. She didn't have to. He'd assumed from the symptoms William had died of a metabolic disorder.

When Sophie hadn't argued the point, Jack continued. He told her these diseases often went undiagnosed, since they were rare, inherited disorders. Seventeen years ago, doctors weren't even aware some metabolic conditions existed.

It made sense to him. William had had a poor appetite and then became sick after he ate, since the babies with this disorder lack the enzyme that breaks down protein. The pieces fell into place while he was talking. "Why can't the doctors figure out what is wrong with him?" she'd heard her mother say on one of her many visits to the pediatrician. Later, her pleas consisted of "I promise I didn't hurt your brother. You have to believe me."

But Sophie hadn't believed her. No one had, except her father.

Every symptom William had had sounded like the disease Jack had described—what he said was possibly a metabolic acidemia or something along those lines. Sophie had had Jack spell it while she typed it into her phone.

The confusion was that it also reiterated the prosecutor's closing argument because all of those symptoms could have come from poisoning. Sophie tried to keep her emotions in check. Her feelings vacillated from exhilaration to guilt to pure fear. Her mother had been on death row for seventeen years. Not only did the system think she was a baby killer, her own daughter had, too.

Sophie's phone lit up. LOW BATTERY.

Where was her car charger? A frantic search through her glove compartment yielded nothing. In the console between the seats, a black-coiled car charger appeared along with the unopened envelope Ben Taylor had given her from her mother.

She tore open the envelope and pulled out a photo: Sophie, snuggled asleep in her bed with her princess tiara on. Teddy curled up right beside her. Her fingernails were painted with purple glitter nail polish. On the back her mom had written one word: GRATEFUL.

Sophie plugged in her car charger and redialed Ben's number. This time her message said "Ben, I hope you're home, because I'm on my way to see you."

"HEY, BABY, I WAS WAITING FOR YOU." Thomas was sitting at the kitchen table holding a newspaper when Sophie walked in to grab a change of clothes for her trip. The color of his face matched his white oxford shirt. "Come sit beside me."

He was never home in the middle of the afternoon. Sophie's thoughts hurled through an escalating list of worst-case scenarios. *He does love Eva? He found out about my mom? Jack told him about the baby?*

"You feeling okay?" Thomas should've been the first person she called after she left the obstetrician's office, not her mom's death row attorney. What was wrong with her?

"We need to talk. Can you sit down?" By the look in his eyes, she knew what he was about to say was important. Did he mean what he said this morning? Was it his deception or hers? Did it really matter? She put her hand over her stomach.

"Thomas," she said, pulling out the chair next to his. "I am so . . ." Her words fought their way through the thickness forming in her throat. She collapsed into the chair.

"I'm sorry," Thomas said. He put his hands on her legs. "I haven't handled this whole thing the right way."

Eva's alluring painted red lips burst into her mind. "I knew it. You cheated on me with Eva?" She took his hands off her knees and started to stand.

Thomas pulled her back down. "No, not Eva!" His tight face lightened a bit. "I haven't been completely honest, but I have been faithful."

Faithful. Sophie braced herself, not sure if his next revelation would be better or worse.

He held up a section of the *News & Observer.* "Doctor Implicated in Death of Girl," headlined page four. "Do you want to read it or should I paraphrase?" Thomas placed the neatly folded article on the table and slid it over to her.

"Paraphrase."

"A reporter interviewed the parents," Thomas stammered. "They said I didn't even know their daughter's name. They said I didn't care."

"How could they say that? You didn't sleep well for days." She grabbed the paper from the table, undoing Thomas's precise folds. "Who wrote this piece-of-trash story, anyway?"

Thomas rubbed his stubbled cheeks while Sophie scoured every word. "It doesn't matter who wrote it. That's how the parents feel."

"This article makes you sound guilty. It's says you failed to give appropriate post-op care, you didn't take an accurate medical history."

"I know what it says." Thomas gripped the side of the table. "I, along with most of the community, *know* what it says." His chair legs scratched their hardwood floor when he abruptly stood up.

"This baby's a good thing," Jack said. *"It'll take Thomas's mind off everything else."*

Thomas pulled a bottle of water out of the refrigerator while she mulled over when she should tell him about the baby.

Judging by the way he slammed his water bottle on the table when he sat down, today wasn't the best day.

"I've been talking to my dad and my brother, asking for advice on what to do."

"What do you mean 'what to do'?" Her question added weight to his already slouching shoulders. "If you aren't guilty, you should fight it."

"I'm not guilty. Everything I did was standard of care." He leaned in toward her and put his hands on her knee. "Don't you believe me?"

Sophie rubbed his hands. "Of course I believe you."

"My dad and Carter, they're both telling me to make this go away. I should've already settled out of court." Thomas rolled his bloodshot eyes. "For them, it was all about keeping this out of the papers."

Sophie understood their concern. The stench of stale cigar breath assaulted her just thinking about the editor from the *Brookfield Journal* camped out on her porch steps, a bulky camera slung around his neck and a microphone perched in his hand.

"I've thought about listening to them. I have. I want to make this go away." Thomas took his hand from beneath hers and recreased the folded article with his thumbnail. "I could fight this. I could have my attorneys call in expert witnesses. Have them explain to the jury what this little girl died of was a rare adverse reaction to her anesthesia, and that would be totally true. Malignant hyperthermia is rare. Even if I'd been right by her side, given her a different medication—I don't think I could have saved her."

"It wasn't your fault." Why was it so easy to believe he was innocent and not her mom?

"I did all I could think of to do." Thomas scratched the back of his head. "But I can't get her face out of my mind."

The image of her handcuffed mother popped into her head.

She reached over and massaged the back of his neck for him. "What are you going to do?"

"I'm going to do what I should have done from the beginning." He pulled out his cell phone. "I'm going to talk to the parents."

GRACE

The TV is blaring a promo for the Christmas special about to air next. "An angel helps a compassionate but frustrated George Bailey by showing him what life would have been like if he never existed." I'm writing to you from the dayroom, and I'm pretending the protective arms of my dad are wrapped around me.

As I've told you before, Granddad Joe lived for December. Before the turkey turned cold on Thanksgiving eve, he had my mom and me pulling out all things snow-related and planning our early-morning trek up the winding mountain roads deep into the forest so we could chop down the perfect Christmas tree.

He inspected each Douglas fir for symmetry and branch strength, preferring the fat and short tree to the long and skinny one.

"I like that one, Daddy," I said every year, pointing to the tallest one I could find.

When I became old enough to understand the ritual, my mom and I would bait him just to hear his response: "Trees always look much bigger when you get them home, sweetheart."

She'd wink at me as we watched him pull out his black-and-yellow tape measure and say, "Put your foot on the bottom of this, Gracie."

He'd stretch the tape measure as far as it would go, then guestimate. "About eight inches too tall for our living room." He'd look to see if we were disappointed. "You want to have room to put that star on, don't you, Gracie girl?"

We decorated the tree as soon as we pushed and pulled it through our front door. My dad, still drenched with sweat, turned the screws in the tree stand. "That look straight to you, sweetheart?"

He held me on his shoulders while I threaded the electric star through the top of the tree. My mom made chicken and noodles (I'm going to write that recipe down for you—four stars!) in the kitchen while Dad and I gazed at our lighted glory. We ate our meal in front of the television and watched A Christmas Carol.

Earlier today, Roni's disciplinary hearing officer stood outside her cell and read the consequences of her altercation with Carmen.

"You are sentenced to disciplinary segregation for a period of forty-five days for the class-one offense of causing physical injury to another inmate."

Roni said nothing.

The hearing officer continued: "You have given up your right to testify on your own behalf or to call witnesses."

These disciplinary hearings always happened out of our housing unit and in front of a panel, but Roni had refused to leave her cell.

"I'd like to do this without having to extract the inmate from her cell," I'd heard Officer Jones say to someone on the phone.

Me, too. Extraction meant gas. I'd prayed whoever she was talking to would bend the rules, but I made sure I had a clean wet towel to put over my face just in case. My eyes burned for three days the last time Roni refused an order.

The hearing officer had agreed, on the condition that Roni pleaded guilty and forwent her right to testify. "I don't have anyone I can trust to tell the truth," she'd hissed at Officer Jones.

I could see Roni's face plastered up against her window now as the hearing officer read from his paper. "You will be remanded to your cell for twenty-three hours per day. You will lose all accrued good-behavior credits."

I bit the corner of my lip. No recreational time, no phone calls, and no visitors. She could receive mail, but I wouldn't be allowed to read it to her.

The hearing officer pushed a piece of paper through the slit in her door. "Sign your name stating you have heard and understand the penalties for committing a class-one violation."

"Screw you, cowboy. Screw all of you," she screamed. She spit on the paper and tore it up before shoving the individual pieces back through to him. She slammed herself against the door and sobbed. "I hate you," she shouted to whoever would listen. It was the first time I'd heard her cry since she'd been in here.

Carmen hadn't poked her head out of her cell all day. I hoped she was down on her knees asking God to forgive her like I'd done every other minute today. God might wipe this sin away, but I doubted Roni would ever trust me again.

Jada joined me in the dayroom just as the movie was about to begin. She handed me an opened envelope. I took out a silver card. A white dove with open wings spanned the front. Written inside the card in gold scroll was a standard greeting: *Merry Christmas from Our Home to Yours*.

Underneath, written in red ink, were three simple words: *I forgive you*.

"It's from my mother-in-law," Jada whispered. She curled her legs up to her chest and started to rock. Her wet, dull eyes opened and shut while we watched the TV.

I returned to my cell and opened my *Woman's Day* menu planner. *December 23—Crispy Honey Mustard Chicken Thighs and Spinach Salad with Pears, Walnuts, and Goat Cheese*. I drew a big red *X* and then counted. Fifty-four days until I die.

SOPHIE

"What about your dad? Your brother? What about chief of surgery?" Sophie questioned Thomas while he looked up the number for the girl's parents.

"I don't care about being chief of surgery. I'm happy right where I am, and as far as my family goes . . ." Thomas stroked absently at the sides of his arms. "I don't care what they say or think anymore. A little girl is dead, my fault or not—I have to let the Campors know I did care, and I'm sorry."

Sophie watched him walk slowly but deliberately into the study. "Mr. Campor," she heard him say before quietly shutting the study door.

"There are some things I have to make right, too," she said out loud. Starting just as soon as Thomas got off the phone.

A CONVERSATION LIKE THIS REQUIRED a more comfortable chair and a cup of warm coffee to improve Thomas's mood, so Sophie asked him to sit down in the living room. She put water in the Keurig while he called in to his office. "Can you let my first few afternoon patients know I'm running a little late?"

Sophie heard her cell phone buzz as she put the K-Cup into the machine. Two missed calls from Ben Taylor. She didn't take time to listen to his voicemail, but hit redial instead. Before she could check to see if Thomas was still on his phone, Ben answered.

"Ben Taylor." His voice sounded quick and hurried.

She saw that Thomas had hung up from his call and appeared to be checking his e-mail on his phone. She slipped into the garage.

"Ben, this is Sophie."

"I'm glad to hear from you. Your message sounded urgent."

"I need to see you. Are you in town?"

"In court until tomorrow evening. Leaving on Christmas Eve to go out of town for a few days. Can it wait until I get back?"

"I think my mom may be innocent." She spoke the foreign words softly so Thomas wouldn't hear. "I think my brother may have been sick."

"I'll change my plans. How soon can you get here?"

THOMAS SIPPED HIS COFFEE, his long muscular legs crossed and his back relaxed up against the sofa cushions. A little bit of his smile returned when Sophie joined him in the living room.

"That wasn't an easy phone call to make, but I'm glad I finally did it."

"How'd it go?" Sophie asked, almost scared to hear his answer.

"I explained what I think happened and then I apologized. I sincerely apologized." Thomas moved a magazine from a basket and set it and then his coffee cup on the side table. "I could hear him choking up as I talked."

"Are they still going to sue?"

"I don't know. I didn't ask him. His daughter died and I needed to make sure he knew how sorry I really was."

She put her hand on the side of his face one last time before she confessed her shortcomings and gambled away the life they shared together. The baby growing inside her had a father full of courage. She pulled his face into hers and kissed him. "You know you mean everything to me."

"You mean everything to me," he answered, wiping a smudge of lip gloss off the corner of her mouth. "My life made sense the second I met you."

"You rescued me and you didn't even know it."

Thomas's pager beeped before she could continue.

He looked at Sophie and then put his pager back down. "It can wait."

"I need to tell you something now." She stopped and tried to summon the strength to say the next words that were sure to risk everything. "It's about my—"

Thomas's cell phone rang before she finished. If the phone rang right after the pager went off, it was undoubtedly urgent. He grabbed her hand before he answered it.

"Dr. Logan," he said gruffly. He squeezed Sophie's hand in apology. "I'm in the middle of something."

Sophie watched him as he listened, grateful for this interrupted moment that might be their last. After a series of uh-huhs, Thomas relented, "Call the OR and get me a room. I'll be there as soon as I can."

He apologized several times as he made his way out the door. "Dinner tonight? That quiet place with the candles on Third Avenue. We can talk for as long as you want."

Sophie wrapped her arms around him like he was being deployed overseas. "I love you," she told him when she finally let him go. "Never forget that."

He walked out and she watched through the wrought-iron door frame as he jogged to his car. *If only I could have done this better,* she thought. *Thomas and a whole lot of other things.*

She packed a bag with more clothes than she needed for a quick trip. She had no idea when she'd be back or how things would be with

Thomas once she was. She e-mailed Thomas a note she guessed he would open about the time she'd be headed to Brookfield.

> *I need to leave for a few days and make a few things right myself.*
> *Merry Christmas, sweetheart.*
>
> *Love, Sophie*

She pictured his face when he read the e-mail. Running his fingers through his dark hair, questioning what she could possibly be up to and what he'd done to deserve her running out on him. If only he was ever free for her to explain. For now, she had to get on the road and find out the truth, but before she did, she had to make one more stop.

SOPHIE TUGGED A LARGE BLACK TRASH BAG over her shoulder and down the hall of the pediatric ward. Max's Christmas needed to be special, even if they had to celebrate it a couple of days early.

"Where's my little man?" she said cheerily as she opened the door to his room.

"Sosie," Max hollered back. He held his hands out for her to pick him up. A frail woman wearing camouflage pants and a gray hoodie held him on her lap in the mauve recliner. He squirmed to get down.

"Hi, I'm Sophie." She extended her hand to the woman, who appeared much older than she probably was. Open sores scattered across her forehead and at the corners of her mouth.

"Ruby." Her hand didn't reach out, but she tightened her grip around Max's waist. "I'm Max's mom." Her dipped-in cheeks made her mouth crooked.

"Oh." Sophie set the plastic bag full of toys down in the corner of his room. "I'm glad to meet you."

"Sosie, hold me." Max tried to push away his mother's hands.

"Mommy's holding you." She bounced him up and down on her knee, but he became even more frustrated.

"This used to work." She tried to stand with Max on her hip, but she lost her balance and fell back into the chair.

"What's wrong?" Sophie said to Max. His lip puckered and he started to cry.

"You can take him," his mom said without making eye contact.

Max leaped off her lap and into Sophie's arms. His oxygen tubes became twisted and his monitors started to go off.

"I need to go smoke," she said, before Sophie had a chance to untangle him or ask questions. She bolted out the door just as Mindy entered.

"I see you met Max's mom," she said to Sophie once Ruby was out of hearing distance.

"Yes, I did." She tried to make Max feel like that was a good thing. "Your mommy came to visit. Yayyyy!"

Mindy took off his oxygen for a second while Sophie spun him around. Belly giggles came out of him like she'd never heard before.

"You my mommy," he said when the spinning stopped.

"I'm your Sosie." She poked his belly.

She looked at Mindy for advice on how to handle this one. Mindy, with her pen hanging out of her mouth, shrugged. "She wants to take him home."

"Can she do that?"

"Court papers say she can. Our hospital attorneys are reviewing the documents as we speak."

"What about his health, all his medical needs?" Sophie pointed to the oxygen tanks and monitors. "Does she realize the amount of care he needs?"

"She says she does," Mindy said while pushing buttons.

Sophie put Max back in the bed while Mindy positioned the nasal cannula over his nose. He was already panting.

Max pointed over to the plastic bag. "Puzwles?" he asked. His blue lips framed his wide toothy grin.

"Maybe," she teased.

After Mindy left, Max opened package after package of presents: crayons, markers, coloring books, and puzzles with bright colors and pieces that fell into place. Sophie laid down beside him in bed and read him a book about a man who lost his large purple shoe, and then another one about a caterpillar who refused to move, all with one eye on the door. Was his mother coming back?

"And the stubborn caterpillar started to shake as his twelve eyes dripped with fear. What is happening to me?" Sophie said in her best obstinate insect voice.

"You silly, Mommy," Max said to her through his giggles. His tight arms were still wrapped around her when his real mom walked through the door.

GRACE

"You might feel a little sting," the infirmary nurse said as she pinched my stitches with tweezers before cutting them out. "This looks great."

She pulled out a black compact from her white coat pocket, opened it, and handed it to me. "Normally, on the outside"—she pointed the scissors off somewhere beyond the barbed wire—"a plastic surgeon would have been called in to take care of a cut this severe. You're lucky our doctor is skilled with the sutures."

I held the mirror up to my face and examined the thick, jagged line that now spilled down from my right eye. I thought of Roni and tried to feel grateful. I wiped off the brown powder from the outskirts of the mirror the best I could and took a closer look. The reflections from the television screen and the plastic-coated mirror in the beauty shop have been kind to me. Glass mirrors don't lie, and I'm not finding the truth attractive.

I examined the rest of my features before she took my reality away. The black swimming pools under my eyes and the grooves now making their way across my forehead shocked me.

"This place has been hard on you." She held her hand out for the compact.

"Your mirror is hard on me," I responded. I don't have the energy to tell her how I really feel.

"If it matters to you, I think you look pretty good for forty-nine."

"Thanks." I tried to smile. It did matter.

Beauty is only skin deep. I heard myself repeating to Sophie what my mother repeated to me. I felt stronger about that adage when my skin was thicker and my high cheekbones had color.

Paul always told me that when he walked into a room, he noticed me first. "It goes beyond your smoking-hot bod," he'd say to me. "You have a gentle beauty that will never fade."

I wish he could tell me that now. Whisper in my ears and hold me in his arms while I breathe in the fading smell of his cologne after a long day. Soak in his words assuring me my changing hair color and my invasive wrinkles meant I was full of wisdom even if they weren't the lessons I'd have chosen to learn on my own.

"We won't need to do any more wound care for this," the nurse said. "I'll see you . . ."

We both knew when we'd see each other again.

"I hope you have a nice Christmas." I waved good-bye before the officers escorted me out the door.

Ms. Liz and Carmen sat at the table in the dayroom, talking as I made my way back to my cell. Jada sat alone in the corner away from the TV and kept her head down as I passed.

"Did you get your stitches out?" Ms. Liz asked as I shuffled by.

"Looks good as new, right?" I said to her. I still can't say anything to Carmen.

I tried to peek into Roni's cell as I passed by, but an officer prevented me. "Mind your own business," he ordered.

She'd been in isolation for several days. I needed to apologize and tell her why I did what I did. *Do I even understand what I did?*

"Stand for count," he yelled before he took my cuffs off.

Everyone was clearly visible except Roni.

The officers exchanged glances. The bigger of the two officers shouted, "Lock 'em down."

Jada and Carmen walked briskly back to their cells. Ms. Liz stood at the side of the table and looked confused. I could tell she didn't know what was going on.

The shorter officer locked my cell without undoing my feet or arm shackles. The door slammed shut before I had a chance to protest.

"We've got a hanger," the officer shouted.

Within seconds, an announcement boomed over the row's loud-speaker. Four more officers rushed through the cell block and convened outside Roni's door.

I peered out my window, praying they were wrong. "Please, let her be okay," I cried to God and everyone.

One officer stood at the door while three others entered. A twisted white sheet hung from the ceiling, Roni's limp neck draped through it.

The officer cuffed her hands before he cut her loose. I couldn't stand it anymore and turned away. "Why? Why?"

A gurney from the infirmary squeaked its way past my door. I looked again and saw them pick Roni's floppy body off the floor. The sheet was still around her neck.

"Found a faint pulse," I heard someone say as they pushed her past my cell and off death row.

SOPHIE

Sophie planned to drive as far as her fatigued body would let her so she could make it to Brookfield on Christmas Eve. Thomas called her as expected. "Please tell me what's wrong," followed by "What can I do to make you come back?"

She could give only vague answers like "I'm so sorry about this. I wanted to have a real conversation about this before I left, but then you got called in so quickly. You did everything right. I can't tell you something of this magnitude over the phone." She begged him to trust her, but had no idea why he possibly should.

She considered telling him she was pregnant, thinking that bit of news might soothe his discomfort and solidify a bond between them no amount of previous deception could break. But she wasn't exactly sure if he'd be happy about the baby. The last time his partner's wife delivered, Thomas had made some offhanded comment as he and Sophie left the maternity ward. "So glad," he said while they stepped onto the crowded elevator, "that you and I don't have any kids to tie us down." She didn't know, for Thomas, if the time would ever be right.

Sophie couldn't judge him too harshly, because motherhood—well, the idea actually terrified her. *What if I inherit my mother's coping style?* That fear had faded some when she met Max, a little more when she'd heard the sound of her baby's developing heart shuddering inside her.

After miles of unanswered questions, Thomas finally stopped asking.

He made her promise to call him as soon as she arrived and "keep in touch" as to when she'd be back.

"How can I explain this to my parents?" he asked before she hung up the phone. "My wife leaving me on Christmas." His grief cut through the line.

"Tell them it's my turn to make something right."

He hung up the phone without saying good-bye.

Sophie rolled down all four car windows, begging the ice-cold December air to keep her awake. When it didn't, she pulled her car off the interstate and onto an exit ramp about ninety minutes from Brookfield. Right off the exit, a green sign instructed cars to turn right for Lakeland State Penitentiary or left for gas, hotels, or if you wanted to eat at Cracker Barrel. A truck driver honked his horn after Sophie sat at the intersection long after the light turned green.

She fought the urge to turn right, drive to Lakeland, and stand outside the thick, twisted barbed wire, shouting: "Mom, please tell me what happened to William. I need to know how I should feel about you."

After the truck driver blared his horn for the third time, Sophie turned left and pulled into the parking lot of a Holiday Inn she and her father had stayed at the evening of her mom's conviction. This time the deserted parking lot had no reporters armed with bulky cameras and flashing bulbs posturing themselves to ask the first question. "Mr. Bradshaw, do you still believe your wife is innocent?" Her dad's silver wedding band had pulled a piece of her hair as he shielded her from them.

"Why do these news people hate my mom?" she had asked him after they checked into their room. He didn't have an answer. Sophie sat at the windowsill and watched a normal family swimming in the concrete pool while her dad locked himself in the bathroom. "Jump, Johnny," a young mom instructed her toddler, his orange floaties secure around his arms. "Mommy will catch you."

Her dad came out much later, after Sophie's growling stomach had her pounding on the bathroom door. "Dad, I'm hungry. Let's get Mom and go home." She could hear him crying.

"In a minute, sweetheart," he told her as he turned on the water in the small hotel bathroom sink. "We need to talk."

Throughout the trial, her dad had tried to protect her. He kept the news off after school and shuffled her to stay with various members of the church during the two long weeks of her mom's trial. An elderly neighbor filled in when the congregation wasn't available.

Her dad believed, he later told her, that right after the jury deliberated he'd scoop his handcuffed wife off and whisk her home where she belonged—home, where he could protect her and she could be Sophie's mother. They'd deal with William's death as a family.

He never imagined the foreman of the jury would stand up and say, "In the matter of the people versus Grace Bradshaw, we the jury find the defendant guilty." The judge had agreed: "Mrs. Bradshaw, you are an attention-seeking liar whose maternal instincts have gone awry."

Later, at sentencing, the prosecutors hugged each other when the judge said, "Your premeditated actions were the ultimate act of betrayal and hereby warrant the death penalty." They'd won a case. Her family had lost everything.

A sixth-grade Sophie sat beside her dad on a stained brown-and-coral comforter in room 330 at this very hotel while he robotically told her the news. "Your mom has to live at Lakeland now."

Sophie pulled her suitcase through the desolate parking lot. When she checked in, she told the clerk at the front desk, "Any room but room three-thirty is fine."

BEN TAYLOR HAD LEFT AN ENVELOPE on the front door of his office building. The note inside read: *Sophie—Call me when you get here.*

Sophie took off her brown leather gloves and pulled her phone from her coat pocket. No texts from Thomas. He was off today and tomorrow because she'd asked him to be so they could do some shopping and buy a tree. Last minute, but their Christmas Eve tradition. "You know we'll eventually have to do this tree thing earlier when we have kids," she'd said to him last Christmas.

"Ben. It's Sophie."

"Hi." He sounded out of breath.

"I'm here. Outside your office." The wind started to pick up, so she held the phone with her cheek and put her gloves back on.

"Did you keep any of your mom's old files?"

"They should be at my parents' house." They were in the white cracked laundry basket pushed up against the wall in the laundry room. Newspaper articles and yellow legal pads buried under stacks of dirty towels and bed linens.

"I'll meet you there in fifteen." He hung up before she could protest. She hadn't been inside that house in years. The thought of wall-climbing mold spores and the hefty cockroaches that probably resided there made her want to throw up. Old pizza boxes and dirty pots stuck with ramen noodles and Campbell's tomato soup had cluttered the countertops the last time she'd locked the door. She hadn't washed a dish the last semester of her senior year.

Ben was already sitting on the front porch swing when Sophie pulled into the driveway. He unlocked the front door while she walked up the cracked sidewalk. "I need your dad to fix this," she could hear her mom say. "Someone's going to twist an ankle."

"You have a key?" she asked Ben after she slid her hand under the old mailbox and felt the spare key still stuck there.

"Yes. Your mom asked me to change the locks and look after the place after it became evident . . ."

"That I wasn't going to do it," Sophie finished. "It's okay. I left this part of my life behind me when I left for college. I never intended to come back."

Ben held the screen door open for her. The place was neat and organized. It looked exactly like it had before her mother left. Sophie fought the urge to cry.

"How?" She turned to him.

"No offense, but the place was quite a mess after you left. When you stopped paying for the upkeep, the city made some complaints."

Sophie walked over to the fireplace and stared at the mantel. It was full of framed photos of her holding newly born William, her dad grilling corn and pork chops on the Big Green Egg he received for Father's Day, and her mom standing in front of the first three-tiered wedding cake she'd ever decorated. Sophie pulled down a plaque that read *Suffer Well, for It Shapes Your Soul*.

"When we couldn't find you, your mom asked if I would hire someone to clean the place."

Sophie looked down at the recently vacuumed brown shag carpet. Her dad had saved for months to buy her mom this carpet. In the corner of this room, under the now-outdated rug, was a heart that read *Paul + Grace = Forever* carved into the dented hardwood floors.

"My mom always made sure this place looked good." Sophie ran her palm over the handmade draperies framing the windows in the living room. "Look at this silk fabric I found on sale," she remembered hearing her mom say to her dad. "I negotiated with the saleslady and bought this for almost nothing."

"No place like home," Ben said.

A part of Sophie agreed. The other parts still needed to gather evidence.

"I had the housekeeper box up everything you left lying around. She said she put the boxes in one of the bedrooms. Shall we look?"

The house had only two bedrooms, so Sophie led the way to her parents' room first. William's crib, still assembled, stored box upon box of their lives' paperwork.

"Let me get these," Ben said, grabbing the first box of the stack. The housekeeper had written SCHOOL PAPERS ETC. on the lid. Ben put the box on her parents' double bed and Sophie started sorting. Lying on top was some of her kindergarten artwork. A stick-figure girl with orange pigtails holding what Sophie thought was a kite. Written beneath in messy large print: *I want a puppy!*

Ben grabbed the next box, which read *MISCELLANEOUS* and opened the lid. On the top of the stack were unopened envelopes from Duke Power, water bills from the City of Brookfield, and various other ignored letters from Sophie's days home alone.

"I guess these have been paid." She smirked and tossed the envelopes back into the box.

"All taken care of," he responded, pointing to the lights on in the room.

"My dad's life insurance?"

Ben nodded.

"This looks like the right container," Sophie said, pulling out some file folders that read TRIAL TRANSCRIPTS.

"Your phone call made me start thinking," Ben said as Sophie moved the box over to the bed, "I have all the transcripts from the trial, all the depositions from their expert witnesses, but what I should be looking for is anything your dad might have discovered after your mom's conviction."

Sophie pulled all the papers out of the box. Three yellow legal pads filled the bottom. "This is what he worked on every night after dinner." She handed them all to Ben.

"Why the change of heart?" Ben asked after he'd been flipping through the pages for a few minutes. "Why'd you call me?"

Sophie started to feel light-headed and stood up. "I think I'm going to go grab some water," she murmured.

"I'd run that awhile before I'd drink it," Ben said, following her into the kitchen. "The water's on, but I'm not sure how good it'll taste.

"You feeling okay?" he asked as they sat down at the table.

"A little hungry, I guess." She didn't have an appetite at all, but that reason seemed easier than trying to explain how she really felt.

He dug into his coat pocket and offered her a peppermint.

"Thanks." She unwrapped it and popped it into her mouth. "You must think I'm a real prize." Sophie couldn't look him in the eyes. *Why does every moment have to be so hard?*

Ben looked at her in silence and Sophie felt even sillier about being such a wreck every time she saw him. "How's my mom?" Sophie asked him. She moved the mint around in her mouth while tracing the three overlapping water rings on the oak table. *"Use a coaster, Sophie. This table cost your dad a lot of money."*

Sophie had made herself stop thinking about how her mother was doing a long time ago. She forced herself not to worry about whether her mom had enough blankets, or if she had money for snacks and stamps in her commissary account, justifying this callous decision by saying things to herself like, *Who cares if she can buy a candy bar? William never tasted one.*

Now, since the possibility of her mother's wrongful conviction had crept back into her consciousness, so had the overtaking feeling of guilt. Even when she tried to occupy her thoughts with Max, or the fund-raiser, or Thomas, the feelings of failed responsibilities always lurked below the surface. Visions of her mom watching the other inmates eat micro-waved popcorn in the dayroom, or her mom's cold toes turning blue when the temperatures dropped because Sophie didn't care enough to send her money to buy thicker socks.

Justice for William used to help her forget, but now . . . Sophie hadn't fully processed that yet.

"She's hanging in there. Never been one to give up."

"Does she know you found me?"

"I haven't told her yet. I didn't know how, especially if you don't want to see her?" The last part of the sentence was phrased more like a question. She felt him studying her face for clues.

"I'm pregnant," Sophie blurted. Her mom's death row attorney was the first person she's told.

"Is that why you're here? You want to tell your mom?" Ben drummed his fingers on the table.

"That's why I think my mom may be innocent. I . . . found out my brother, William, he had all the symptoms of a rare metabolic disorder."

Ben closed the file he had brought in from the bedroom. "Go on," he said.

"I told my OB that I had a baby brother who died. No one else knows the truth." Sophie's cheeks started to burn. "I've been ashamed to tell anyone."

Ben skated a box of yellowing tissues over in her direction. "You handled things the best way you knew how."

She gave him a smile that wasn't really a smile. "I messed up and I need to make that right. That's if it's not too late."

"I can arrange a visit—most definitely—but I don't know if we should share your theory with your mother yet."

"What do you mean? You said you think she's innocent. We may be able to finally prove she didn't kill my brother."

"I stayed up all last night after I received your phone call, scanning through years of documents for the one hundredth time. Your mom's first attorney did a terrible job, but I worry it's not bad enough to get your mom a new trial."

"They didn't know," Sophie said. "They had no idea at the time about this disease my brother may have had. No one did. My doctor said they didn't have any diagnostic tests back then."

Sophie dumped the rest of the contents of the box Ben had brought out on the middle of the table as if to prove to herself and to Ben that there was something in there that would clear her mother's name.

Ben shuffled through dated legal pads while Sophie looked through the pile of stamped papers for anything official from the coroner's office.

"When did your dad die again?" he asked while shuffling through some dated pages.

"End of November." Sophie set her stack of papers on her lap and massaged the corners of her eyelids. "My dad died sometime after I went to bed on November twenty-eighth. My senior year in high school."

Ben put down one legal pad and quickly picked up another. "Thursday, November twenty-eighth." His finger ran down the page. "I think I may have found something."

Sophie stopped rubbing and scooted her chair closer to his. "Where? What'd you find?"

"Friday, November thirtieth," he read before looking up. "Dr. H. Robinson. Your dad was supposed to call a Dr. H. Robinson?"

GRACE

Did you know the day you were born there were twenty-six babies in the nursery? You were number twenty-seven. Our number twenty-seven. We watched you from the window after they took you back. Daddy held his arms up in V for Victory and I glanced around the hallway to see if any other mothers were experiencing this incredible feeling of amazement.

Most of the babies were crying, but not you, Sophie—you were perfectly content. No matter what was happening around you, you were at peace. All bundled up in a pink-and-white blanket. Your boppy, you later called it.

I wish you could have seen your daddy. He had his thumbs hooked through his belt loops and his chest puffed out. "Out of all the babies in here, how'd we make the very best one?"

If you only knew how much those little moments mattered to me.

xoxoxo

December 24, Enjoy Shrimp Lo Mein and Spring Rolls from your favorite Chinese takeout while you wrap those last-minute holiday presents.

Would I have been better off never being born? I've asked myself that question more often than I probably should share. I keep replaying the minutes leading up to William's death. My squirmy baby full of explosive giggles, then drained of it all, right before my helpless eyes. Maybe if I'd been a better mother, a more intuitive one, a more attentive one, I would have known the right thing to do. If only I'd taken him to the doctor one more time . . .

I don't understand his death. I guess I never will. Why he started refusing my breast and sucked only from the bottle. Why when I fed him his bottle he became deathly ill and threw up his food, his tiny chest struggling to rise and fall. The doctor said not to worry, he'd be fine and that he'd gained some weight. He promised me William's sleepy eyes would wake up and his giggles would return.

My actions, or inactions, were not intentional. A mother could never love a child more than I loved William. But my love wasn't enough. My inadequacies failed him, failed you and Paul, too.

Carmen noticed my pleasant demeanor and told me to cheer up. She yelled, "You're not dead yet," when I walked to the dayroom. She and Jada were sitting at the table opening Ziploc bags of items sent in from the outside. Sample-size Close-Up toothpaste, Pert shampoo, and Jergens hand lotion, along with peanut-butter crackers and a bag of Skittles, lie within the clear packaging. A red bow adorned the top.

"I guess these church ladies didn't get the memo about the tooth-brushes," Carmen said, referring to the regular-size toothbrushes that had been confiscated and were now lying on the officer's desk. "Maybe now he'll brush his teeth"—she raised her voice so he'd hear her.

Every year we received a package from the women at Lake Terrace Lutheran Church. I imagined them sitting around and stuffing the bags.

"Walmart had a sale on peanut-butter crackers and shampoo. Great deals on everything."

Carmen threw my bag at me. "You must be special. You got a hand-written note this year."

I still haven't said a word to her since she faked the fight with Roni. I know, I should remember my own advice to Sophie: choose love and forgiveness.

Instead, I sat at a different table with my back toward her.

"You don't blame me for what happened to Roni, do you, Grace?"

Her sharp words startled me and I had to respond. I think it scared Jada because she scurried to the other side of the room.

"You lied." I tried to keep my voice calm and low, but I refused to back down.

Carmen started to come toward me. "You bitch!" Her pencil-thin lips flattened.

I stood and realized my legs finally felt free.

"Call me whatever you want, but take some responsibility. You lied, and because of you Roni may never get to meet her dad."

"I didn't hear Sister Grace tell any truths," she spewed back. We were so close I could see her tongue. She'd been eating orange Skittles. "Holier-than-thou baby-killer kept her judgmental mouth shut."

Jada cleared her throat. The officer by the door watched us with one hand on the side of his belt.

"You're right. I'm as guilty as you."

Carmen tossed her head back and claimed victory.

"We both owe Roni an apology," I said.

The officer made his way over. "Sit down, ladies, or return to your cells."

Carmen grunted at me and then at him. We all sat down at different tables. I put on hand lotion. Carmen ate more Skittles.

Choose love and forgiveness. Sometimes I hated Paul's sermons.

No one would tell me if Roni survived. The officers refused to answer when I asked, and Ms. Liz had not been back to visit.

I watched the local news report a break-in at the Motel 6 located right outside the gates and a car-jacking that happened late last night involving an elderly woman pumping gas—but no mention of a twenty-five-year-old woman who'd attempted suicide all because she wanted to meet her biological father for the first time this Christmas.

I'm praying Roni's okay. That she's lying in a hospital bed outside these confined walls watching reruns of *Friends* and dreaming of a better life. That maybe, just maybe, a kind nurse will take pity on her, notify her next of kin, and sneak her father in for a visit. His hand rubbing her hair. "It'll be okay now, Daddy's here. I'll figure a way to get you out of this mess."

I CAN MAKE ONE CALL on Christmas. My attorney's office won't be open, but I might call anyway. If only to hear the phone ring.

I twist the top off the last peanut-butter cracker before I open the note left for me by some faceless woman who'd taken the time to remember. My name is written in calligraphy on the folded white envelope stuffed inside.

> *I wanted you to know that you are not alone this holiday season.*
> *Or at least not in spirit . . . I've been praying for you since I read the*
> *denial of your latest appeal in the newspaper. Don't give up hope.*
> *The same God who was with you then is with you now.*

I reread that last sentence at least three times before I folded the note and stuck it between the pages of my Bible. A book I no longer felt worthy to hold in my hands.

"God, if you can hear me at all—please help Roni."

And then I begged him to watch over Sophie.

SOPHIE

Sophie found herself sitting in baggage claim of an airport located forty-five minutes outside of Brookfield on Christmas Eve. Ben left to get her a decaf coffee and came back with two sugar cookies and a chocolate double-fudge brownie.

"You're eating for two," he said as he held up the choices.

I bet he's a good dad, Sophie thought as she grabbed one cookie and half the brownie. "Guess I'm a little hungry."

A few hours earlier, he'd listened to Sophie go over in detail the conversation she'd had with Jack. "It may be nothing or may be everything," he said after she finished. He punched the number her dad had written under Dr. H. Robinson's name in his cell phone. After the first ring, an automated voice said, "The number you have dialed has been disconnected. If you think you have reached this number in error, please hang up and dial again."

"Thought that might happen," Sophie said.

"Let me put a call in to a detective I know in the police department. If Dr. H. Robinson is still kickin', this guy will find him."

Within minutes, Ben had a new cell phone number for a gentleman from Seattle, who may or may not have run a lab on this side of the country seventeen years ago. "Pray this is the guy," he said to Sophie as he dialed.

"I already have." She held her clasped hands up for him to see.

"This is Henry." Ben put the phone on speaker.

"My name is Ben Taylor. I'm looking for a Dr. H. Robinson."

"This is he, but I just go by Henry now. I've been retired for the last five years."

"Can I ask you if you ever knew anyone by the name of Paul or Grace Bradshaw?"

"Bradshaw?" he asked. "That name sounds familiar. Who'd you say is calling?"

"Ben Taylor. I'm an attorney who represents Grace Bradshaw. She's on death row, convicted of poisoning her infant son."

"Oh, a long time ago. South Carolina case. I remember now. Her husband, uh, what'd you say his name was again?"

"Paul," Ben repeated. "Paul Bradshaw."

"Oh, yes, tall guy with glasses. He asked me to run some independent lab tests. I had the results, but I never heard from him."

"What lab tests?" Ben tapped his fingers on the outside of the phone. "Do you remember anything about them?"

"You bet your reindeer I do." Ben rolled his eyes and shot Sophie an "I hope this guy isn't crazy" look. "Ethylene glycol. I tested the baby's bottle."

Ben gave Sophie a thumbs-up. "How soon can I interview you? In person, I mean?"

Dr. Robinson sighed and clicked his tongue into the phone. "I'll be back in a few weeks. Flying my Cessna to Florida to see family for the holidays."

"I'm afraid we can't wait that long," Ben said. "Grace's execution is scheduled for February."

Sophie could hear the doctor muttering something to someone in the background. *On Christmas Eve?* a female voice shrieked.

"I'm headed out tonight. I'll need to stop and refuel somewhere." *Tell them we have plans!* "How close is the nearest airport?"

When Ben told him, Dr. Robinson said, "Can you meet me around eight?"

BEN DUNKED HIS COOKIE in his coffee while Sophie flipped through a Chamber of Commerce pamphlet on "Brookfield's Top Attractions." A glossy magazine's way of making the run-down covered bridge located on the outskirts of town sound like a must-see.

Ben stood to stretch and checked his watch: 8:27 p.m.

"Thanks for canceling your plans," Sophie said to him. She thought about asking him how his kids had taken the news, but that might make him ask her about Thomas. For that question, she didn't have an answer.

"Thank you for giving me a good reason to." Sophie could tell by his sincerity that he truly cared for her mother.

"Mr. Taylor?" A man with a silver-trimmed beard and a tucked-in green-and-white-striped golf shirt approached them from behind. "Sorry I'm late. The wind's a little stronger coming in this direction. I'm Henry Robinson."

"Ben Taylor." He held out his hand to shake. "This is Sophie, Grace's daughter."

"Nice to meet you both," he said. "I brought all the notes I could find, but as I told you on the phone—this was a long time ago."

"Anything you can give us is appreciated." Sophie noticed the Augusta National logo on the polo he was wearing. "The Masters?" she asked.

"We go every year," he said. "You play golf?"

"My husband does. We've been a couple times." She and Thomas might have stood next to him at Amen Corner.

"I tried to get in touch with your dad to go over the results, but he didn't return my calls."

"He passed away," Sophie said. "From a heart attack. Ben found your name on some of his notes."

"That explains it, then," Dr. Robinson said. He opened his briefcase and pulled out a file.

"He didn't know?" Sophie asked him after reading the summary confirming her dad's suspicions. *No evidence of ethylene glycol (the active ingredient found in antifreeze) was present in the bottle.*

"He didn't know," Dr. Robinson said.

Sophie's dad had never wavered in his belief his wife was innocent. He didn't need a piece of paper to prove otherwise.

"I sent the results to the DA's office, but no one ever called me. After a while, I just stopped trying."

"Grace hired me after Paul died to handle her appeals," Ben explained. "I have a copy of the tests the prosecutor's office had done. It showed trace amounts of ethylene glycol in every bottle tested—the police found the windshield-wiper fluid under the sink in the Bradshaws' kitchen."

Sophie didn't know where he was going with this, but he continued. "The autopsy on William's brain concurred. The experts testified to it and it's what pointed to murder."

Sophie tried to get the picture of William's open skull and dissected brain out of her head. This all sounded so convincing. Had her mom poisoned William?

Ben saw her clench her fists. "I'm playing devil's advocate here, but we need another explanation."

"I tested the same bottle the prosecutors did. I can promise you there was no trace of windshield-wiper fluid." He handed a second report to Ben.

"I looked at the court transcripts your father gave me. Your mom's defense attorney did a terrible job. The test the hospital lab performed on

William's blood"—Henry pulled another piece of paper from his file—"was totally unacceptable."

He shook his head while Ben studied the findings. "Hell," Dr. Robinson said, "what you see and what you find depends a great deal on what side you're standing on. You could find antifreeze in my cup of coffee if you used these outdated chromatographic techniques. I'd have retested William's blood if I'd had any, brought in another medical examiner—something to point the jury in another direction."

Sophie closed her eyes and took a couple deep breaths to calm herself.

She wanted to hit something or blame someone. No matter how she spun it—all fingers pointed back to her. She shouldn't have given up on her mom. She should've finished what her dad had started.

"I should've looked through my father's papers more carefully." She pushed the rest of the words out. "Maybe I could have found your number and gotten in touch with you much sooner. My mom went through seventeen years of hell. This is all my fault."

Ben tried to comfort her before turning on himself. "You were a kid. For that matter, I should've investigated this."

Sophie stared at Ben and then shrugged. Easier to forgive someone else than it is to forgive yourself. No time for what-ifs or "Why'd we stop?" now.

"My mom needs us now."

"You're right," Ben said to her. "We have to be strong for your mom and strong for her grandbaby."

Sophie nodded and put her hand over her stomach. "Dr. Robinson, do you think my brother could've died because of a metabolic disorder?"

"A metabolic disorder?" The lines that crossed his forehead thickened. "I hadn't thought of that possibility, but it makes sense." He put his hand over Sophie's hand. "I may know a way to find out."

GRACE

A tray with a hard-boiled egg, a cup of mixed fruit, and a single sausage patty slid through my door to help celebrate my seventeenth and last Christmas Day on death row. I decided I didn't have much of an appetite. Instead I spent my time in my cell, forcing myself to remember every Christmas since Paul and I met and we started a family.

Daddy putting together your pink Schwinn bike after I tucked you in bed for the night and made you promise to go fast asleep. The white instruction pages spread across the floor in different languages, his hammer and every size screw and Allen wrench aligned in a row across the coffee table.

I stayed in the kitchen, gnawing the ends of carrot sticks in imitation of Rudolph's teeth marks, then took a bite out of the two Oreos you had laid out before going to bed. I poured half the glass of Santa's milk down the drain.

Paul or I would yell the next morning from the kitchen while you made a beeline to the tree, "Looks like Santa and his reindeer sure enjoyed the snack you left for them." You'd rush over to look.

If I had enough energy left, I'd pull apart a cotton ball and leave small bits of fuzz stuck in the fireplace cover. "Poor Santa must've ripped the bottom of his pants again." You jumped up and down, giggling. "Silly Santa," you'd say.

I dreamed last night we were all in the same bed. Me on one side, you and William in the middle, and Paul on the other. The house made no sounds and the TV wasn't on. Just us, lying there. I could hear you breathe and feel William's arm brush up against mine. I felt like time stood still, like nothing could ever go wrong. I was in perfect peace.

When I woke up this morning, alone, still on the row, the noise of guards shouting and cell bars clanging, I felt as if the last bit of life I had in me had been sucked out. The peace from my dreams was gone and the chaos of my reality rushed in to take its place.

I used to pray God would let me be with my family each night when I closed my eyes. Those brief dreams helped me survive and helped me through the long moments when my eyes were forced to be open.

For a moment, I envied Jada. She stays to herself. She hoards her bread slices at mealtime and molds them into zoo animals. The giraffe knows more about her than I do. Her mind creates her reality, and her family lives with her there.

I've heard it said that right before you die, your life flashes in front of your eyes. Snippets of big and small, like "It's a girl," then "He has your nose," to "Of course I'll marry you" and "Don't give up. We'll get through this." All the occurrences that elevate and deflate us and bore us to tears, all melted together to become the story of our lives.

Most people tend to remember the significant. The "I dos" and the "I will no longers," or the exhilaration they felt the first time they pulled themselves upright on water skis. I do, too, but as I look back on my forty-nine years the most important moments are not the events but the seconds right after. When I'm snuggled in bed next to you at the end of a long Christmas Day, the floor overtaken with *crumpled wrapping paper and torn boxes, the mashed potatoes glued to the side of the pan, all my earlier energy depleted, and you look at me and say, "Mommy, did you have a nice Christmas?"*

Relationships that messed me up are the ones that kept me going. Circumstances that made me crazy challenged me to be better. Those moments shaped my soul and energized my spirit. These are the things I want to remember, these little pieces embedded in me so deeply they've become a part of who I am. They will follow me to my eternity.

Don't live your life for the big events. Pause and enjoy the moments after.

SOPHIE

Right now, Sophie guessed, Thomas was probably sitting around his family's breakfast bar while his mom fixed him the traditional Christmas-morning sausage and three-cheese quiche and crème brûlée French toast casserole. The smell of freshly brewed cappuccino lingering in the background was always Sophie's favorite part.

Vivianne would be asking, "Where's Aunt Sophie? She promised to paint my fingernails." Knowing Thomas, he'd probably tell her that Aunt Sophie wasn't feeling well, needed to rest, and had asked him to go to Charleston without her. She pictured his mom raising her eyebrows when he explained, his dad looking over his bifocals.

She resisted the urge to call or text him because she didn't know what to tell him. "Hey, I have great news. My mom, the one you thought was dead, isn't, but she may be innocent." No text seemed close to appropriate. Soon, though, she had to tell him about the pregnancy. He deserved to know he was going to be a dad.

AFTER THEY FINISHED THEIR MEETING with Dr. Robinson, Ben offered a spare bedroom for Sophie to stay in. The idea of returning to the only bed-and-breakfast in Brookfield, sniffing kitty litter and greasy bacon on Christmas morning, made her decision for her. *Who cares what this looks like,* she rationalized when she gave him a quick yes.

They needed to move forward with a plan if her mom had any hope of being exonerated. "Even though you and I both believe your mother is innocent," Ben cautioned her, "we have to get the governor to agree to even hear our evidence." He exhaled. "This is a long shot that may not be possible."

"One hundred percent failure rate if we don't try," she said back to him. This time she smiled.

And it was a long shot—that much Dr. Robinson had made clear. After he had the chance to do some research on the disease, he gave Ben and Sophie a call. "The kind of metabolic disorder William may have had, isovaleric acidemia, or IVA for short, is rare—about one in seventy-five thousand. No one diagnosed it around the time your brother was born."

He asked if both of them were following along before he continued.

"Both of your parents had to be carriers for William to become sick. Since you don't have the disease, you have a fifty percent chance of being a carrier like your parents, or a twenty-five percent chance of having perfectly normal genes. Babies born with IVA have a hard time breaking down protein. I suspect that's why William threw up after he had a bottle. Without treatment, seizures and loss of life can occur. Today, it's treatable by simple diet changes and medication."

A carrier. Could my baby be sick? Jack mentioned something about additional testing, but Sophie hadn't asked him to clarify. She started to twist her hair.

Ben must have read her worry because he grabbed her hand and asked Henry, "Where do we go from here?"

"I'd love to test William's blood. Any chance the DA's office would allow us to do that?"

"I've already tried. No blood was left. All of the evidence had been discarded, believe it or not." He tapped his pen rapidly on his thigh. "Could we exhume William's body for testing?"

The thought of disturbing William's final resting spot made Sophie twist her hair even faster.

"I don't think we'll have to." Static interrupted the clarity of his voice.

"Can you repeat what you said?" asked Ben.

"I said I don't think we'll have to. We can test Grace. I don't suppose the prison has any state-of-the-art genetic-testing facilities available?"

"Even if they did, the mounds of paperwork that would be required to push that through—it would never happen in time."

"Since your dad is not alive," Dr. Robinson asked Sophie through the speakerphone, "how do you feel about giving me some blood?"

SOPHIE FOUND BEN IN HIS KITCHEN, scrambling eggs. "How'd you sleep?" he asked her.

"Not too good." She pulled out a chair and sat at the kitchen table. "Innocent and on death row all these years."

"It happens more often than you think," he said. "Wheat or white?"

"Wheat, please."

Ben popped two slices into the toaster. He had on faded blue jeans and a navy pullover sweater. His kitchen countertops, free from clutter, held a family of painted ceramic roosters on the end closest to the refrigerator. His wife's touch before she passed away, Sophie guessed.

"I'm thinking this isn't what you thought you would be doing on Christmas morning," she said to him.

He handed her a glass of ice-cold orange juice. "My gift will be an innocent Grace Bradshaw walking out of prison." He whisked the eggs and then put some link sausage in a frying pan. "Hope you're not a vegetarian."

"I'd eat a twelve-ounce sirloin right now if you had one. This baby's making me hungry."

"I called a friend who's an ER doctor at the hospital. She's out of town right now, but she told me the outpatient lab at Brookfield General is small and understaffed. And it's not open today, anyway." He scooped some eggs onto a plate. "She suggested we go to a larger facility with special lab technicians who are well versed in genetic testing. I plan to call a genetics expert to interpret the results."

"Where'd she have in mind?"

Ben handed her some butter and blackberry jam. "Duke. Isn't that right in your backyard?"

"Sure is," Sophie said. Her two worlds had finally collided.

Ben turned off the stove and gave Sophie three link sausages and two generous scoops of scrambled eggs.

"So, if I understood Dr. Robinson correctly . . ." She started to take a bite of eggs and stopped. "If I have normal genes, we can't prove William had the disease." She put her fork down and pushed her plate aside. "And my mom will die by lethal injection."

She then put her hand over the place where her baby was growing. "If I'm a carrier, then my baby could have exactly what William did."

"I know." Ben turned from wiping off the stove. "That's a real catch-22."

After a few moments of silence, she picked up her orange juice to toast. "Merry Christmas to me."

Ben ignored her sarcasm and pulled out a chair across the table from her. "Either way, you'll need to find out. What'd your husband say?"

"He doesn't know."

"About the testing?" Ben questioned.

"About anything." She fought back the tears. "About the pregnancy, anything."

"You want to surprise him?" Ben widened his eyes. Sophie could tell he hoped that'd be her reason.

Sophie knew she was about to disappoint him. "It'll be a shock, all right. He doesn't know I even had a brother. Thomas thinks my mother's already dead. Cancer. I blurted it out when we first started dating."

Ben tore off a paper towel and held it for too long over his mouth. Sophie tried to read his expression. Did he understand, or was he appalled by her?

"How'd you keep that a secret"—he put the paper towel in his lap— "for all these years?"

"Lies," Sophie responded. "Lots of lies."

Ben's cell phone rang, but he ignored it. "That must've been a heavy burden for you to bear all by yourself."

"It was." She picked up his cell phone from where it was ringing in the center of the table and said, "Here, talk to your kids."

Sophie watched Ben's face brighten as he heard his five-year-old granddaughter's excitement as she told him all the things Santa brought her. "I miss you more," Ben said.

"Wish I could be there, too," he said when his son picked up the phone. "I'd have to have a pretty darn good excuse to be away from my kids on Christmas morning."

When he hung up, Sophie said to him, "Ben, can you do me a huge favor? Can you please take me to see my mother?"

GRACE

Bear with me. I don't want to forget anything that happened, so I'm writing it all down. You'll understand why when you get to the end.

Christmas Day was interrupted by Carmen . . .

"I need to shower," she yelled at whoever would listen. "My husband will be here soon and I smell like dirty toilet water." No one answered. Shower day was yesterday, and she wasn't getting another one.

"Grace," she screamed through the locked doors, "when are you gonna cut my hair?" I didn't answer. I forgot to tell her my beauty-shop privileges had been revoked.

Inmate is no longer permitted to work outside the current assigned housing unit due to impending status change. *Fancy prison talk that means I can't work in the beauty shop anymore.*

The cell doors unlocked and Carmen was still ranting. She flew out the door with a plastic comb in her hand and said, "Can you help me do something with this?"

"Merry Christmas," I said to Carmen and then to Jada, who was watching from inside her cell.

"Right back at ya, Grace," Carmen said in the most unjoyful tone she could muster. "Now tease my damn hair before my husband gets here."

I took the comb and followed her to the dayroom. I glanced inside Roni's empty cell. Maybe today we'd hear some news.

"Jada, you wanna join us?" I asked her as I walked by.

"No, I'm going to stay in my cell and get ready. In case my kids get a chance to visit."

I gave her a "why, sure they will" smirk.

"Hurry up, Grace!" Carmen waved her hands all around her head. "He's waiting on me."

I put the comb to Carmen's head and pulled her bangs straight up in the air. Her hair was thinning, making it difficult to get any height on it at all. After a few minutes of failed attempts, I said, "You look lovely."

She grabbed the comb and walked over to the turned-off TV to study her reflection.

"Get ready for body search," the officer informed us after he put down the receiver on the phone.

Carmen squealed like she won the lottery. "I'll go first."

I ignored her. No body search needed for me and Jada. No one was coming to spend Christmas with me.

Carmen disappeared behind the curtain and I settled myself in for whatever TV shows I could find that would help pass the time. A rerun of the Westminster Dog Show. I covered myself up with a gray blanket I dragged from my cell and decided to cheer for the Portuguese water dog. He reminded me of Teddy, and he had a nice sass in his step.

xoxoxo

"Bradshaw, don't got all day," the officer shouted at me from across the room.

"Get over here right now if you want to see your visitor."

I turned down the TV and made sure he was talking to me. "I have a visitor?"

"Not if you don't move faster."

I almost ran across the room to be searched. This must be a mistake.

Maybe Ben? I hadn't heard from him since my phone call to him disconnected.

Two officers escorted Carmen and me down the hall and through the series of automated checkpoints. My ankle shackles felt tight, as did my chest. I had to remind myself to breathe.

"Where are you taking me?" I asked the officer after we passed the checkpoint for the attorney-client room.

"Visitor area," he said. I couldn't remember the direction. I hadn't been there in years.

COULD IT BE YOU?

I needed a drink of water.

The officer buzzed us through a few doors I'd never seen before.

"Number sixteen," the control room man said to the officer escorting me.

"Number nine," he said to Carmen's.

"You look mouthwatering," she said through the glass to her husband as soon as she sat down.

The officer unlocked my ankle shackles and pulled out the blue chair for me to sit in. He clamped them back to the chair legs and took off my handcuffs.

No one was seated across the glass from me.

I looked at the officer and he shook his head. "No idea. I just do what I'm told."

The black phone had been taken off the wall. Thick glass and mesh grates now separated me from whomever.

After a few long minutes, I heard an officer say, "Sixteen. Bradshaw is in sixteen."

My hands started to tingle like they were falling asleep. I closed my eyes and prayed that when I opened them, I'd see you sitting in front of me.

I heard a chair being pulled out. When I opened my eyes, a young man sat down. He glared at me through the glass.

I dropped my head. I didn't want to give interviews. About my life or about my death. Especially not on Christmas.

"I'm not interested in being interviewed." I tried hard not to sound rude. "I don't have anything to say." I scooted my chair back, turned, and raised my hand for the officer.

"She has your dimples," the young man said.

I turned back around and studied his face. I had no idea who he was.

"Your high cheekbones, too." He didn't look happy when he spoke those words, but he didn't look mad, either.

"Who are you?"

"I almost didn't get in," he said, tilting his head in the direction of the control room. "My brother pulled some strings." He had on a tweed sport coat over jeans.

"Are you related to Ben, my attorney?" He didn't look like Ben. Taller and wider at the shoulders, but much thinner. I think he exercised.

He didn't respond but kept staring at my face. I couldn't remember if I'd combed my hair.

"I didn't believe it was true when I first heard it," he said to me. "I had to call the district attorney's office myself."

"Do I know you?" I asked the same question in a different way.

"I didn't know you were alive," he said slowly; articulating the words seemed to cause him pain. "Until yesterday."

I sat with my back straight up against my chair and glanced over to make sure the officers were still watching. He pulled out a picture from his wallet and pressed it up against the smudged glass. He and his wife in front of a church with hand-cut stained-glass windows and steep arches. Him in a black tux. Her in a fitted white beaded gown with an angel-cut wedding veil.

"My name is Thomas Logan. I'm married to your daughter."

SOPHIE

Ben drove ahead of Sophie on the way to Lakeland, slowing down through every intersection. He wanted to make sure Sophie didn't get stranded behind a red light. *I know the way to the prison,* she finally texted him when they were stopped behind an accident. He texted her back a thumbs-up emoticon.

Sophie dialed Thomas's cell phone as soon as she realized the cleanup for this four-car pileup might take a while. She pushed speakerphone on the steering wheel, just in case, since multitasking with her hormonal brain was no longer a safe option.

"Leave a message," Thomas's voicemail said after the third ring.

"Call me" was all she could get out. He must be really hurt. She pushed the Bluetooth button again and started to say "Call Margaret Logan," but her phone beeped before she could.

"Sophie?" Mindy said.

"Hi, Mindy. Merry Christmas." She tried to sound natural.

"Where are you? Thomas is worried sick about you."

"I needed to get away for a few days, you know, clear my head."

"On Christmas?"

"I know it's weird, but I needed to take care of a few things."

Mindy didn't respond, but Sophie could hear one of the twins whining for waffles in the background, so she knew she hadn't hung up.

"I'm worried about you, Sophie. People don't disappear on Christmas without something major going on." Mindy's voice was lowered, but she sounded sincere.

Something major is going on. I'm on my way to see my mother, who's about to die from a lethal injection. I've done nothing over the years to help her because I didn't believe in her. I didn't trust her. If she dies, it'll be my fault. All my fault.

"I'll tell you everything when I get back," Sophie finally said. As much as she wanted to confide in her, she couldn't tell Mindy before she confessed everything to Thomas.

"Okay," Mindy reluctantly agreed, after another awkward pause.

"How's my boy?" Sophie asked, trying to change the subject.

"I didn't work today, but the nurse before my last shift said his mom came to visit. Hasn't missed a day."

"Is that a good thing?" Sophie didn't know how to feel.

"Not for us to decide, unfortunately."

Sophie started to tell her the people who do decide those things suck, and that they don't gather all the facts before handing down permanent decisions, and that those well-intended evaluations screw up innocent children's lives, but she didn't. "Tell Max his Sosie sure misses him."

"Will do," Mindy promised.

"Thanks for checking on me."

"You're welcome," Mindy said. "Promise me you'll come home soon."

Sophie decided not to call the Logan house after she stopped talking to Mindy. She didn't want to answer any more questions.

The only conversation she needed to concentrate on was the one long overdue. The conversation she was about to have with her mother.

BEN ROLLED DOWN HIS WINDOW and flashed a badge to gain entrance into Lakeland State Penitentiary. Sophie had to step out of her vehicle and let the officer visually search her front and back seats. After she showed the uniformed officer her driver's license, he waved her through.

The enormity of this place still intimidated her. She used to have dreams about standing on one side of the tall chain-link fence with her mom on the other, bleeding from cuts inflicted by the circles upon circles of sharp wire. "I can't find the Band-Aids," Sophie remembered crying out in her sleep.

Ben met her at her car and walked with her to the door that read VISI-TORS' ENTRANCE. A long line of women and small children stood outside the door designated for the men's section of Lakeland. Sophie watched a young mom shove a bottle into her crying baby's mouth while ordering her toddler to "hold on to my leg." She handed the child an open box of Cheez-Its.

The processing time was what took the longest. In the past, Sophie had stood for more than an hour in the freezing rain while waiting to get inside the door, when she didn't have her dad around to remind her to wear her gloves and take an umbrella.

"Bring back memories?" Ben asked when he noticed her looking around.

"Too many."

"The visitor line always this long?" He flashed her his laminated attorney's badge that read SPECIAL ACCESS in bold letters across the bottom. "I normally walk right in with this, but who'd believe an attorney was working on Christmas Day?"

"On holidays, my dad and I would get up before the sun came out to make sure we'd be the first in line. My dad bribed me with a Peanut Buster Parfait from Dairy Queen when I tried to roll over and go back to sleep. 'C'mon,' he'd tell me. 'Your mommy's waiting on us.'"

A man wearing faded blue jeans and a black jacket stood in front of them. He turned around several times and started to speak, but didn't.

Sophie knew by the way he kept rubbing his palms on the front of his jeans that this must be his first visit to Lakeland.

"I guess we should've gotten here earlier," Sophie said to Ben. "One-forty-five p.m. on Christmas Day puts you at the back of the line."

"Better late than never. Don't think your mom's going anywhere."

Not yet, anyway.

"You here to visit your mom?" the man in front of her asked.

Sophie nodded. She hated sharing personal information, but this guy seemed to need a friend. "Your first time?"

"Very first," he answered. "That obvious, huh?"

"A little."

He held out his hand and with callused fingers shook Ben's hand, then hers.

"Carl," he said. "I drove all the way from Alabama to get here, and I had to close down my gas station—first time in twenty-seven years."

The line stopped moving. The three of them stood in a tight circle as the wind picked up.

"I'm here to see my daughter," he said. "The drive about killed my back." Years of pumping gas in the hot sun made his leathery skin look older than he probably was.

"I'm sure she'll appreciate the effort," Ben replied.

"I lost touch with her several years ago." He put his hand in his jeans pocket and pulled out a pack of gum. "Her mom got messed up real bad with drugs and took her away from me, out of the state." The deep lines around his eyes curled. "She changed her last name and said she wasn't my kid. I could never track her down."

He offered Sophie and Ben a piece of Juicy Fruit.

"No, thanks," they both said.

"After the TV news media grabbed on to the story, people started talking. I knew I had to find out the truth."

"Make sure you have all identifying paperwork out and ready," a female voice said over a loudspeaker. The line started moving forward again.

"She's mine." Carl reached in his back pocket and pulled out a piece of paper. "I have her birth certificate. Veronica Mae Cooper. Born on July thirteenth, 1993."

He beamed like he'd found a precious treasure.

"She goes by Roni now."

TWO HOURS LATER, the red digital numbers at the front of the visitors' area said 312. Sophie had 314. "Getting close," she said to Ben.

He put down the newspaper he was reading. "You look pale. Are you feeling okay?"

Sophie glanced at the time on her phone. "I probably need to eat. It's after two."

Ben pulled out some change from his pants pocket. "May I buy me lady a candy bar?" His bad British accent broke the monotony.

"Is that the best you can do?" Sophie teased.

Ben scoped out the vending-machine selections in the corner of the room. One machine claimed to have "Fresh Deli Meat" sandwiches, but Ben said he didn't trust that. He came back with a Snickers bar and a Sun Drop.

Number 313 flashed across the screen.

Mr. Cooper shouted, "That's me," and darted to the window.

Sophie unwrapped her candy bar while she stood to stretch. Her lower back started to cramp and she contemplated using the restroom. Three women, two with small children, stood in line for the one-stall facility.

"What do you mean my daughter has been transported to another facility?" Carl Cooper's already slouched posture sunk even more. "She sent me letters from this facility."

Sophie couldn't hear what the woman behind the glass window was saying to him. "I can't come back. I need answers now."

Someone in a brown uniform came out from behind the closed door and escorted him out of the visiting room. "Let's talk in here." The officer pointed to a desk behind the check-in window.

Sophie watched Carl walk away, his small eyes glossed over.

Number 314 flashed across the display. Sophie picked her purse up off the chair and threw it over her shoulder. She waved the slip in the air to Ben, who was holding a cup under the water dispenser over by the bathrooms.

Sophie walked up to the window and slid her driver's license through the slit.

"Inmate's name," the intake officer said through the glass. She typed without looking up.

"Grace Bradshaw."

"Date of birth?"

"Mine or my mother's?" She felt like a scared little girl again. The cramps in her back started to intensify.

"The inmate's," the lady behind the glass replied, making Sophie guess the question should've been self-evident.

"October twenty-first, 1960-something," Sophie said. "She's forty-nine."

The intake officer looked over her black-rimmed reading glasses. "Grace Margaret Bradshaw."

"Yes, that's her."

The officer continued to type, then picked up the phone beside her computer.

After a few "that's what it says" and "that's what I thought," she put down the phone and said, "Prisoner 44607 has already had a visitor today. No more allowed."

Sophie put both hands on top of the shelf jutting out from the window. The room felt stuffy and hot.

Ben pushed his attorney badge up against the glass. "I'm her lawyer. It's imperative that we see Mrs. Bradshaw today."

Sophie squinted and tried to look at what was behind the window. Carl was bent over a table while an older woman with arthritic fingers rubbed his back and squatted down beside him. He didn't move as the officer spoke.

Her vision started to blur as she watched Ben argue with the intake officer. She squinted again at Carl. Something on her legs felt warm.

"Sophie, are you all right?" Ben said. She felt his arm around her back as she started to slide down to the floor.

"Call an ambulance," he shouted.

The little girl holding on to her mom's leg said, "Look, Mommy. That lady is bleeding."

GRACE

I MET THOMAS TODAY!

Sophie, I met your husband. My son-in-law. I felt like embracing everyone I came in contact with when I shuffled back to death row. The shackles on my arms and feet couldn't even hold me down.

"Thank you, God. Thank you, God," I kept repeating. The officer must've thought I was crazy.

You could imagine how surprised I was when he sat down. He looked mad at first. Most people meet their in-laws over a grilled steak and baked potato, so I totally understood his initial reaction.

I could tell by the look on his face he was sizing me up. Could I be as evil as the papers called me? How could you have been loved by someone like me?

I let him ask me anything he wanted. All the whys and the what-ifs. The floor was his. I answered his questions the only way I knew how—with the truth.

He didn't know, but I was doing the same thing to him. Sizing up this handsome man who holds your heart. I like him. I really like him.

I don't care that he's a doctor; he could pick up trash off the streets, but what matters to me is the tenderness he gets in his eyes when he says your name. At first he was reluctant to talk about you—"I'll let Sophie tell you what she wants you to know"—but after a while when he realized he didn't need to protect you from me, he opened up.

"Just tell me if she's happy?" I asked him before he had to leave. That's all I wanted to know. That when you lay your head down on your pillow at night, next to his, you feel peace.

Thomas said he thinks you are, but he doesn't really know. Sometimes, when he looks at you, you smile, but you're not always there. Your body is, but your laugh is not complete, like your joy is held back.

He did tell me the closest you are to total happiness is when you are holding a little boy named Max who doesn't have a family. He told me about the fund-raiser and how hard you've been working on it.

I am so proud of the woman you've grown up to be. My heart feels like it's about to BLOW UP.

I can live my final days in peace because I know without a doubt you have someone who will carry you through. I love you, my daughter. And I know without question Thomas does, too.

xoxoxo

"Publishers Clearing House find you today or something?" Carmen asked me later.

"Something better. I found my daughter." My lips stretched. I hadn't smiled this big since I've been here.

Jada didn't say anything. She picked up her magazine and walked back to her cell.

"Bet your visit wasn't as good as mine," Carmen said. "My hunk of a man hired me a new attorney. He says I'll be out of here by Easter."

"I'm happy for you." I didn't expect anyone in here to be happy for me or to understand. I didn't care. Ms. Liz would be back soon. She'd be happy.

As soon as I entered my room and my shackles were off, I did something I haven't done in seventeen years. I danced.

SOPHIE

Sophie heard what she thought was Thomas's pager go off and felt relieved to be finally back in her own bed. She rolled over to put her arm around him.

"Hold on," Thomas said, "your IV will get caught."

"Thomas?" She saw him push a button that made the blue machine stop.

"Everything's okay. I'm right here." He straightened out the tubing trailing from the top of her hand and then kissed her forehead.

"Where am I?" The tape on her arm started to pull as she shifted in the bed.

"In the hospital. You've been out for a while."

"The hospital? What day is it?"

Thomas took his cell phone and checked the time. "About eleven-thirty-seven p.m.—the day after Christmas." He pulled up a chair close to her bed and sat down.

She picked at the tape on her hand and tried to make sense of what he was saying. *The prison. Our baby.* Sophie started to put the events together, but nothing felt right.

"What happened to me? Is the baby . . . ?"

"So you did know?" Thomas put his hands behind his neck, then dropped his head.

"I was going to tell you. Things just became complicated." She tried to sit up but felt weak and queasy. "I needed time to process everything."

Thomas scratched his jaw. His wrinkled shirt and scruffy face told Sophie he'd been with her for a while.

"Is the baby okay?"

"The heartbeat's strong." He shifted forward in his chair. "Which means you probably won't miscarry."

"What happened, then? Why am I here?" Sophie put her hands between her legs to see if there was any blood.

"For one thing, you're significantly dehydrated and you're anemic." He leaned over, picked up the clipboard hooked on the end of the bed, and checked something. "Not sure why you were bleeding, but your blood pressure is extremely high." Thomas glanced at the monitors by the side of her bed, then read some papers.

"You have to rest and stay calm." His authoritative tone made him seem like her doctor.

Sophie nodded.

"For yourself and for our baby." This time he spoke from a different place, more vulnerable, like a dad.

"I'm so sorry, Thomas." She reached her arm out to him.

He tossed the chart on the end of her bed without responding.

"How'd you know where I was?"

Thomas grabbed the pink pitcher from the nightstand. He filled a cup with water, stuck in a bent straw, and handed it to her.

"I was there," he said to her after she swallowed.

"Where?" She pulled the straw out of her mouth and tried once again to sit up.

"I saw her." He took the cup from her and set it on the nightstand.

"Who?" Sophie asked. She could feel the blood draining from her entire head and settling in her stomach.

"I met your mom."

For a minute she thought he was playing a cruel joke on her. Payback for the lies, for not telling him about the baby. "My mom?"

Thomas nodded.

She'd never seen him look this way before. His body seemed unnaturally stiff and his words deliberate. "You should've told me."

She watched him contract his shoulders and his neck while she struggled with how to reply. He watched her, too, confusion seeping from his eyes.

"I didn't know how." Her breath snagged as she tried to explain. "One lie turned into another. I was ashamed."

Thomas started to reach for her hand, but he pulled back.

"Can you ever forgive me?"

Before Thomas could answer, someone opened the door.

A nurse walked in with her stethoscope slung around her neck. She was carrying something. "I'm glad to see you're awake and talking. How you feeling?"

"I'm not sure," Sophie said to her, but she meant it for Thomas. She couldn't be sure until he answered her question.

"The doctor wants you to try to eat something. Anything sound good?" She placed a tray with a bowl of tomato soup and packaged crackers in front of her.

Sophie shook her head. "I'll try the crackers."

The nurse took the package off the tray and opened it for her. "I can order you something else. A sandwich, maybe?"

Nothing Sophie could think of sounded good, but she was thirsty. "Do you have any root beer?"

"WHAT'S SHE LIKE?" Sophie asked Thomas after the night-shift nurse left the room.

Thomas had already stretched out on the empty bed closest to the window. His back was turned to her, and she thought he might be asleep.

"Your mom?" he asked. He sat up and pushed back the peach-striped curtain that semi-divided the room.

"Does she hate me?"

Thomas swung his legs around and sat on the side of the bed. He straightened the bedsheets before answering. "No, she doesn't hate anything about you."

Sophie picked at the lint balls on her blanket. "After my dad died, I was all alone. Our church brought me food for a while, but no one knew what to say to the poor orphaned girl whose mom was on death row."

Thomas didn't say anything.

"When I left for college, I realized no one knew me, knew my story. I could be anyone I wanted. Before I knew it, I'd become someone else."

"Why didn't you tell me?" The word *me* shot right across the room.

"I wanted you to accept me. I loved you from the first moment you walked into Starbucks. You knew where you were going, what you wanted. I didn't. I drifted into your life by accident, and it was by pure luck you decided to love me."

He stood up and walked over to her bed. He pulled the covers down and slid in beside her. "You drifted into my life because you were supposed to." The tenseness in his posture had started to fade. "There was nothing accidental about it. I looked in the window and watched you make dozens of lattes before I had the nerve to ask you out."

Sophie rolled over and laid her head on his chest. "You watched me? Why didn't you ever tell me?"

"I guess there's a lot of things we didn't tell each other."

She wrapped her arm around him. When she finally let go she asked him, "How'd you find out about my mom?"

"It took some work. I didn't understand why you left. Nothing made sense. At first I thought maybe you didn't believe me about Eva, then

I thought maybe you were disappointed in me about the whole malpractice thing. I called Carter to talk it through. He did a background search and found some information."

"So Carter knows?"

"My whole family does."

Sophie adjusted the neck of her hospital gown to make sure it was covering her. "I suppose that went over well."

"I don't know how well it went over." He rolled over so he was facing her. "It doesn't matter." He pulled her hospital gown up and put his hand on her bare stomach. "All that matters to me is you and this little baby."

"No," Sophie cried out. "Stop. You're hurting her!"

Thomas jiggled her shoulder. "Wake up." He put a wet washcloth over her sweaty hair. "Everything's okay. You're having a bad dream."

Sophie opened her eyes, glad to be out of her nightmare, then realized she wasn't.

"All these years," she blurted, "I blamed my mother for something she didn't do." She took the washcloth off her head and threw it across the room. "Her baby died. My little brother. People in my small town hated her. Called her all kinds of horrible names."

She buried her face in her blanket.

"You need to calm down." Thomas gently scratched the side of her arm. "For our baby."

"I scoured the court records looking for anything to prove my mom didn't poison William, but all the evidence said that she did." She pulled the blanket away from her face. "I was with her when she bought windshield-wiper fluid."

Thomas hesitated. "You had no way of knowing."

"How will she ever forgive me?"

He put his index finger on the dimple under her lip. "She already has."

Sophie looked out the door and saw Ben pacing the hallway. "Would you please come in and sit down?" Sophie yelled to him. "Tell him to get in here."

Thomas shut off ESPN and stepped out into the hallway. By this time, Ben felt like family. Thomas told her how a worried Ben stayed by her side in the emergency room until he could get there and arrange to have her transferred to Duke. "He cares about your mom and about you," Thomas told her. Ben had explained to him the need for the genetic testing before Sophie had the chance.

"What's wrong with you?" she said to Ben when he appeared in the doorway. "You're making me nervous."

"What's wrong with me?" He waved his arm at the IVs still attached to Sophie's arm.

"What's your gut telling you?" she asked him.

"My gut's telling me the geneticist is going to tell us exactly what we already know."

"My mom's innocent?" Sophie looked at Ben and then Thomas for confirmation.

Ben was heading for the hallway to pace again when Dr. Blakely, the geneticist, met him at the door. "We have the results of your test."

Thomas held out his hand. "Thanks for rushing these."

Sophie raised the head of her bed while Thomas and Ben stood on either side of the doctor. He laid out the lab sheets on the overbed table.

"This metabolic disorder is mapped to a mutation in the gene." He pointed to a number value on the paper. "This is your wife's sample."

Thomas picked up the paper and examined it more closely. "She has the carrier mutation."

"So that means her parents had to be carriers, too, right?" Ben said with cautious excitement.

"Sure does," Dr. Blakely replied.

"What about my baby?" Sophie couldn't celebrate until she was sure her baby would be okay.

"That's some more good news. Thomas has two normal genes. Your baby will not be affected."

After the doctor left, and Sophie gave Ben a long and overdue hug, he gathered his coat and packed up his briefcase. "We have the evidence. Now we need to pray someone will listen to it."

GRACE

A metabolic disorder. William died of a metabolic disorder.
I'm trying to process all of this, but I don't understand.
Ben's roller-coaster visit confused me. One minute I'm
feeling elated and hopeful, the next vindicated but disgusted.
Why couldn't anyone save my baby?
Ben told me you were here. YOU WERE HERE! That
news makes me jump up and down. Thanks for coming
back to me!

The tiny lines on the corners of Ben's eyes pointed upward when he told me the news. "Sophie and I came to visit you on Christmas Day." His presence felt lighter than it had the last time I saw him.

"What are you talking about? I didn't see you."

"Sophie and I came."

"Soph . . . Sophie was here?" I, on the other hand, stuttered. My spine cracked against the back of the metal chair. I felt like I might topple over.

"That's what I tried to tell you when you called. I found Sophie."

"You found Sophie, and her husband found me?"

"Something like that." Ben shrugged in disbelief. "She came to see me because she had some information."

"Information? What in the world are you talking about?"

"I'm talking about your husband and your daughter. They may have saved your life." He talked fast, but paused long enough to emphasize the word *may*. "Remember you told me Paul kept working on your case after you were convicted?"

I nodded. "That's all he did when he wasn't working or taking care of Sophie."

"Sophie came to visit me on Christmas Eve. We visited your old house and dug through his paperwork. To make a long story short, we talked to Dr. Robinson. The person Paul hired to test the baby bottle."

"Test the baby bottle?" I took a quick look around the room to make sure the officer wasn't going to cut our time short. "Who did what?"

"I had no idea, either, but we found his name."

"How'd you find his name?" I tried to scratch my forehead, but the chain holding my wrist to my waist was too short.

"We'll fill you in on that later." Ben stared at the clock on the wall. "The point is, the tests were negative. No windshield-wiper fluid."

"I know."

"Sorry," Ben said. He reached across the table to touch my hands, but they were in my lap.

"Wrap it up," the officer notified. He held up his spread hand to indicate we had five more minutes.

"Why am I just now hearing this?" Was I missing something?

"Paul died and he never received those results. He didn't tell you because he didn't know."

Paul knew. He always knew. He didn't need a lab to tell him I didn't kill William.

"That's not the best part. Dr. Robinson thinks William died of a metabolic disorder."

"A metabolic disorder?"

"Some type of metabolic acidemia."

"Is that why he threw up? Is that why he wouldn't wake up?" I felt sad and relieved at the same time. "His pediatrician? Why didn't he know?"

"It's rare. They didn't know much about it when William was an infant."

I tried to take hold of what he was telling me. "What does this mean?" Would it change anything?

"It means we have a genetic test providing evidence that you didn't kill William."

"From a baby bottle?"

"No. From your daughter. Sophie is a carrier for the same disease."

"She is?"

He might as well have been speaking in Japanese, but at least it sounded like good news. "Will she be okay?"

I couldn't stand it if you were sick.

"She's fine. Her—" He stopped. I could tell he wasn't telling me everything.

"Grace, this is all good news. I'm just sorry it took so long to discover."

"Me, too." I knew it wasn't his fault. And I didn't know who to blame.

"I have a lot of work to do. The only hope we have left is executive clemency."

"The governor?" My newfound hope started to sink. "Is that even a possibility?"

"I hope so. We've exhausted all our appeals. We're throwing a big Hail Mary."

Ben crossed his fingers and placed them over his heart. I closed my eyes and prayed.

When I opened my eyes, he said, "Your daughter is lovely."

"So I've heard."

"She's a phenomenal young woman. We waited to see you. When we finally got to the window, the officer wouldn't let her through."

"Because of Thomas?"

Ben nodded. "She had to leave town. How about setting up a phone call?"

"Do you even have to ask?"

"I didn't think so." He reached into his pocket and pulled out a yellow piece of paper. Typed beside Sophie's name was her telephone number.

SOPHIE

Sophie's phone buzzed all day with texts about the Secret Chef fund-raiser. Eva, Mindy, then Kate. Then two more from Eva. *I need to talk to u.*

Since she'd gotten home from the hospital, Thomas had done nothing but wait on her. He'd even learned to cook. She heard him on the phone with his mother: "So how long do I stir the flour to make the roux?"

After eight days, he finally returned to work.

"Promise me you'll stay off your feet." He kissed her on the head and pulled out the ottoman for her to put her legs on.

"I promise," she said. "I can talk on the phone from my chair."

No one in West Lake knew about Sophie's mom, but it was all she thought about. She begged her doctor to let her off bed rest ("I have this big fund-raising event I'm in charge of!"), but Dr. Johnson wouldn't budge.

"Not until your blood pressure stabilizes." She'd taken over her records from Jack when she returned from the holidays. Sophie would eventually have to confide in Dr. Johnson, but then Dr. Johnson might "confide" in Jack. She'd tell the world about her mother, but she needed to come to terms with everything herself first.

Can u come over? Sophie texted Mindy. She hadn't told her about the baby and needed to share some good news. Eva's texts, she ignored.

Mindy arrived with Starbucks and two cherry-frosted cupcakes from her twins' birthday party.

"Can't believe how big they're getting." Mindy handed the one with the most icing to Sophie. "You need this more than me."

Sophie stuck her finger in the icing. "Delicious. I'll have to pass on the coffee, though. No caffeine. Doctor's orders."

"You're pregnant!" Mindy shouted. "That explains your weird behavior!"

"Part of it, anyway." Sophie unwrapped the cupcake and took a bite. "I'm on bed rest. High blood pressure."

Mindy scrunched her nose. "Already?"

"Already. I need to stay calm—if I'm good, I hope the doctor will let me get back to normal. Can't have a successful fund-raiser while I'm sitting on my ever-expanding bottom."

Mindy laughed and then stopped. "Are you happy about the baby?"

"Of course I'm happy about the baby. Why wouldn't I be?" It was a sassy rhetorical question Sophie immediately regretted the moment she asked it. Mindy was asking the kind of questions close friends ask each other when they care to know more.

"Well . . ." Mindy paused.

Sophie put down her cupcake and pressed her hands together, holding them close to her lips. "I'm sorry, Mindy."

"No, I'm sorry. I didn't mean to imply you didn't want the baby," Mindy said while picking cupcake crumbs off Sophie's ottoman. "It's just weird, that you left and all, over Christmas."

Sophie grabbed Mindy's hand so she'd stop with the crumbs. "It was weird," she said, beating down all the boards and bricks she used to put up. "Sit back, because my story gets even stranger. I went to visit my mom."

GRACE

To be honest, Ms. Liz didn't have many words to make me feel better. She couldn't give me any answers with certainty or make any promises that would take my fear away. There was just something about her, though, that made me feel safe. Recognized. Significant. Valued. With her, my feelings never felt judged, and my fears never felt minimized. And today I got to share with her a part of me she's never seen before.

"Exhilaration is what I'm feeling most of the time." I fought the urge to hug her as I filled her in on the latest news. "I'm so full of joy, these walls, the noise—I barely notice."

Ms. Liz squinted like she didn't fully recognize me. "Have you talked to her?"

"Not yet. Ben gave me her number." I ran the words over in my head. I HAVE MY DAUGHTER'S PHONE NUMBER. I actually pinched the top of my thighs to make sure I wasn't dreaming. "I'll call the second I'm allowed. The warden suspended my phone privileges until I get my execution paperwork filled out."

"What are you going to say to her?" Ms. Liz asked, biting down on her smile.

I've thought about our first conversation so many times. What I'd say. What she'd say. I closed my eyes to relish the thought of that moment. Finally, I said, "I just want to hear her voice."

"And I'm sure she wants to hear yours." Ms. Liz placed her hands close to her heart. "Have you talked to Ben?"

"Not since he left last week." I hoped that wasn't a bad sign.

"I'm sure he's busy."

"They have to let me out. Don't they?" My wide eyes pleaded with hers to say yes.

"I'd think so," Ms. Liz said. "How could they not?"

"I'm sure Ben is doing everything he can as fast as he can." I refuse to give up now. "Have you heard anything about Roni?"

Ms. Liz straightened her skirt and then glanced around the room to see how close the nearest officer was. "You know I'm not supposed to tell you information about another inmate," she whispered.

I nodded, but encouraged her to continue.

"She's alive. She's in intensive care, but she's alive."

The officer on duty seemed engrossed in whatever paperwork he was doing, so Ms. Liz leaned in and carried on. "I couldn't stand the thought of Carl Cooper not seeing Roni on Christmas. So I waited for him in the visitors' area on Christmas Day. I told him what happened."

"Visit's over," the officer shouted before I could ask her any more questions.

"I took him to meet his daughter," Ms. Liz whispered, then winked. "Mr. Cooper finally got to meet Roni."

"Ms. Liz," I said before the officer escorted me away, "if you see them again, will you tell them I'm sorry?"

WHEN I GOT BACK TO MY ROOM, I made myself sit down. I thanked God for Roni and the time she got to spend with her dad. I prayed they'd have many more visits and that Roni would finally feel what it was like to be loved.

After I finished praying, I forced myself to fill out the warden's papers. The task seemed much less daunting when I reminded myself I might be going home soon. I'd fill out anything if it meant I'd get to talk to Sophie.

Ben had taken the application for executive clemency. "I want to make sure we dot our *i*'s and cross every *t*. We don't want to give the governor any reason not to intervene."

I asked Ben to make sure I get buried in Brookfield, in our family plot—next to Paul and William. He promised he would.

The only forms left for me to tackle were my execution witness list and the last meal. Ben took my will and hand-delivered it to the warden's office.

"Put my name down." Ben tapped his index finger on the witness list before he left. "If this happens—I want to be there for you. Put Sophie's and Thomas's names down, too."

I adamantly shook my head. I didn't fear dying, but I did fear Sophie watching me do so.

"I can't put Sophie through that." No good mother would ever ask her child to do that.

"Let her make the decision. Put her name down and then let her make the decision."

I'd spun this conversation around in my mind several times since Ben left. Would Sophie be mad if I put her name down? Would she be mad if I didn't? I wished I could ask her, but mostly I wished I didn't have to.

I decided to listen to Ben. I used my left hand to steady my right as I wrote: *Ben Taylor—my attorney and friend. Dr. Thomas Logan—my son-in-law. Mrs. Sophie Logan—my daughter.*

SOPHIE

Two people in Sophie's immediate circle had her right where she once feared they wanted her—exposed and open to attack, with no refined skills to mount an effective defense. But to her surprise, her worst-case scenario had become a welcomed Utopia.

"I can't imagine the pain you must be going through," Mindy said after Sophie finished summarizing her past seventeen years without a mother.

Mindy pressed her hand into Sophie's thighs. "This must have been tough for you to carry all alone. Please let me know what I can do. Day or night, I'll be there for you."

The wounds in Sophie's filleted chest healed some when she heard her friend make this promise.

"I know your mom will be okay. I promise you. This will all work out."

Sophie felt her heart rate slow down for the first time in a long time.

Mindy appointed herself co-chair of the Secret Chef fund-raiser, keeping Sophie busy with smaller details, anything that could be conquered from a chair, like who should sit next to whom or whether the Oxstyle rose or the lotus with purple flowers might inspire a prospective donor to give more money.

Ben and Sophie exchanged phone calls every evening at 6 p.m. If he didn't have anything new to report, he'd call anyway, "just to see how the pregnancy's going."

Sometimes Thomas answered. When Sophie held out her hand, he'd reluctantly give her the phone and say, "I'm just trying to relieve some of your stress."

The truth was, Sophie had never felt better. Sure, she agonized over the possibility the governor would decide not to grant clemency, but what were the chances of that? Her mom was innocent. She pictured the governor at a press conference flanked by her mom and Ben. "What we owe this woman can never be repaid." The crowd would roar and cameras would flash. Her mom would hug Sophie and say, "I can't wait to hold my new grandbaby."

"When am I going to get to talk to her?" she asked Ben every time they talked.

"Whenever the warden says she can call," was his pat but polite answer.

Ben warned her not to get her hopes up, for a phone call or for anything else. "Plan for the best, but prepare for the worst." Sophie didn't even want to think what that meant in this case. She sat on the deck off her bedroom with her laptop and ordered new linens for the guest bedroom. "Lavender and yellow are my mom's favorite colors," she explained to Thomas.

He agreed without hesitation to let Sophie's mom come live with them after she was released. "She can stay with us as long as she likes," he said, rubbing her lower back at night. "Anything to make you smile."

She was grateful beyond measure for Thomas's quick and unexpected forgiveness. She knew her lies didn't come without consequences, but she'd yet to see them. When she'd asked if he was upset with her, Thomas had said, "We'll talk later, after your health stabilizes."

He hadn't said it in an alarming way, more in a manner that let Sophie know his rock-solid reality was off-balance. His life's checklist jumbled and out of order. The woman he'd been sleeping next to for all these years was not who she'd advertised. Like the optical illusion that appears to be a beautiful young lady until you tilt your head and squint your eyes and the picture becomes an old woman. Sophie imagined all kinds of things when she caught Thomas staring at her.

He didn't answer her when she asked what his parents thought. Instead he said, "It only matters what I think." But the way he snuck into the garage when Carter called told her all she needed to hear.

She overheard him on the phone one evening after he thought she'd gone to bed. "You're looking at this from only a prosecutor's angle. If anyone is at fault, it's the doctors and the hospital." She tiptoed closer and angled her ear to the door. "Somebody should've figured out this baby was really sick."

Before Thomas slammed down the phone, Sophie heard him shout, "Screw my status at the hospital. An innocent woman does not deserve to be executed."

Sophie pretended to be asleep when Thomas snuggled up against her in bed. She hated to see him caught in the middle. She'd have to see his family and explain to them why she'd made up a past to gain a future, but that wasn't going to happen today or tomorrow. In the meantime, nothing could derail her concentration or dampen her enthusiasm. Every moment from here on out would be spent on what she should have been doing all along—helping her mom get off death row.

GRACE

The warden had received my papers eighteen days ago, but I still hadn't been cleared to make a phone call. I didn't know what was worse—worrying you'd refuse to talk to me or worrying you'd think I didn't want to talk to you. I prayed today would be the day I heard your voice.

"Did you hear Roni's coming back?" Jada said to me.

"No." I put down my journal. "How do you know?"

"I heard Jones and Mackey say so."

"Is she okay?"

"Okay enough to return to death row." Jada stood up and flipped the television on to *The View*.

I slid my pen inside my journal and walked back to my cell. I took the box of handmade Christmas ornaments from under my bed. All seventeen of them wrapped in toilet tissue and stacked in cushioned rows, waiting to be one day opened by Sophie. One of my favorites lay triple-folded for extra protection.

I took it out of the box and told myself Sophie would understand. On top of the paper I wrote: *Please forgive me. Love, Grace.*

While the officers chatted about NCAA basketball, I snuck over to Roni's cell and placed the white ceramic ornament in the center of her bunk. Under the impression of my handprint, in blocked-stamped letters, was the word FAMILY.

Carmen ran to the telephone to begin her fifteen-minute phone call. I decided to stay in my cell and forgo the torture of hearing her exchange sloppy kisses and sentiments like "I wanna wrap my arms around you, too, baby." Some things are better off left unimagined.

I wet some brown paper hand towels and started to scrub my toilet.

"Your turn, Bradshaw," Officer Mackey shouted.

"Me?" I yelled back. I threw the wet towels in my sink and wiped my hands on my pants.

"Hurry up," he called. "Clock's a-ticking."

I searched my room for Sophie's number. I found it right where I left it. Under the cover of my Bible. I've prepared myself for this conversation a million times. Now I couldn't remember anything I'd rehearsed.

"Give me the number," Officer Mackey said as I approached the phone.

I handed him the small yellow piece of paper. For the first time, my mouth didn't feel dry because of him. He dialed the number and then handed me the phone.

"I'll give you an extra five," he whispered.

"Thank you." I put my hand over my heart to show him my appreciation.

And then I prayed you'd be home . . . Please, God, let Sophie be home. Please let her answer.

SOPHIE

"The invitations have been mailed and the clubhouse confirmed," Mindy said. She sat across from Sophie in her living room. The smell of sausage and shrimp jambalaya drifted over them as they worked. "The only thing left to do is make sure the chefs show up and the people of West Lake bring fountain pens to write big fat checks."

"No kidding." Sophie tried to pay attention to Mindy, but when Mindy was going over the secret-auction items, Sophie read the blog on the Innocence Project's website. *Three hundred sixteen inmates exonerated and counting.* She'd sent them three letters about her mom's case since she came home from the hospital. She made a mental note to send the fourth.

"Yoo-hoo." Mindy waved her hand in Sophie's face. "Earth to Sophie."

"Sorry, I'm having a hard time concentrating." Sophie picked up her checklist. "Thank God the clubhouse was open. Much less work than having it here."

"You've been having much more important 'events' in your home," Mindy said, pointing to Sophie's stomach. She air-quoted the word *events*, and then raised her hand to give Sophie a high-five.

Sophie laughed. "You're such a guy." She appreciated Mindy's attempt to lighten her mood.

"Give me some credit," Thomas interrupted as he walked in from the kitchen.

Mindy held her fist to bump his.

"The cornbread will be done in about ten minutes," Thomas said. "Do you want to stay for dinner?"

"Smells delicious, but I have to get home to the twins."

"What's gotten into him?" Mindy winked at Sophie as Thomas went to stir something on top of the stove. "Quite the chef."

"He loves to cook now. Home by six and meal on the table by seven-thirty." Sophie glanced in the kitchen to make sure he couldn't overhear. "He does everything for me. I think he's scared something's going to happen to the baby."

"Your doctor said everything's okay, right?"

"Yes. I saw Dr. Johnson today and my blood pressure's fine. Baby's heartbeat is strong. I'm about fifteen weeks."

"Are you still on bed rest?"

"Modified, I guess. The doctor told me my first priority has to be the health of the baby. I'm not supposed to worry."

"Easy for your doctor to say." Mindy scrunched her forehead and nose. "Doctors can be so blunt sometimes," she whispered, so Thomas couldn't hear her. "At least the fund-raiser is on autopilot now. Don't worry about a thing. Just show up on February fourteenth and enjoy."

Sophie pulled out the calendar on her iPhone to count the days.

"Twenty-four days until the fund-raiser." Twenty-five days until . . . *That won't happen. That can't happen.*

The phone rang as Thomas was taking the cornbread out of the oven. "I'll get it."

Sophie prayed it was Ben with some good news. She helped Mindy gather the last of her papers and gave her a quick hug.

"Can I use your restroom?"

"You know where it is," Sophie told her.

Mindy closed the restroom door just as Thomas said, "Of course we'll accept the charges."

GRACE

*You know all of what happened next, but I had to write it down.
I had to make sure every moment we shared was documented. I
couldn't bear the thought of forgetting even one second.*

*"Of course we'll accept the charges." My son-in-law's deep voice
reminded me of your history I hadn't been a part of.*

*"Hi, Thomas. It's Grace." I willed my cracking voice to be
strong.*

*"How are you?" His voice sounded anxious. I don't think
he expected this phone call to be from me.*

"Did Ben tell you I was going to call?"

*"No. I mean, yes. He said he gave you our number, but not to get
our hopes up you'd be allowed to call."*

*"I'm surprised, too." I fidgeted with the cord. He wasn't the only
one anxious. "I don't have much time. Is Sophie there?"*

He hesitated, so I asked again. "Is she there?"

"She's saying good-bye to a friend. Let me get her."

*Thomas covered the receiver, but I could hear his muffled voice.
"Take this in the study. I'll get rid of Mindy."*

*My darn legs started trembling so much I had to brace my back
against the wall. Breathe, I told myself. A large part of this moment
felt as foreign as the first time I met you. Mom, meet your new baby*

girl. The masked doctor placed your red-blotched skin on top of mine. Look, she has your long fingers.

I didn't know that baby any more than I know you now. Did you want to talk to me? It's taking forever. Did you have company? Did they know about me?

The recording announced, "Thirteen minutes." I looked for Officer Mackey. He's at his desk, reading the newspaper.

Finally, I heard a click on the other line.

"Mom?"

Your voice sounded fragile, but I'd have recognized it anywhere.

"It's me," I said.

Your next words sounded like they could break. "I can't believe I'm finally talking to you."

"I can't believe it, either."

"I have so much to tell you. So much to apologize for." Your voice faded, and I could barely hear you.

"Sophie, it's okay. It's all okay. I understand. I'm not mad at you."

"I talk to Ben every night. He's going to get you out."

"I know he's doing everything he can, but, Sophie, I want to hear about you. Tell me about your life."

I heard you take a few deep breaths, and then I think you started to cry.

"Please, stay calm. Your blood pressure . . ." I could hear Thomas in the background.

"Are you sick?" I asked. Like William? The automated voice reminded me of my dwindling time.

"Not exactly." Stay calm, Thomas told you again.

You sniffled, and I heard you ask him to get you a glass of water. After you took a drink, I heard the most magnificent words I'd ever heard.

"Mom, I'm pregnant. You're going to be a grandma."

SOPHIE

"You're going to have a baby?" her mom shouted into the phone.

"I'm due in June."

"My love runneth over."

Sophie closed her eyes. Suddenly she was six again. "Mommy, see my picture. It's our family." Her mom had placed the picture up against her heart and said, "My love runneth over."

"Are you feeling okay?"

Sophie kept her eyes closed. She could feel her mother's tender arms around her, shielding her and stroking her hair.

"I'm feeling great, Mom. The doctor's watching my blood pressure, but I'm fine, I promise."

Neither of them said anything for a moment. Sophie could hear her mom sniffling into the phone.

"Are you happy?" her mom asked. Sophie could tell from her tremulous voice that that was all she cared about.

"I try to be." Sophie answered that question honestly for the first time since her mother left her. "I tried for as long as I could to pretend everything was okay. I became good at it, but I can't do it anymore. I miss you. I need to see you and bring you home."

"I want to see you more than you know," her mom said, her voice now barely above a whisper.

"It'll happen, Mom." Thomas stroked her hair while she talked.

"I like your husband."

"I thought you would. He reminds me of Daddy." Sophie reached up and held Thomas's hand. "I wish you could have been there. On my wedding day, I mean."

There was quiet on the other end.

"I didn't mean to make you feel bad," Sophie interjected.

"You only make me feel good," her mom finally said. "Everything about you makes me feel good."

The phone beeped, indicating their time was almost up.

Sophie took her hand off Thomas and gripped the phone. "I love you, Mom."

For the first time in eleven years, her mom whispered back, "I love you, too, Sophie."

GRACE

We just hung up the phone and I have so many things I still want to ask you. Big questions, like "Do you want a boy or a girl?" and "How are you decorating the nursery?" but mainly I'm curious about the small details most mothers know about their kids, like "Do you still need to hear the dryer running when you fall asleep?" and "Do you still eat your toast with cinnamon sugar sprinkled all over it?" The observations mothers store in the back of their mind that no other person would even care to notice.

I want to be able to run to the grocery store and buy you lemon drops because sucking on them will help your nausea (are you having morning sickness?), or make you thirty different freezer meals just to have on standby when you're too tired to cook. All the tangible favors moms are privileged to do for the ones they love. Since Lakeland won't let me out to run those errands, I'll have to concentrate on the intangible gifts that only come deep from within a mother's soul.

I can't explain how amazing it was to hear you say "I love you." Parts of me that hadn't been alive since the last day I saw you breathed again. I floated back to my cell.

I know Thomas loves you, too. He told me so when we met, but he showed me when I overheard him caring for you when we were on the phone. I can sleep, like never before, because I know you have someone else in your life who adores you.

I don't know how many phone conversations we have left or if I will ever get to see your face again. Those are the decisions I can't control and you can't, either. No matter what the governor does or doesn't do, please know I will be fine and in a much better place surrounded by love.

You will be fine, too. Every morning when you look into the ever-changing expressions on your newborn's face, know I am with you.

Guard against letting any more of your moments be soaked in regret. I'm choosing to let go of any resentment and make a conscious effort to let my enemies bring out the best in me—not the worst. I'm praying you will have the strength to do the same.

I asked myself over and over throughout my years in here . . . Was I a good mom? Did we bake enough cookies?

I wasn't able to teach you everything you needed to know to make it in this unpredictable world. I don't even know if you can balance a checkbook or have proper table manners, but as I go over the "good mom" checklist in my mind, I realize only a few things really matter. Are you loved, and do you love others well?

As I looked back over my life, I realized my purpose was to give you yours. To show you the way, to tell you the truth, and to give you everything I had to give.

Slow down and enjoy. Fish sticks and macaroni and cheese always taste better at a happy table.

I can't believe my grandchild is growing inside you.

SOPHIE

"I'm doing everything I can think of," Ben said.

Sophie had waited until Thomas left for work to call him. The execution date was two weeks away and her impatience was growing as fast as her stomach was. While they spoke, she cut tags off of the new elastic-waist pants she'd ordered online.

"Why haven't we heard anything?" Deep down she knew he didn't have an answer, but she couldn't stop herself from questioning him every time they talked. He'd explained to her and Thomas, in depth, the death row appeals process. This new information could be heard only if the governor's office would listen.

"The governor's office has assured me they have received the petition, but that's all they will tell me. I have no idea when a decision will be made."

Sophie felt like she was pulling a rug with an enormous armoire on top of it. "I'm starting to lose hope. I feel like no one in the whole world cares my innocent mother is rotting in jail but you, me, and Thomas." She hurled her scissors onto the middle of the bed.

"We knew this would be a long shot," Ben said.

The Internet searches she repeated late at night when her mind refused to shut down told her Ben was probably right. History wasn't on her mother's side. A South Carolina governor hadn't stopped any of the forty-three executions since the death penalty had been reinstated more than thirty years ago.

"I don't know what they'll do," Ben finally said.

"We can't give up."

"I'll never give up on your mom, but we have to prepare ourselves." He paused, then exhaled.

"For what, Ben? Prepare ourselves for an innocent woman who has already spent over a third of her life in prison to die there?" She bent over the best she could and started picking lint off her bedroom floor.

"This new information may have come too late." Ben stated what Sophie knew. *I waited too long to help my mom. She's going to die because of me.* Sophie picked up a broken gold tube of Elizabeth Arden's Beautiful Color Maximum Volume Mascara that had fallen off her dresser and chucked it at the wall.

"Well, you can do that, Ben. You can prepare yourself, but I'm not going to. My mom is coming home, and I won't let anyone tell me otherwise." She hesitated for a minute, but then her words erupted while her shame turned to anger: "Maybe you're not the one for this job."

Ben didn't respond to her threat. "I know you're frustrated. I am, too." When she didn't reply, he said, "How are you feeling? How's the baby?"

She knew he was trying to change the subject to get her to calm down. The truth was, she could never fire Ben. He'd become her family and the only connection she had to her mother. His concern reminded her of that.

"The baby's doing fine. My doctor said I can do limited activities—go to the grocery store and get my hair cut. She won't clear me to travel yet."

"I know your mom understands," Ben reassured her. "She's not allowed visitors right now, anyway."

"Why? Did she get in some kind of trouble?" Sophie fixated her gaze on the newly black stain she'd created on her wall.

"I received a fax earlier this morning," he said reluctantly. "Two weeks prior to the scheduled execution, the inmate is moved off of death row and to a death-watch cell for observation."

GRACE

This part of my story gets difficult to read. I'm compelled to write the end of my story, but please don't feel obligated to read it. (Forgive the plain white paper; I'll explain in a minute.)

Before the morning sunlight had a chance to slip into my cell, I was awakened by the sound of officers shuffling their feet. Several of them (whose voices I did not recognize) congregated outside my door.

Six hours before, I'd overheard a similar noise and had gotten out of bed to see what the commotion was about. Officer Mackey had been pushing a wheelchair down the row. Its crooked front wheels clinked on the concrete, refusing to roll straight. At first I thought we might be getting a new occupant, but when he moved closer, I could see it was Roni.

She held her head down and cocked to the side. Her back was secured to the back of the chair with a thick white belt. I wanted to shout, "Welcome home. I'm glad you're back," but she didn't look like she was awake enough to hear. And would that be the greeting she'd want to receive?

I wanted to tell her in person I was sorry for what I did, for what other people had done, and that if she'd give me another chance, I'd never let her down. I knew she didn't really want to die, to take her own life as she'd tried to do, but that she just didn't want to go on living THIS life. There was a difference, and I made a promise to myself to help her feel better.

From outside my door, I heard someone yell, "Prisoner 44607— Grace Bradshaw." The chaos, this time, was for me.

I immediately jumped out of my bed and stood facing my door. I bit the inside corner of my lip, but the rest of me stood completely still.

My cell door opened and before me stood five officers. Three of them had protective shields over their faces. Two others carried long sticks.

A female officer threw in an orange jumpsuit and ordered me to change. My body stiffened at first. I tried to shuffle through reasonable explanations for this early-morning intrusion.

"Hurry up," she said, after I didn't make any attempts to undress.

"What's going on?" I asked.

A male officer carrying a clipboard made his way into my cell. "You're being transported to another part of the prison."

"What for?" My execution was still a couple weeks away.

"To begin preparations." His reply sounded as matter-of-fact as a flight attendant reviewing safety instructions before takeoff. "Get undressed."

I did as I was told. I turned so my back faced the officers and I braced my arm on the bed while I bent to pull my pant legs off.

While the female officer examined me, I fixed my eyes on the pictures hanging on the wall above my bed. Paul and you. You and William. Me and Paul.

"Am I coming back?" I asked as she finished her final sweep across my bare chest. She didn't answer.

Two of the officers were reading over paperwork on a clipboard, while the other three watched my every move. I attempted a polite smile to let them know I wasn't planning to give them any trouble.

I started to peel the pictures off my wall, but one of the officers stopped me. "No personal belongings allowed."

"What will happen to . . . ?" I patted the top of my blanket to feel for your journal.

Two of the officers rushed over to my side. I put my hands where they could see.

"Can I take anything?" I felt as though I couldn't get any air. "My Bible?"

I was leaving forever and I couldn't take a thing.

Officer Jones pushed her way through the wall of officers blocking the cell. "For God's sake, let her take her Bible."

The officer with the clipboard shifted his feet, then nodded. "Bible, but nothing more."

Officer Jones stood to the right of me while I bent down and grabbed my Bible off my table.

"Sophie's journal?" I said quietly to her.

"I'll make sure she gets it."

I found it under the covers at the end of the bed. There was so much more I needed to tell you.

I kissed the top of the unfinished worn brown leather journal and handed it to Officer Jones.

"Don't give up," she said to me. "Don't give up."

The officers shackled my hands and feet as I took one last look at the pictures hanging on the wall. The photos that documented my life and had kept my heart beating for the past seventeen years.

As I walked out of my room I heard one of the officers say, "Throw this stuff into a box and label it for her next of kin."

SOPHIE

Sophie couldn't wait any longer. She contemplated asking Thomas what he thought, or if he would be mad, but didn't. When she picked up the phone to dial, she prayed Thomas would have a smidgen of understanding still left inside of him.

"May I speak to Carter Logan, please?" Sophie said with the sweetest southern tone she could muster.

"Mr. Logan is unavailable at the moment. Would you like to leave a voicemail?"

"Yes, please."

After an extended period of silence, Sophie heard Carter's recorded message: *"You have reached the voicemail of Carter Logan, the District Attorney for Charleston County. I am grateful for the opportunity to serve the people of my community and welcome your phone call. Please leave me a message and I will get back to you."*

Sophie took a deep breath before she began. "Carter, this is Sophie. I didn't want to call you at home. I didn't want Vivianne to hear. I know you're aware of what is happening with my mom. If there is any way you could help her, and help me, I'd appreciate it."

After she hung up the phone a small part of her felt empowered, but other, larger portions of her felt desperate—raw and exposed, like a homeless person begging for food at the corner of a busy intersection or an already thin model being told she needed to lose more weight before a photo shoot.

If the truth be known, she'd walk naked through the streets of West Lake if it meant her mom would be free. But would she in front of Thomas's family?

Sophie checked the pregnancy-tracker app on her phone. Seventeen weeks and four days into her pregnancy and still no acknowledgment from Thomas's side of the family that she was going to have a baby. Not to her, anyway. She knew Thomas had talked to them. She could hear him whispering in the study in a serious voice, not the kind of exchange one would expect when you were talking about happy events, such as the impending birth of a new grandchild.

Still, she had no one to blame for their abandonment except herself. Relationships built on dishonesty were sure to come tumbling down at some point. *Welcome to some point,* she told herself, flipping through the various daytime talk shows, trying to fill another day with productive activities while sitting on the sofa.

She'd started to doze off when her telephone rang.

"Sophie, it's Mindy. You have a minute?"

"I'm trying to decide whether to watch reruns of *The Price Is Right* or take a nap. So I'd say you caught me at a bad time."

Mindy laughed. "Well, not to interrupt your busy day, but I thought you'd like to know."

"Know what?"

"Max's mom has cleared all the hurdles with social services and she plans to take him home."

"What? When?" Sophie tossed the remote on the couch beside her. "Can I see him?"

"She's planning on taking him home this evening. If you want to see him, you better hurry."

GRACE

"Can I tell them good-bye?" I asked the officers escorting me. Two of them are in front of me, two of them are flanking me, and the other two are trailing behind me.

Carmen's and Jada's faces stared at me through their narrow windows.

"This is as good as it gets," one told me.

I turned my head to Carmen's door. Her eyes met mine and neither one of us broke eye contact for several seconds. I raised my hands as high as I could to say good-bye. She gave me the thumbs-up sign.

Jada's face blended in with the ashen paint color on her door. She wiped something out of her eye before she disappeared.

Roni's window was empty.

I started to walk over, but the officer grabbed my arm and turned me around.

"Time to go."

I bowed my head and said a prayer for Roni. I pictured her lying helpless in her bed with the wheelchair across the room.

"Wait a sec," Officer Jones said. "Somebody wants to say good-bye."

I opened my eyes and saw Officer Jones pointing to Roni's window. Half of Roni's face appeared. Through the other part of the window, I saw the ornament I'd given her. She held it flat against the window. I could read the word FAMILY.

SOPHIE

At 6 p.m. on the button Sophie walked faster than she should have through the doors of the hospital carrying a JCPenney bag. Thomas, who she promised she'd wait until he returned home so he could at least drive, trailed behind.

"Slow down. You're supposed to be on bed rest," he shouted.

She waved her hand in the air and kept moving, praying Max was still in the room when she walked in there.

"Max?" she said, when she finally arrived.

His bed had been stripped of sheets and his old monitors taken from the room.

"I've missed him." No evidence was left of any circus puzzles with happy elephants or a single character from *Toy Story*. "He's gone."

Thomas walked into the room just as Sophie sat down in the mauve recliner that had held her and Max so many times. She'd never see her little man again.

"I'm so sorry you missed him," Thomas said. "Let me go see if I can find Mindy. I'll see if we can get an address or phone number for him."

Sophie tried hard to remain calm. *Stress is not good for the baby,* she heard Thomas say in her mind. *But losing Max is in no way good for me,* she rebutted.

"Someone wants to tell you good-bye," Thomas said, pushing the door open.

Max, dressed in a navy blue winter coat, threw his arms out to greet Sophie. "Sosie, where you been?"

Sophie bent down and scooped him up in her arms. "Missing you."

Max's mom walked into the room behind Thomas. "Tell her good-bye. We need to get you to your new home." A John Deere hunter-green stocking cap covered most of her hair. Her gaunt cheeks were covered with peach blush and she smelled like cigarette smoke mixed with an evergreen car freshener.

"Do you mind?" Sophie asked, pointing to the bag beside her on the floor.

Max's mom reached down and tightened the gold nylon shoelaces on her steel-toed work boots. "Sure, I guess we have a minute."

With Max still on her lap, Sophie opened the bag and pulled out a pastel blue-and-pink-and-yellow crocheted blanket. As she wrapped it over Max she said, "This was my baby brother's. He was very special to me, just like you are. I want you to have this."

GRACE

"Everything okay in there?"

I had no idea where I was or who was yelling at my door. My orange top was twisted around me. It stuck to the skin on my back. This place was dark and hot.

"Bradshaw, you okay in there?"

I blinked, but nothing looked familiar. *Where am I?*

The door opened and in walked the person calling my name. I tried to adjust to the light that had followed her.

"You okay, Bradshaw? You seem to be having quite the nightmare."

A blue uniform stood over me.

Death-watch cell. I've been moved to a death-watch cell.

"What time is it?" I asked the slightly built female officer. Her spiked hair added an inch to her short frame.

"Several hours before you need to be up." She wiped her forehead with the back of her hand.

I rolled over and tried to untwist my shirt and untangle my thoughts. My head and neck felt fixed, like someone had taken plastic wrap and coiled it around me, winding and winding until my cells were no longer mobile.

"Take some deep breaths." The officer watched me squirm. "Try to breathe. It'll help calm you." Her words stayed soft and steady as her stance widened. She took a few steps back before glancing out the door for backup.

"This is not unusual. It happens to everyone on their first night here." She put her hand up and signaled to someone that she had the situation under control.

I fought my urge to stand and run, knowing full well any sudden unauthorized movements I made would be met with a swift and severe response. I searched the room for a focal point and tried to remember the relaxation exercises Ms. Liz had taught me. At the end of my metal bed frame, where the top met the sides, the paint was chipped. The exposed metal formed sharp, jagged lines.

I stared at them and counted to ten. *Visualize, Grace,* I could hear Ms. Liz whisper into my ears. I tried to remember what Paul smelled like after he splashed on his cologne, or how Sophie's long arms felt wrapped around my aproned waist as I stood washing the dishes. Nothing would come to me.

The sharp lines began to grow, moving up and down, forward and back. I put my head in my hands and started to weep.

The officer walked over and gently put her hand on my damp back. "Deep breaths," she repeated.

I inhaled again and counted to five before exhaling slowly. This time changing my focal point to the shiny handcuffs dangling down from her belt.

One, two, three . . . The name on her laminated name tag read *I. Kollins.* Ida? Irene?

"Guess it would be a stupid question to ask you what you were dreaming about."

I finished exhaling and started my count again before I could answer. *Four, five* . . .

"My husband died." My words were interspersed with raspy inhalations. "After I was convicted." The vision of Paul in his natural oak coffin without flowers floated in and out of my dreams as if it were announcing an impending tornado warning. A plain, unadorned coffin set smack in the middle of my repeated nightmares.

I left you all alone. You had to be at your father's funeral all alone.

The officer took her hand off my back and watched me gasp for air.

"Is there a problem in here?" A bald officer with a bushy mustache appeared at the door.

"No problems whatsoever," Officer Kollins answered, after my wheezing subsided.

"Then finish up the girl talk," he barked. "We have some procedural issues to take care of."

Officer Kollins put her hand back on my shoulder and squeezed before she left my room. "Try to get some sleep. I'll talk to you in the morning."

After she left, my mind finally quieted enough so that I could see William's long eyelashes fluttering as he slept, his chest rhythmically rising up and down, dreaming his sweet dreams. I laid beside him, watching him breathe for the rest of the night.

SOPHIE

Dr. Johnson removed the measuring tape from Sophie's expanding mid-section. "Eighteen weeks and three days," she said. "The baby's growing right on schedule."

Sophie pulled down her shirt. "So I can resume normal activities?"

"Normal activities, such as . . ." Dr. Johnson finished winding the tape and tossed it into a drawer. She pulled out a fetal Doppler. "Pull up your shirt again for me, please."

Dr. Johnson pressed the Doppler low on her abdomen while Sophie fumbled for any combination of words that made "visiting my mother before her execution" fall under the umbrella of normal. After a few seconds, she gave up and closed her eyes to take in her new favorite sound, the rushed thumping of the baby's heartbeat.

"The baby's heart sounds good." Sophie breathed the same sigh of relief she did every time.

"Listen, Sophie," Dr. Johnson started, "your blood pressure has stabilized and you have no protein in your urine, but . . ."

Sophie prepared herself for what was next.

"If you want me to give you permission to go see your mom, I can't do that." Dr. Johnson held out her hand to assist Sophie up and off the exam table. "That's a decision only you and Thomas can make." Her baby, their baby, meant everything to her, but so did her mother. And now that she'd finally figured that out, she couldn't believe she might be forced to choose.

"I understand," Sophie said, "but you're saying I'm off bed rest?"

"I'm saying you still have to take it easy." Dr. Johnson tucked her flatter-than-usual shoulder-length bob behind her ears. A long call night, Sophie conjectured, after noting the tiny smudges of eye shadow caked on her eyes. "But you can increase your activities."

"Okay." Sophie considered reassuring her doctor by saying facts like "Thomas can borrow a wheelchair for me" and "The visiting room on death watch is close to the parking lot," but she opted to leave well enough alone. "So—two weeks."

"Yes, but call me if you need me." Dr. Johnson put her hand on the doorknob and then stopped and turned around. "Sophie," she said; her tired eyes spoke compassion. "I know you're going through an unimaginable time right now . . . with, uh, your situation."

Sophie fiddled with the thin white crepe paper crumpled beneath her. "With my mom, you mean?" The word *situation* did seem to flow a little better than "I'm sorry about your mom's lethal injection."

"Yes, with your mom," Dr. Johnson responded softly.

The clinical instructions, Sophie gathered, came more easily for Dr. Johnson than the personal ones.

"I can't begin to know what you're going through." Her pager went off, thankfully interrupting before Sophie had to respond. "But try to remember, you have a complicated pregnancy."

Back in the waiting room, Sophie's cell phone rang just as she finished scheduling her next two-week visit.

"Hey, Thomas," she said, getting ready to put a positive spin on Dr. Johnson's cautionary advice.

"Sophie. It's Carter."

"Oh." She hadn't checked the screen before she answered. It had been four days since she'd left the message at his office and she'd given up hope he'd call her back. "Hi, Carter. How are you?"

"The bigger question is how are you?"

"I'm okay, I guess. Just finished seeing my doctor. The baby is fine." She almost said, "Your niece or nephew is doing fine," but she thought better of it.

"Glad to hear that. Thomas told us the good news. Congratulations. Caroline's been planning to call, but she's been busy with Vivi."

"I understand," Sophie said, but they both knew she didn't. "I guess you're calling about my voicemail."

"Yes, I am," he said, his words morphing awkwardly professional. "I'm afraid I'm not going to be able to do much."

"Why is that, Carter?" She pushed her challenge through her suddenly dry mouth.

"Because Mrs. Bradshaw has had seventeen years to prove she's innocent. She's had all her appeals. This looks like a last-ditch effort by a small-town defense attorney, and frankly, Sophie, the governor is not going to buy it."

Sophie held the phone under her chin while she fished through her purse for her car keys. *Mrs. Bradshaw, really?* She dumped the contents of her purse onto the hood of her Land Rover. The keys were nowhere.

"We have proof, Carter." Sophie put her makeup bag and her billfold back in her purse while searching the parking lot for her keychain. "We have a genetics test."

"The D.A. has evidence, too. He found ethylene glycol in William's blood," he said, more sternly than she'd heard him speak before. She pictured a sixteen-year-old version of Vivi tiptoeing across the maple hardwood floors twenty minutes after curfew, praying, "Please don't let my dad wake up."

Sophie walked around to the back of her SUV and leaned against the bumper while Carter continued.

"The test on the baby bottles and your brother's blood samples were sound scientific evidence. Even if your brother had some kind of metabolic disorder, that still doesn't negate the fact your mother poisoned him."

"No one ever tested his blood for a metabolic disorder. We have a test on the same baby bottle, and the results were completely different. His blood was tested *with antiquated techniques*. Please, Carter, I know my mother is innocent."

"I'm sorry, Sophie. I am." His voice softened a little. "But I'm not sure I can always believe what you say, not enough to stick my neck out, anyway."

Sophie knew she deserved his second sentence. "You're right, I lied. I was ashamed. I wanted to fit in with your family. You can distrust me all you want, but please don't take it out on my mother."

The door to the obstetrician's office opened, so Sophie walked around to the more discreet side of her SUV. "My mom didn't kill my brother."

As soon as the words left her mouth, Sophie heard the faint sound of keys jingling behind her. A lady wearing pink scrubs laid Sophie's keys down on the curb beside her. Sophie recognized her as the nurse who'd scheduled her next appointment. "You left these," she mouthed, before rushing away.

Sophie watched her scurry into the office. Probably already gossiping about what she'd overheard. Let the Google searches begin.

"I wish I could help you, but I can't," Carter continued, with as much sincerity as he could muster. "You better prepare yourself, because the governor won't, either."

GRACE

My cell door unlocked before anyone yelled "Stand for count" or a breakfast tray inserted itself through the slit in my front door. Officer Kollins walked in with a chair and a clipboard.

"Did you get any sleep?"

I knew her question was her way of trying to put me at ease, because the video camera mounted in the corner of my cell recorded my every move.

"Not much."

"I don't think I introduced myself last night. My name is Officer Kollins."

"Grace Bradshaw." I held my hand out like we were making introductions at a PTA meeting.

She shook my hand.

"That's a first," I joked, when the shaking ended.

"Not my regular practice, either." She glanced up at the camera. "Officer Jones is a friend of mine. She asked me to help you with this transition."

Transition—is that what they're calling it these days?

"Thank you for helping me. Will I see Officer Jones again?"

"I'm not sure," she said as she skimmed through the papers on her clipboard. Her lack of eye contact told me probably not.

"I need to go over the procedures with you now that you are on death watch."

"Okay." I straightened the wrinkles on my pants while she began.

"With the exception of fifteen minutes that will be allowed for your shower, you will spend all your time in this cell." Officer Kollins put the end of her black ballpoint pen in her mouth and pulled off the cap. "You'll be visited by a nurse, a psychologist, and a spiritual adviser daily. You're not allowed to have any personal belongings other than these."

She placed a sheet, one pillowcase, a change of underwear, and some thin gray socks at the foot of my bed. She held up bottoms of the now all-orange prison uniform next to my waist and said, "These look three times your size. I'll send the property sergeant up to laundry and see if we can get you something that fits."

I started to tell her not to bother. I knew full well how to twist and tie and make something that fell off me stay in place, but the consideration of waking up tomorrow without red marks from the excessive fabric knots swayed me to keep my mouth shut.

"The property sergeant will bring you down some toiletries before your shower this evening. Anything else you would like needs to be re-quested in written form."

"Can I have some more paper?"

Officer Kollins nodded. "I'll bring you a form."

My Bible lay open at the end of my bed. "Can I keep that?" I hesitantly tilted my head toward the book.

Officer Kollins flipped through the papers on her clipboard. "That's allowed."

"Can I have visitors?"

"Visitation is allowed on the day of"—Officer Kollins cleared her throat and made some quick check marks with her ballpoint pen—"your execution."

She left after telling me she'd try to get me some reading materials. "Do you like any particular magazines?"

"*Woman's Day*," I told her, but wished I hadn't. I didn't need the month of menus anymore. I could count the days I had left on my hands.

SOPHIE

Despite the doctor's cautions and Thomas's worries, nothing could have prevented Sophie from going to see her mom on what could be her final day. Although Thomas made a show of telling her to be careful, she knew he understood her reasoning.

What she didn't tell him was that she had to see her mom face-to-face to gauge for herself whether she held on to any trace of blame or of anger toward her. Being unsure about her mother's true feelings would crush Sophie in a way she'd never recover from.

She watched the cable news networks pick up the story with increased intensity as her mom's execution date approached. "South Carolina woman Grace Bradshaw will be executed in two days unless she receives executive clemency. She will be the first woman to be put to death in the state in twenty-four years."

Ben continued to do what he could. He even landed an interview with a sassy former prosecutor on her late-night talk show.

"With all due respect," the impudent TV host questioned, "your client had seventeen years to come up with this 'metabolic theory,' and at the last minute, you throw this out. Why, sir, didn't you investigate this sooner?"

Ben combated her aggressiveness with his southern warmth and stuck with the facts. "Grace's husband passed away before the new evidence could be pursued. William Bradshaw died of a metabolic disorder. We have genetics tests from his sister to prove this."

During commercial breaks, Sophie decided to make a Facebook page: *Free Grace Bradshaw—South Carolina Plans to Kill an Innocent Mother.* She called Thomas in from unloading the dishwasher to preview what she'd written.

"Are you sure you're prepared to go public with this?" He looked over her story, and the family photos she'd uploaded that he'd never seen. "I took them from my house when I visited Brookfield," she explained.

"That's me, holding my mom's hand after I was born." She had studied every detail of that picture, again and again, since she'd brought it home.

She watched her husband for his reaction. He touched her picture on the computer screen. "I've never seen a picture of you as a baby."

"Neither had I. Not for a long time, anyway." Sophie dropped her chin to her chest and exhaled before looking Thomas square in the eyes. "I'm proud to be Grace Bradshaw's daughter. My mistake was not realizing that sooner."

Thomas enlarged the picture. "Why didn't you trust me enough to tell me?"

The ache in his words tore through her.

"I feel like this"—he swiped back and forth between them—"has all been one big lie."

Sophie took his hand. "None of this is a lie. I thought if you knew, if your family found out, you'd leave me. My family is nothing like your family. You're nothing like me. I needed you to love me."

Thomas moved his face closer to hers. "I do love you." He gripped her face harder than she thought he intended to. "I don't want what my family has. I want what your family had, what our family can have."

"I want that, too," Sophie whispered. "I want that, too."

Later that evening, Thomas logged on to his Facebook page. "Between us, we have a lot of contacts," he said while scrolling through. "We might as well share this page with them all."

Margaret Logan called Thomas's cell soon after. He took the call in the study, but Sophie knew by the way he pined around the rest of the evening that his mother hadn't offered much support. "I know what it feels like to be accused of something you didn't do," he said to Sophie after they'd gone to bed. He wrapped his arms around her and slept with her close to him.

He hadn't told her any details about the pending lawsuit when she asked ("We'll worry about that later!"), so she texted Mindy.

Parents dropped lawsuit ☺, but newspaper article destroyed his bid for chief of surgery. A row of yellow sad-faced emoticons followed Mindy's reply.

The morning before the scheduled execution, Thomas called his office and told them he needed a few days off for personal reasons, while Sophie unsuccessfully dredged through the maternity blouses hanging in the upper rack of her closet. *Has any employee handbook in the history of employee handbooks ever stated that a valid reason to use a personal day included attending the murder of your mother-in-law? Likewise, did the designers from A Pea in the Pod say to one another, when sketching my beige peplum-and-lace button-down, "Why, Jane, this will look especially good on a pregnant woman if she has to attend an execution"?* When she didn't emerge after several minutes, Thomas finally made the decisions for her and selected a long-sleeved, cream-colored crocheted tunic and khaki leggings.

Sophie saw the florist truck parked in front of the clubhouse as they drove past. Thomas pulled to the side of the road when Mindy ran from behind the delivery truck and waved them over.

"I need to give you a hug." Mindy pointed to Sophie through the rolled-up windows. Sophie opened her door as Mindy darted over.

"I'm holding you close," Mindy whispered in her ear before they drove away. "You'll never have to go through anything alone again."

———————

THOMAS BOOKED THEM INTO A HOTEL close to the prison. He mentioned the name of it after they were already on the interstate. He didn't know it was the one Sophie and her dad had stayed at the night her mom was locked away. She decided not to tell him yet, but she would. She had learned the hard way that one secret leads to another, and that part of her life was over.

Instead, to help her endure the long car ride, she chose to close her eyes and let her mind go to a place that calmed her. Her mom, sitting cross-legged on the kitchen floor, holding Sophie's tiny hands. She could smell the polish as her mom painted her fingernails a purple glitter color, blowing each coat dry, until her polished nails looked just perfect.

GRACE

Forgive me for not writing for a while. I ran out of paper. Finally, after I filled out another request form (eight days ago), Officer Kollins brought me a three-inch pencil and single piece of unlined paper. I'm writing small so I won't run out of space.

I knew this time would come and I think I have prepared myself well. I've promised myself not to waste another moment focusing on what may or may not happen; instead, I'll concentrate on all the good days that have come before.

Amid the crazy circumstances, I NEED you to know I'm okay. It's been an adjustment trying to acclimate to my new "room" and different schedule, or lack thereof, but second by second I'm doing just that. The hardest part is not being able to talk to you again.

I know I've missed out on a lifetime of moments with you that an "I'm sorry" won't go far to fix. I've had to forgive myself for not being with you when you needed me. I hope you can forgive me, too. After your dad died, you had to navigate through some pretty monumental life changes alone. No one was home to guide you when you filled out your college applications. No one cheered when you opened the thick letter that meant you got in. No one helped you pack your bedroom or stood on the front porch and waved when you drove away from your childhood home, praying you'd make it safe and stay protected.

I can't change any of that, but I'm choosing not to give another second to regret or "I wish I could have." I do need you to know I am puffed up with pride. You are worthy of the tallest trophy, the fattest A+, the bluest blue ribbon, and the shiniest tiara.

All the landmarks, from moving yourself into an empty dorm room to picking out the perfect way to wear your hair on your wedding, have not gone unrecognized by me. In my imagination, your dorm room was decorated in wildflowers with curvy stems and funky-shaped leaves. Am I right? Your hair on your wedding day had soft, pulled-back curls, and, from the picture Thomas pressed against the glass, you wore a veil clipped in the back, accentuating the high cheekbones on your heart-shaped face.

No milestones recorded in the books of other mothers went undocumented in the heart of your mother. You were not forgotten. In case I don't get to tell you in person—I need you to know how amazed, impressed, and on-my-knees grateful I am to be your mom.

I realize there are millions of minutes I'm leaving out, significant events that deserved to be mentioned, like parents' weekend at your college (Did you stay in your room that weekend or did your roommate's family invite you to dinner?) and whether you had enough money to plan the wedding you wanted. I've already used most of the first side of the paper, though, so I guess enough will have to be enough.

On the back side, if you don't mind, Sophie, I need to write some reminders for me. I'm forcing myself to be positive, and I think this will help me.

I asked Paul one day, after witnessing a particular "scratchy" interaction he'd had with one of his parishioners, "How do you stay so kind to these people?" I pointed to the back of the nasty gentleman who'd just finished yelling at my husband. Paul had accidentally left his name off of the donor plaque for the new pews in the sanctuary. "How could you do such a thing after all the money I gave to this congregation?" the man had spewed out his car window before speeding away.

"God doesn't always give us the people we want in our lives," Paul said to me, as I held my tongue and fought the urge to sling some revenge. "He gives us the people we need. Each ugly encounter I view as a gift. A chance to make me kinder, or an opportunity for me to build more patience."

I'm reflecting on your daddy's wise words, and I think I'll make me (us) a little visual aid.

NAMES	THE GIFTS THEY GAVE ME
Ms. Liz and Officer Jones	*They treated me with kindness despite the horrible acts they thought I'd done. They helped me feel real in here.*
Roni	*She helped me develop X-ray vision. The ability to see beneath her flesh and muscle and understand her configuration—the foundation of who she'd become and why. She handed me the most vulnerable parts of herself, all shrouded in stained and trampled gift wrap. I'm glad she can now experience the all-encompassing love that can come only from a parent.*
Jada and Carmen	*They gave me the opportunity not to understand, but to accept. Not to condone, but to acknowledge and to love anyway.*

You and William	*Gave me the most precious gifts of all. The endowment of being a mother. To love you without counting the cost, and to adore you so much my insides jumped. You are also giving me the gift of being a grandma. (Can I see him/her grow from heaven?)*
Paul	*I know in a few days his face will be one of the first I'll see. He and William will be waiting for me. He gave me the gift of never doubting me and of seeing me for the person he knew I was meant to be. I'm so grateful to have experienced such love.*

Before I forget . . . Grandma Pearl's Chicken and Noodle Recipe.
Boil four or five chicken breasts with just enough water to cover.
When the chicken is cooked, remove it from the broth and shred.
Then throw a package of Frozen Egg Noodles (I hope you can find those, but if you can't, another short, dry, wide noodle will do) into the chicken broth. You can add some water or some canned chicken broth, if more liquid is needed. Boil until noodles are done. Here comes the good part . . . Drain most, but not all, of the broth from the noodles, then add one can EACH of cream-of-chicken soup, cream-of-mushroom soup, and cream-of-celery soup. Stir together, add some salt and pepper, and ENJOY! (My mouth and my eyes are watering—I'm smelling the creamed soups, and I can picture my mom whipping up this delicious dinner before me.) If it's too thick, add some milk or more chicken broth. You can't mess this one up.

SOPHIE

Ben met Sophie and Thomas at the breakfast buffet in the hotel lobby. No one felt like eating, but Thomas insisted Sophie at least have a piece of fruit. Ben detailed today's plan while Thomas grabbed a banana off the counter.

"The governor has not said no," he assured them after Thomas sat back down. "We just haven't gotten a response."

"Is this normal?" Thomas asked while he peeled the skin off of the banana and handed it to Sophie.

"Like we talked about before, nothing's normal, so to speak, in these situations. We just have to wait and see what the governor will do."

"We will be allowed to visit your mother for some period prior." He didn't say prior to what, but they knew what he meant. "Then, if the governor doesn't grant clemency, your mom will be taken to the execution chamber, where they will begin the procedure."

Thomas put his arms around Sophie's shoulders. A family with a young daughter hovered around their table while waiting in line for the wafflemaker.

Ben lowered his voice. "Have you decided if you would like to be present during the execution?"

Sophie couldn't answer. *Is this really going to happen?*

"Sweetheart, your chocolate-chip waffles are ready." The little girl jumped and her pigtails flew up and down.

Thomas tightened his arms around Sophie and squeezed. "We'll figure this out together once we get there."

PROTESTERS HAD ALREADY FORMED opposing camps outside the heavily barbed wire fence in front of the penitentiary when Ben turned his car toward the guarded gate. He'd suggested all three of them ride together because "the prison is a real madhouse on execution day." The minute the words had come out of his mouth, he'd realized how callous they sounded.

"I'm sorry," he said. "That didn't come out the way I meant it to."

"It's okay." She flipped down the sun visor and checked her eyeliner for smudges. She guessed to most prison employees today was "execution day." It was similar, she supposed, to a teacher who had "parent conference day" or a medic who had "CPR recertification day." Something they didn't particularly care to do if given the choice, but since they weren't, they made the best of this bothersome and troubling job requirement. She knew Ben didn't deserve to be lumped into that category; he was just trying to be practical and efficient with their time. None of that mattered to Sophie, because today, until proven otherwise, was not an execution day, but the day the governor would finally set her mother free.

Clusters of death penalty opponents sat outside the pointy fence in lawn chairs, slipping candles into paper holders. A lady wearing a navy blue hoodie and had her brown hair pulled back in a scrunchie blew into her hands as Ben drove past. When she saw them, she picked up and waved a piece of torn cardboard. In red letters, she had written: STOP KILLING TO STOP THE KILLING.

A small church bus bearing the name Lake Terrace Lutheran Church sheltered the growing crowd of protesters from the cold February wind. Sophie waved to the lady kneeling in front of her chair as she passed by.

On the other side of the road, only a few protesters "for" the death penalty had started to congregate. "It's early," Ben pointed out to Sophie when she made mention of the large discrepancy in the number of pro-testers against and in favor of her mother's execution. "It's still early."

"I need driver's licenses of all people in the vehicle," the uniformed officer instructed Ben after he rolled down his window.

"What is the reason for today's visit?" the officer asked Ben after he handed him back his license.

"I'm the attorney for Grace Bradshaw."

The officer nodded. "And you, Mrs. Logan?" He examined her license picture and then examined her face.

"I'm Grace Bradshaw's daughter."

The officer studied her face again before handing her license back to Ben.

"And you?" he said to Thomas.

"I'm Grace's son-in-law."

The officer opened the gate and then waved them through.

GRACE

*I'm writing down my time on death watch with the pretense that
"not knowing" may be more torturous on you than the "knowing."
If that's not the case, please ask Thomas to read through first and
filter.*

*This morning, Officer Kollins walked into my cell to collect my
breakfast tray. "You're not going to eat any more than this?" she
asked after noticing the unpeeled spotted brown banana and the clear
plastic lid still on top of my gray cream-of-wheat bowl.*

*"Not much of an appetite today." I knew she knew that, but
small talk didn't come easily in this situation.*

"How'd you sleep?"

*"Not so good." She must not have been watching me on video
last night.*

*In fact, I wasn't sure I'd slept much at all. I kept vacillating
between feeling up, then down; excited, then distraught. In hours,
I knew I would see you—a face I hadn't seen in eleven years.
I imagined smelling your hair and the sound of your beating heart
so close to mine, but as quickly as the good came, the bad did, too.
I saw you sobbing and pleading as the officers shackled me and took
me away. "Say good-bye to your daughter," I heard them say as
soon as I started to doze off.*

"I want to go over your schedule today so we don't have any confusion." Officer Kollins pulled out a form and put it on the table beside me. "This morning, you will be visited by the nurse and prison psychologists. You can address any medical or psychological needs you have with them at that time." She looked at me for confirmation I heard and understood before checking the box.

"After those visits are concluded, you may have visits from your legal and spiritual advisers. Do you understand?"

"I understand, but when can I see my daughter?"

"Visitation for family members will be between three and four this afternoon."

A square digital clock outside my cell displayed the time as 8:37 a.m. I counted the time on my right hand. Eight hours and twenty three minutes.

"What time is . . . ?" I couldn't bring myself to say it, so Officer Kollins said it for me.

"If the governor doesn't intervene, your execution will be at six p.m. tonight."

SOPHIE

Ben punched numbers into his phone while Sophie and Thomas paced back and forth around the small private visiting area.

Ben said, "This is Ben Taylor again. Can you please tell me when the governor will issue his response?"

Someone knocked on the door right as Ben started to call his office to see if Louise had heard anything.

"May I come in?"

Sophie stood still as a small woman with gray hair pulled into a tight bun entered the room. Her stiff legs and curved spine made her introductions slow.

"Hi, I'm Sophie." She held her hand to greet the woman who was carrying in a stuffed tote bag embroidered with a name Sophie couldn't quite read.

"Sophie, I'm Ms. Liz." Her bent handshake felt warm. "I'm your mother's spiritual adviser."

"How's my mom? Have you seen her today?" Sophie didn't exhale as she waited for her to answer.

"I have not," Ms. Liz answered slowly. She nodded a greeting in Ben and Thomas's direction.

Ben hung up the phone and Sophie could tell by his defeated expression that Louise didn't know any more than they did.

"Please sit down." Ms. Liz motioned to them.

Ben pulled some folding chairs from out of the corner of the small room. Two out of the three metal folding chairs had wobbly, uneven legs, so Ben and Thomas stood, debating which of the other two women needed the most stability.

"Give Ms. Liz this one," Sophie told him.

Ms. Liz sat down while Ben pulled his handkerchief from his pocket and put it under the leg of Sophie's chair.

"Do you know how she is?" Sophie asked.

"I'm sure she's being incredibly brave as usual," Ms. Liz said. "I'm going to see her as soon as the nurse is finished with her."

"Is she sick?" Sophie asked.

"No, this is all just normal protocol," Ben interjected.

"I've been meeting with your mom for some time now," Ms. Liz said. "We've become quite close."

Sophie felt her eyes start to burn. "Then I guess you know?"

"Know what?" Ms. Liz asked her. The lines around her eyes tightened, but her face seemed safe and soft.

"That I've been a terrible daughter." Sophie controlled her voice, but she couldn't keep her shoulders and hands from shaking. All of a sudden the room became cold.

Thomas took off his suit jacket and placed it around her. He kept his hands on her shoulders.

"I do know one thing," Ms. Liz said as she pulled some tissues from her coat pocket. "Your mom's entire countenance changes when she talks about you. It's like these walls"—she swirled her arms in the air—"just don't exist."

Ben's cell phone rang as Sophie was about to exhale. Both she and Ms. Liz chose not to move.

"Ben Taylor." Pause. "Yes, yes, that's correct." Pause. "Okay. Thank you."

Ben held his phone close to his chest. "The governor has issued a response. His office is faxing it to mine by four p.m. His assistant said he's holding a press conference around the same time."

"Is that good news or bad news?" Sophie stammered, her eyes begging Ben or Ms. Liz for some kind of reassurance.

Ben shook his head. "I have no idea what it means."

Ms. Liz patted Sophie's hand. "We have to just wait and see."

A tap on the door interrupted their discussion. "Ms. Liz?" An officer opened the door. "You can see Mrs. Bradshaw now."

Sophie buried her head in her hands. She could feel her baby adjusting itself inside her.

"Sophie," Ms. Liz said. She reached down to get something out of her tote bag. Sophie could see the name *Elizabeth* scrolled in deep purple cursive. "Your mom asked me to give you this." She handed her a brown leather journal.

Sophie grasped it with wobbly hands. Tears started trickling down her face as she held the worn book close to her chest.

Ms. Liz rose from her chair and ran her bent fingers over the top of Sophie's hair.

"Ms. Liz," Sophie cried. "I need you to do me a favor."

GRACE

By 12:17 p.m. I'd been visited by the nurse and the prison psychologist. Both asked me questions with no good answers, like "How are you feeling?" and "Do you want to talk about anything?" I answered the best way I knew how. "My feelings fluctuate" and "My daughter will be here soon, so I can talk to her." My polite way of saying, "Weigh me, take my vitals, and leave." Who cared what the numbers on the scale read, anyway?

"Can I see her now?" I heard Ms. Liz's frail voice outside my cell.

"When Officer Kollins finishes with her," I heard whatever male officer was on duty say to her. "She'll have to escort her to the visitor's area."

I didn't have a mirror and I desperately wanted to make sure my hair was at least combed before I saw Sophie. I didn't know if I'd be returning to my cell or not, so I quickly ran my brush through and pulled my hair, maybe for the last time, into a ponytail.

Ms. Liz waited outside my cell while Officer Kollins made me cough and squat, then placed my arms and feet in restraints. "How you holding up?"

I looked at the clock again. "I'm okay, I guess."

Ms. Liz braced herself against the wall outside my cell. "Hello, Grace," she said as soon as my cell door opened. "I have a surprise for you."

Ms. Liz walked beside me as we made our way through two locked metal doors and to the death watch visitor's area. "The warden granted you permission."

"Permission for what?"

"You get to visit with Sophie in the visitors' room. A contact visit."

I had no idea this was even a possibility. I'd prepared myself to see her through smudged glass.

"Let's get you into the visitors' area," Officer Kollins said when my legs started to buckle. She and Ms. Liz took hold of me.

After I regained my balance, we started to walk. And then I saw Sophie. It was the back of her head, darting into the restroom. I think Thomas was behind her.

"Was that her?"

Ms. Liz smiled and nodded.

"She'll be out in a minute." Officer Kollins had one hand on my back and the other on my arm, leading me forward.

"Sophie," I wanted to yell. I wanted to run to her. "I'm here. Your mom is here."

"Take some deep breaths," Ms. Liz told me. "You'll see her in a second."

Officer Kollins pushed some buttons on the keypad outside the visitors' area. I turned around to see if I could catch a glimpse of her coming out of the bathroom.

"Hello, Grace," Ben said to me as soon as the door opened.

He had his suit jacket off and it was tossed on the seat of a folding chair. His gray-and-black-striped necktie seemed crooked.

"Hi, Ben."

Officer Kollins pulled out a chair for me and I sat down. I looked at Ben, ready to hear him tell me clemency had been denied. But he knew that wasn't what mattered. Instead, he said, "Are you ready to see Sophie?"

I thought I was ready. But when he said the words, I couldn't make my lips form a reply. I'm not sure I inhaled or exhaled. I thought for a second my heart might have stopped pumping. My body understood what my mind could not comprehend. These moments with my Sophie would probably be my last.

Sophie felt it, too. When she walked into the room and our eyes once again found each other, we both knew. We understood the significance of time, so much so that nothing else mattered, nothing else existed. We could talk about what might have been, but we chose not to. We did the only thing we could do—cling to each other.

"Can you uncuff me?" I asked Officer Kollins when I finally found my voice.

Officer Kollins had been joined by Officer Mackey; they glanced at each other before Officer Mackey pulled out his keys. "Don't make me regret this."

"Your hair," I said to Sophie once my cuffs were off. "It smells just like I remembered."

She put her hand up to her shiny blond hair, secured neatly to one side with a sequined bobby pin. "I still use the same shampoo you used to buy me. It makes me feel close to you."

I didn't know where Thomas or Ben stood; all I knew was that for this instant, my little girl sat beside me. I held her hand and she rubbed mine. I even touched her stomach and felt my first grandchild shift about. Sophie moved my hand, then put hers over mine. "Feel here, Mom. Your grandbaby's kicking."

I reminded myself, when I could calm down enough to isolate a thought, that I had to be strong. I needed to protect Sophie and let her know—no matter what happened—I would be okay. She would be okay. *Please, God, make me strong.*

I can't explain the peace I began to feel, or the strength that washed over me. It was like all the moments that had come before faded away, and this was the instance, the minute, the second I'd been moving toward. No particular words needed to be said, no regrets spoken, because

Sophie and I understood. We shared something. A love that refused to go away.

I knew this tranquillity didn't come from me. It came from a God who, for all these years, had heard my prayers. An angel stood over this room, with his huge outstretched arms protecting Sophie. I'd never felt more loved.

SOPHIE

As soon as the officer removed her mom's handcuffs, Sophie felt them again—the top of her mom's hands. Her fingers were now thinner, and her veins a thicker blue, but her velvety skin was as silky as she remembered. The same hands that had put the syrupy green aloe on Sophie's scorching red back—"This should be better by tomorrow, sweetheart"— or added cold milk to her overly microwaved oatmeal were still as comforting as Sophie pictured.

"I'm sorry," she tried to say, but her mom stopped her.

"We are together now," her mom whispered. "We are together now." Her mom closed her eyes and put Sophie's hand over her heart.

"Tell me about your dreams?" Her mom asked her after they both settled down. "Thomas told me about your work with the fund-raiser, but what are you passionate about? What makes you excited to get out of bed?"

Sophie thought for a moment. No one, not even Thomas, had asked her questions in such a way that bore straight through her. "Do you remember Thomas telling you about Max?"

"I do. The little boy in the hospital, right?"

"I'm crazy about him. I love him, Mom. I really love him."

Her mom put her hands on the sides of Sophie's face. "I was waiting to see something that lit up your face."

Sophie put her hands over her mother's and then moved them to her lap. "His mom took him home, though, so I'm not sure I'll see him again."

Ben's phone rang and he answered it. Sophie tightened her hands over her mother's and watched Ben's face for any clues. Her mother didn't take her eyes off her.

"Ben Taylor," he said into the phone. "Okay, okay, uh-huh. What channel?"

GRACE

"In 1997, Grace Bradshaw was convicted of murdering her infant son, William Joseph Bradshaw." The governor stood behind a wide mahogany lectern in the garden of the governor's mansion. The misty pink tea roses that once flanked his side in late spring lay frozen in mounting piles of new dirt.

"I have reviewed the facts of this case and the applicable laws pertaining to her sentencing. Despite the evidence presented at the eighth hour by the defense, there is no question in my mind Grace Bradshaw committed this heinous crime."

I knew what was coming next, so I forced myself to focus on what I couldn't see. Future buds, hidden beneath him, waiting to see the light so they could bloom.

"Since there are no substantial new facts in this case, I see no reason to grant clemency. As your governor, I have the duty to see that justice prevails and the laws of the great state of South Carolina are fulfilled."

Thomas held up one side of me, and Sophie the other. Ben stood behind me with both of his hands gripping my shoulders. Officer Kollins had shackled my hands and feet before the press conference came on. "It's protocol, Grace. I'm sorry."

Sophie started weeping soon after the governor started to speak. After he finished, I laid my head on her shoulder and wept, too.

SOPHIE

"Why won't anyone help us?" Sophie heard herself yell after Ben shut off the television.

Her mom tried to comfort her. "I'm going to be okay," she repeated over and over. "This wasn't a surprise to God."

Sophie touched her mother's soft face. "How can you be so calm?"

"I'm going to see my husband. I'm going to see my son." Her mom's eyes overflowed with tears. "Please know—I will never leave you." She put her hand once again over the center of her heart.

"Ms. Liz is here," Ben said to Officer Kollins when he saw her standing outside the door. "Is it okay if she comes back in?"

Officer Kollins walked over and unlocked the door. "I have what you wanted," she mouthed to Sophie.

Officer Kollins pulled out her keys and freed Grace's hands while Ms. Liz sat down with two frosted glasses overflowing with foamy fountain root beer and two scoops of vanilla ice cream.

"Please stay with me, Mom," Sophie cried out. Her mom grabbed her trembling hands and pulled them to her chest. She then reached over and touched the pronounced dimple that appeared right below Sophie's mouth when she begged for something.

"You can't leave me," Sophie pleaded. "I need you to teach me how to be a mom."

GRACE

"Grace, it's time," Ms. Liz said. The warden allowed her to walk with me down the short cinder-block hallway from my holding cell to the execution chamber. She steadied one of my arms and Officer Kollins stabilized the other.

> *"It's time," I heard my mom say, when the big gold school bus crunched the gravel in front of our house. Her eyes looked scratchy and red. I thought she might be getting a cold. "Your first day of kindergarten. I couldn't be more proud of you."*
>
> *"It's time," my dad told me as he slipped his arm under mine. He wiped his wet forehead with the back of his black tuxedo sleeve. My white satin pump pinched my left heel. Paul stood at the end of the aisle. He put his hand over his heart when he saw me.*
>
> *"It's time," the OB doctor said to me after eight long hours of labor. "You're ready to push." He snapped the stirrups into place. I could feel Paul's hand gently squeezing the back of my neck as baby William's head emerged.*

"Do you have any last words?" Warden Richards asked after I'd been strapped down and positioned on the stainless-steel gurney. He squeezed the bridge of his nose. I heard one of the officers sniffle and I saw Ms. Liz lift a tissue to her eyes. I turned my head one last time to Sophie. I could see her sitting between Ben and Thomas and I knew she'd be okay. I mouthed to her the words I'd said a million times before: *I love you*.

"No," I told the warden quietly. I'd said everything to those who matter.

I looked up at the ceiling and counted the ceiling tiles. I felt something warm seep deep and fill my veins. I closed my eyes and did the only thing that calmed me when I couldn't stand this place anymore. I pictured the faces I had learned by heart.

EPILOGUE

A pile of crisp burnt orange and yellow sugar maple leaves rattled up and down in the fall wind. "Max. Max! Come out wherever you are," shouted Thomas.

After many minutes of pretending he had no idea where Max was hiding, Thomas fell into the moving pile right next to a giggling Max. Shortly after Gracie was born, Mindy had called and told Sophie that Max was back. His mom had dropped him off at the pediatric ward when his care became too much for her. Thomas saw Sophie's face light up when she spoke on the phone to Mindy. "Let's go see our boy," he said as soon as she'd hung up the phone.

Sophie sat on a park bench, taking in the smells of the fall leaves and her warm apple cider, never taking her eyes off the faces that played before her. Gracie, now six months, snuggled close beside her inside her stroller. Her head, full of twisted blond curls, was protected from the chill by the snow-white hat with misty pink lamb ears Ben had mailed to Sophie shortly after Gracie's birth. *I think she'll like this*, he'd scribbled on the card.

Sophie bent over and kissed her sleeping Gracie. Then she dug deep into her diaper bag and pulled out her own worn brown leather journal. Inscribed inside the front cover was a version of the words from Psalm 91. *Father, thank you for letting me sit beside you and for listening to me as I talk to you about my Gracie and my Max. I trust you with my babies. I know your huge outstretched arms are protecting them, and they will be perfectly safe. . . .*

ACKNOWLEDGMENTS

To Lauren Lo Pinto, Sofie Brooks, and the team at Putnam: Thanks for finding this novel a home. It has truly been a dream come true to work with you.

To Jill Marsal of Marsal Lyon Literary Agency: You top my list of shocking phone calls. Much gratitude for representing me and for embracing this story.

To my husband, Greg: I prayed I'd find someone I'd love my entire life. I'm so grateful I found you.

To Taylor, Lukas, Gracie, and Olivia: The most significant moments in my life are those that include you. I hope you've noticed the way my face lights up when you walk into the room. Do the one thing only you were created to do. I'm crazy happy I'm the one who gets to be your mom.

To Mom, Dad, and my baby sister, Tonya: You made our two-bedroom, one-bathroom house feel like a castle. Thanks for always pointing me in the right direction and for showing me how to love others well. I couldn't have asked for anything more.

To Scottie Barnes (www.forgivenministry.org): It's a rare and priceless gift to meet someone who sacrificially serves others as you do. Your faith, courage, and bravery inspire me to do more and to be better. Thanks for letting me tag along with you and your team at Forgiven Ministry. You're making an eternal difference in the lives of children who have incarcerated parents.

ACKNOWLEDGMENTS

To Caitlin Alexander and Susanne Scheppmann: Your encouragement gave me the confidence to keep writing. Your well-timed words kept me going when I needed that extra push. Thank you for using your voice to help me find mine. I'm forever grateful.

Last, but most noteworthy . . . Thank you to those of you who took the time to read *With Love from the Inside*. It's a privilege to write a story for others to read. I'm humbled you took the time to read mine.